A Collection of Short Stories

by
Lincoln M. Hanks

Edited and Cover Design
by James Van Treese

Northwest Publishing Inc.
5949 South 350 West
Salt Lake City, UT 84107
801-266-5900

Northwest Publishing Inc.
5949 South 350 West
Salt Lake City, Utah 84107
801-266-5900

ISBN #1-880416-48-4

Printed In the United States of America

Dedication

To those from whom my inspiration comes:
my wife, Carolyn Stevens Hanks,
a loving family
and the folks of my time,
in the Gentle Valley of the Tetons.

C. S. TWINING
14819 43RD PL. N.E.
LAKE STEVENS, WA. 98258

C. S. TWINING
14819 43RD PL. N.E.
LAKE STEVENS, WA. 98258

TABLE OF CONTENTS

1

Speck, The Princess

She was a holstein. We called her Lilly. Nice name for a bovine; nice bovine for the name. With giant white splotches on a black coat, or black splotches on white, whichever one may prefer, she was a typical holstein cow. Typical, that is, in spots and splotches, but far from usual in the production of milk. Lilly was a champion. As we carried three-gallon buckets and ten-gallon cans to the milking corral mornings and evenings, we provided one such can for Lilly alone, for on a day during the summer months, this classy bovine would provide sufficient of the creamy, white liquid to all but fill one ten-gallon container by herself. With twenty-five Lillys, which farmer couldn't live securely? With fifty, wouldn't he be rich? So, why not build up the milk herd with Lilly's offspring? She could provide us with a new potential milk producer each spring, and she was young. And her spotted children, wouldn't they, in time, grow up and provide offspring also? After, say, ten years what a dairy business we would have.

As those years came and passed, we observed anxiously each late March as Lilly's flanks bulged with pregnancy, and there was pent up excitement at that annual event when the prize cow presented her offspring. But the black and white queen was given to producing males. One, two, three years running, she brought forth infant gentleman bovines.

It was during the fourth year of her maturity, on a bright spring morning, that Lilly presented us with a delicate, spotted girl child, a beautiful female with markings picked up from somewhere in that vast array of hereditary genes which all creatures possess, markings rather different from those of her noted dam. The little one's spots were actually speckles, black polka dots on a white coat.

So, we named her Speck. And as she grew to maturity, we watched with anticipation as her body assumed those fine angular proportions of her breed. Speck was a special animal; we knew it. She possessed that queenly quality which set her apart from the others. We mentioned this difference as we observed her in the corral or as she browsed in the pasture. She would ably perpetuate Lilly's high blood.

At length Speck became pregnant; her flanks rounded and her udder began to swell as the natal day of her first offspring approached. Her speckled teats extended themselves and her nature seemed more placid, as though she sensed the coming event.

It was a week before the anticipated day of her freshening that I was left at home, a twelve-year-old, as the family motored to town. I was instructed to drive the cows to the corral in the evening and to assemble the buckets and cans for the evening milking ritual, which would begin upon the family's return.

In the pasture, the spring clover stood high and thick, lush pasturage for any herd, and in the field new alfalfa grew velvety green, but ominously alluring. For new alfalfa can produce dangerous gasses in a bovine stomach, which can be fatal.

Evening approached and I made my way leisurely toward the pasture on my assigned errand. Insects flitted about the long shadows of cottonwoods and clumps of willow. My world was at peace. I looked for the holstein herd, for often in the evening they came of their own accord toward the milking corral to have their strained udders relieved. But as I reached the pasture, their black and white coats, easily identifiable against the green and ochre of their surroundings, were not to be seen. Up by the sheep sheds in the east, down to where Big Creek swirled under the barbed wire fence in the west, south to the field gate, my eyes swept across the pasture. I felt an gnawing anxiety, and then alarm, for at a second glance, I could see that the wood-paneled gate to the field had been forced ajar. The herd, every animal, was gone. As I ran toward the gate, I remembered the cautions which had been rehearsed on occasions around the dinner table: If sheep or cattle give evidence of bloat, don't startle or unduly disturb them. Drive them gently; do not let them drink. And I remembered the gruesome details of a hired man's counsel: "If a cow bloats, measure a hand span down from the hip bone, and with a sharp knife . . . " The gory conclusion of his commentary was repulsive.

I soon saw the herd browsing contentedly in a broad expanse of the vibrant green, deadly alfalfa. Running toward the animals, I first observed Lily, the queen. Her flanks were not dangerously distended. That was a relief. And Beauty, and Star, and the others, they seemed in no danger. But Speck, where was Speck? I could not see her easily identifiable coat. I encouraged the animals, gently, toward the gate, hoping the heifer might have gone earlier to the corral. But, to be certain I hadn't missed her, I ran back toward a high, grassy ditch bank, where she might be concealed. I had gone no more than a dozen yards when I caught sight of the familiar back. The young cow was lying down beyond the ditch, alone. I could see in a moment she was in discomfort. Her flanks, already distended from pregnancy, seemed greatly swelled, taut as drum heads. As I approached, she struggled to her feet and trotted awkwardly toward the herd.

"Slow down, Speck," I muttered. Her big, soft eyes gazed toward me with anxiety. She was bloating.

As the herd walked leisurely toward the corral, their rear legs brushing their swollen udders, Speck struggled. She thrust her head from side to side. Her mouth began to gape open and her dark tongue seemed swollen.

When the herd reached the corral, Speck, trailing at the rear, stopped, lifted her white muzzle and shook her head as she desperately attempted to draw breath into her gaping mouth. She sank awkwardly to her foreknees, trembled, and collapsed to her side gasping, straining for breath. The gruesome thought of the "hand span from the hip" terrified me. Speck was dying. I knew it. I reached for my pocket knife, a bone-handled birthday gift. My fingers trembled as I opened the longest blade. Speck's gasps came convulsively as I measured the hand span down from the point of the speckled hip. With difficulty, I thrust the blade to the hilt through the tough hide. There came an issue of green, foamy froth. It ran down the swollen side. But the expected life-saving burst of body gas did not come. Why didn't it come? I thrust the blade into the wound again. The slow ooze continued. For reasons I did not understand, my effort had failed.

So, Speck, the long awaited princess, died before she could give a gift of her lineage to the herd. I wiped the little knife blade between my fingers and rubbed my fingers against the warm, hairy coat, not raising my head as the family car turned in at the gate. I cried at her side, watching the froth bubble from the puncture wound, and then, to be alone with my grief, I ran to the granary.

2

Ice Flowers

It's a hard and memorable cold up here in Teton Basin, this winter of 1935-36. The months have brought a frost that ices up the marrow, dulls ambition, turns good natures sour, and in so doing it freezes the creeks solid, down to their gravely beds. The blizzards narrow our horizons, cover our paths. The incessant sweep of storm and the monstrous cold make of us sullen prisoners in a whitewashed, Arctic wasteland. Unsheltered animals turn their rear quarters windward and wait out nature's hellhound. Manes and tails fly, thick hair on bellies and flanks flutter, cold-stiffened limbs tremble.

After facing the numbing northwester all day, we hope nightfall will bring a calming of the elements, as it often does on a normal winter evening, but now we are disappointed, for with the darkness, the sting of frozen snow kernels against our cheeks and noses assures us that the white onslaught still rides in on the wind, a wind that moans its cold, hoarse moan as it chases ghostly snow plumes across the open fields.

The great drifts grow in height and with the vagaries of the wind, new mounds appear in pastures, across highways, near building corners, around haystacks, before doors. When mornings come, we face new worlds, for communities of strange snow-edifices have risen up out of the night. It is as though aliens from a distant planet have set up their tall, white tents. Roads will have to be rebroken to town, to the haystacks, to the sheep feeding grounds.

Yes, roads will have to be broken and rebroken to those winter feeding grounds. I had turned fourteen in August, and now, with February, my abode is a canvass-covered sheep camp, my companion, a twelve-year-old brother, Clair, and our charges, nine hundred to a thousand docile, hungry sheep. Those bleating, coughing, dull witted bundles of wool are our means of survival as a family during these depression years.

This stern fact is seldom out of our consciousness as we go about the essential duties of our day, which begins with the jangle of an alarm clock before seven A.M. We lay motionlessly, with only thatches of our hair showing from our covers, and think drowsily of the day ahead. Finally we stir and our hands venture from the warm, woolen quilts to retrieve from under the top cover of the bed our shirts, bib overalls, sweaters, and long, heavy sox. The clothing is drawn quickly into the bed with us to be warmed a few moments before we wriggle our long underwear-clad bodies into the apparel, while we still lie under the covers. Now prepared we slide from the bed into our frigid surroundings and push our feet into ankle-high, cold-stiffened leather shoes. We hurriedly pull on our heavy coats and scarves and earlapped caps and mittens, retrieving them from a heap at the foot of our bed, which is a boxed-in mattress extending the full width of the rear of the camp. Finally we wrap our overall cuffs about our ankles, slip on our hightopped overshoes and fasten the cold, metal buckles snugly against our legs. Now we venture through the camp door, with its frost-whitened window, to the outside, where on this morning, the temperature is far below zero.

The faithful horses must be harnessed. They survived the night keeping to the lee side of the loaded hayrack, to which their frozen halter ropes had been secured. The animals acknowledge us with uplifted muzzles and accept their harnesses patiently. Their halter ropes are difficult to untie from the rack. They are stiff as metal cables. Our breath billows into the air as we buckle the leather collar straps. A white, frosty fringe begins to form on our eyebrows and on the folds of our scarves. We press our mittened hands against our mouths, breathing warm, moist breath into the soft material, to take the tingle from our fingers and faces, but once our hands are removed from our faces, the cold pierces sharper than before. We raise our shoulders and draw our heads deeper into our collars. We lift our woolen scarves higher, covering our noses and cheeks. The cold stings our eyes and is sharp against our legs, piercing the thin layers of denim overalls and woolen underwear.

We buckle the hames to the grooves on the horse collars; we fasten the belly straps and the cruppers. The long hair of the animals' coats is tinged with frost. The team stretches their limbs with anticipation. The ton of hay on the rack, towering four or five feet above our heads, provided night provender for the horses. The animals are full.

Before we insert the frigid bridle bits between their lips, we rub the metal bars vigorously in our gloved fingers to take the frost out of them. Not done, the bits will adhere to and tear the moist tissues of their mouths. This ritual completed, we nudge the sensitive lips with our fingers and the horses accept the bits. We slip the bridle straps over their heads, buckle the throat straps and lead the team to their places on either side of the sleigh tongue. We snap the hame straps to the frosty neckyoke, link the tugs to the singletrees, the reins to the bridle bits. But before climbing aboard the rack, we obtain from beside the camp a ten-foot-long pine pole and insert an end of it under the upward curve of each steel-shod sleigh runner. Lifting our end of the pole, we break the frozen bond between the runners and the hard-packed snow surface. Now the team will be able to pull the load free.

The front frame of the hayrack serving as a ladder, we climb to the top of the load. Clair finds his perch astraddle the rack's upright, two-by-four, center post, which extends a foot above the top of the front frame of the rack. He leans back against the hay and turns the team toward the feed grounds. Keeping my balance on the load top, I rub the snow and frost from the pitchfork handle, and as the sleigh is drawn through newly-formed drifts and areas swept clean by the wind, I throw forkfuls of hay down the sides of the load. The sheep, their bells rattling, trot from their darker bedding spots to follow the rack and then greedily feeding, glue themselves to the hay piles.

In twenty minutes the feed is unloaded and the team is turned toward camp. Clair climbs down from his cold perch, attaches the reins to the two-by-four rack post and we dance on the wooden slabs of the rack bed to relieve the tingling in our toes.

Stopping beside our canvas igloo, we quickly unhitch and secure the halter ropes to the rack frame again. We hurry inside our fragile dwelling, supported upon its own sleigh runners, and hover over the small, black camp stove, remove the heavy top lids, stuff inside the fire chamber a crumpled newspaper, place splinters of kindling from the woodbox on the flammable heap, then rub a matchhead across the dark, metal surface. We watch a glowing, orange flame ignite the paper, reach up with more strength into the kindling, and climb higher into the thicker wood. As the fluttering tongues reach upward, we place split wood of thicker diameter upon the fire and the flames rise up out of the lid holes. We replace the metal covers and hear the draw of the damper as it carries the flames along its hidden channel above the oven to the chimney. A life-sustaining radiation of heat reaches up to warm our faces. We pull off our gloves and hold our hands close to the warming stove surface. We remove our caps and throw them back on the unmade bed. The cold floor creaks as we move about.

The warmth reaches out. We feel it penetrate the chilled air. Our toes seem warmer. Soon we remove our coats and toss them on the bed. The air at the rear of the camp, stirred by the flying garments, comes back to us frigidly cold. The heat hasn't reached the rear of the camp. Now the dark, metal stovepipe grows hot, providing a four-foot-long, vertical heat channel to the ceiling, through which the pipe passes to the outside. The frozen water in the teakettle begins to cluck as it melts. Soon, the kettle hisses and an issue of steam rises from the spout.

We pour the warm liquid into a gray, enameled wash basin, which we remove from its hanging place beside the camp door. With a hard, cold bar of soap, we wash our reddened hands and faces. We feel a numbing sensation in our fingers as they encounter the warm water. The towel, removed from its nail near the wash basin, feels shockingly cold. We hold it over the stove to warm it. It feels much better now.

We place a dented aluminum pot on the stove and pour in some hot water from the teakettle. When it comes to a boil, we stir in a cupful of the coarse, "Germaide", wheat cereal, and stir with a tablespoon until the porridge thickens. Clair then crowds the long-handled, black frying pan onto the stove. From a lower shelf in the cupboard, located mid-camp on the stove side, he obtains a hard cube of home-cured bacon, with which he lubricates the bottom of the skillet by rubbing the cold chunk over the dark, warming metal. We let down the table, which, with its hinges at the bottom and latch at the top, serves when not used as a table as a door to a second small cupboard, which is located across the floor, opposite the first cupboard.

I pour a mound of flour into a flat pan and attempt to break an egg onto the pile. The shell must be chipped free, for the egg is frozen. With a butcher knife, Clair chips crumbles of white, iced milk from a gallon can and shakes the crumbles onto the flour. Globules of flour adhere to the damp chunks. I stir the mass. The smaller ice crystals begin to break down into a liquid as I wield the tablespoon. But the egg is stubborn. I spoon it about in the flour, which adheres to the oval ball. We open the oven door, slip the pan inside. While the egg and milk melt, we chip more ice from the milk can into a pot and crowd this container onto the stove. We sprinkle three or four spoonfuls of cocoa powder over the ice in the pot.

Now the contents of the dough pan in the oven are warmed enough to permit stirring. The egg is still reluctant toward the center and the larger lumps of iced milk remain invincible, but we stir, shake in sprinkles of baking powder and soda, and an acceptable batter forms. I spoon into the frying pan two puddles of batter. Bubbles soon form on the surface of the mixture. I turn the cakes with the broad blade of a butcher knife. The bottoms are browned. We are pleased.

We draw from the cupboard, cups, bowls, platters, and tarnished silverware. From a lower cupboard shelf we retrieve a brick-hard mound of farm-made butter and a bowl of sugar. The cocoa is steaming in its kettle. We pour it into our cups, protecting our fingers with a dishtowel. We sprinkle in sugar.

The pancakes are done. We slide them from the pan into our platters and spoon more batter into the frying pan. The wheat cereal cooks with heavy, slow bubbles. It is done, lumpy, but acceptable. We fill our bowls. With our knives we chisel chips from the yellow mound on the butter plate and spread the crumbles across our pancakes. We sprinkle sugar over the crumbles. Breakfast is ready.

From a second milk can, which we had placed at the back of the stove, we pour a creamy liquid over the cereal and sprinkle in a spoonful of sugar. We sip at the steaming cocoa, cut huge triangles of sweetened hot cake, ladle spoonfuls of cereal to our mouths. We fill ourselves, cheer ourselves. The world is brighter. The unbearable Arctic remains crowding about us beyond the thin, rounded canvas walls of our home, but now we forget. Warm life rises in us. We are two ice flowers spreading into a temporary bloom inside a delicate capsule, a tiny island of warmth in a frigid universe.

As I wash the dishes, Clair gathers his books, swathes himself again with sweater, coat, scarf, gloves, cap, and overshoes, and ventures reluctantly into the frozen outside. The school bus will stop at the head of our sleigh trail on the snow-clogged Clawson lane. The bus is a horse-drawn, covered sleigh, warmed by a stove similar to ours. From the window I observe smoke rising from the bus's black stovepipe. The vehicle slides effortlessly behind a black team. I see, even from my distance, bursts of vapor from the trotting horses' nostrils.

Now I begin my long hours alone, alone with two horses, a thousand sheep. The sun makes its appearance into a thin, pale crevasse of sky above the gray-blanketed horizon. I'll make the most of an hour of my own. I tidy up the camp, smooth the quilts across the bed, and wonder what this day will bring down across the five miles of snow fields and creeks, where stand the buildings of home. They seem warm and inviting in my mind. And I wonder about my school mates, who have gone by me. But this is my year to lay out, my turn to give a year to the farm. I'll lay out another year after high school. It's the family way. Even so, I feel left behind and I wonder, feel a little sad, not particularly about school's books and lessons, but about my friends passing me. Maybe someday I'll catch up.

Outside, the wind rises out of the northwest as it did yesterday. I see a lonely snow plume race across the fields east of camp. The thin, pale opening in the horizon fades and I hear snow kernels begin to collide against the canvas protection overhead. It sounds like a sprinkle of driven rain, but sharper. Soon, the horizons begin to narrow, close down, and horizontal vollies of snow sweep over the camp and across the feeding grounds. The blizzard begins its daily rage. The canvas shelter shudders. Through the window in the door I see the horses straining against their halter ropes, attempting to turn their rear quarters to the storm. Today will be a savage one. The wind will double the work required in piling the rack with hay from the mile-distant stack, far out in a snowbound field. This must be done twice, once for the afternoon feeding and then again, a second ton, for tomorrow morning's rounds. The sleigh road across the fields will be precarious. Off the narrow tracks, the snow level is nearly four feet. I must keep the team to the hard-packed trail. But yesterday I accomplished it. I'll do it again today, and tomorrow.

So, at ten-thirty, I hitch the team and drive along the field road, carefully keeping to the fading tracks. Reaching the haystack, I heave pitchfork loads into the wind. I bring the first ton in, and after wrapping the reins about the rack's center post and giving the understanding team their heads, I scatter the feed in broad circles over the snow-swept grounds.

I watered the horses at a distant neighbor's trough. I build a new fire in the camp stove, warm pork and beans, fry frozen mutton, toast homemade bread on the stove top. I stir cocoa and sugar into milk, boil it to a thin fudge. I cook macaroni, open a can of tomato soup, empty it in, add a cup of frozen milk, bring it to a boil. I hear every click of a spoon against a kettle, every crackle of flame in the fire box, rattle of a sheep bell. Noises, even little noises, are loud when one is alone.

I look toward evening, when Clair will return. We'll eat the macaroni soup, what's left of it. We'll fry more mutton and eat the fudge, what's left of it. This afternoon I'll bring in the other ton, unharness, build up the fire, and when he gets here, two ice flowers will bloom again in the warm glow of the kerosene lantern, which will hang from its hook above the table. Its flame will flutter in the drafty camp. We'll hear the wild, low moan as the wind sweeps over the fields; we'll hear the frozen snow pelt our shelter and we'll think of home.

Note: Clair and I lived in the sheep camp until the hay had been hauled from the stack, to the last ton, and then trailed the herd back to the ranch in time for lambing.

3 The Haying Wind

The sun came up pale, uncertain, with a yellowish glow out of it. We keep our hope, an empty hope, for rain, but again, today, the heavens are brass over us and the dry wind rises. We feel the reddened skin of our faces draw in hard against the flesh as we turn into it; we lick our chapped lips and sense a renewed wavering of our spirits.

Over the weeks past, the few clouds that had braved the southwest came up empty, rising in dark, cumulous piles, but then, as we thought we smelled rain, white filmy plumes rose upward at their promising summits and drifted away as smoke from a weed fire on an elevated ditch bank. The great tentative banks were then drawn out into long rainless windows, and finally, fragmenting as froth on blue, moving water, disintegrated, melting away as froth will with a change in the current of a stream.

On the hard land below, a trail of ecru dust begins to sweep up from Emery Adams' hilltop dry farm. The wind, tormenting the summer-fallowed land, has broken the crusted, plowed surface, setting free the under powder. It appears as if the eighty acres, too, are burning, sending up dirty smoke from hidden flames. And in an adjoining expanse of sage brush, a dust devil, born of a brief, swirling turbulence, rises, and dies, leaving a towering column suspended, unsupported, to disintegrate into a spreading dusty smudge over the field.

We hitch up to the hay boats and with pitchforks heave haycocks onto the net chains spread across the flat, wood surfaces. The dry piles, disturbed by the forks, set their withered alfalfa and clover leaves free into the devilish, blustering blow to be dashed up any away, tearing, tumbling to heaven knows where. Our spirits are drawn out to futility as we fork up the stark, dry hay stalks remaining, their greater strength flying away on the wind.

At the stack yard we watch the net-loads rise from the boats, swaying against the buffeting furnace as they are lofted up by the derrick pole. With the pull of the trip rope, the loads fall to the stack, setting free again showering, skittering clouds. We are feeble ants clawing against a great, sweeping destroyer.

Along the dried watercourses in the pasture, their branches thrashing in agitation, cottonwoods strain against the whipping flow. Their long, sleek, frenzied leaves, showing premature yellowing in their veins, are beginning to curl inward from thirst, giving the appearance of opened pea pods. In the high branches, scolding crows cling to their precarious perches, and then, despairing of their security, loft themselves into the air free of their pitching roosts. Clucking and crowing as they are jostled in the sweeping turbulence, they flap and flutter with the great tide, rising and falling with the unstable current as they pump their way toward a distant grove, where the surging branches will likely send them tumbling off into the sky again.

The growth along the ditchbanks stands stark and ambered. Dust-coated stones in stream beds are sterile, bone dry, and the wind blows sand ripples under the banks. Hoof tracks in the long-dried mud are as though imprinted in quartz.

Across the oat field, the strickened growth lies prostrate. The delicate heads, shriveled with premature ripening, whip at the earth. At harvest, we say, the bundles produced by the binder will be a jumble of criss-crossed confusion, producing at the thresher a quarter yield, half of the half-filled heads remaining on the dry, cracked earth. Futility shrinks us.

But toward evening, in the west-northwest, a leaden bank appears, a blue-gray stratum, unaccountable, swelling into the sundown haze. The hot haying wind gasps, trembles for want of direction, and mysteriously dies. By moonrise rain-laden, dark windows roll down the west mountains and the moon and stars wane. The rain comes imperceptibly, stealing out of the sky unheralded, a drop first, growing in the stillness to a soft, pattering drizzle. By morning the cloud banks rest on the valley floor. The parched earth draws the moisture into its dry bowels and the oats in the field lift their heads. The growth on the ditchbanks takes new life, while sullen crows droop under wet plummage on cottonwood roosts. We turn our hard faces upward to permit the moisture, as new life, to penetrate and restore.

4 June Bug Days

I don't know what June bugs are. I don't think I ever saw one, but a soft singing of insect wings seems harmonious in this little glimpse of spring on the Hanks farm in Teton Basin. So it's June Bug Days and it's spring in, say, 1937. That date is far enough away to have gathered a bit of nostalgia, and it's near enough to permit the garnering of a fact or two, one or two, out of memory's mixed bag of distortions and inflations.

I'm about to hitch Ginger and Homer to the farm tool and personnel transport vehicle, which we call the buggy. It's a June morning. The sun is midway to noon. Friendly sun. The horses are gray, of the farm type, comfortable and enduring like old gate posts, bread and milk, and canvas gloves. They aren't excited about this hitching ritual. Their eyes are half closed. They've learned to take life as it comes.

As I lead the animals across the barnyard, I hear the distinct whistling and squawking of long-beaked, long-legged water birds, as they skim along over the grassy edges of creeks and irrigation ditches out in the pasture and fields. My approach to a puddle disturbs a killdeer. It runs off to a safe distance sounding its shrill, nervous chimes. Its dark spindly legs race through the shallow water beneath its body, which, in contrast, floats placidly along. Now a magpie adds its squawking discord. It perches on the bleached rib of a sheep carcass out behind the horse barn. The deceased animal's pelt was salvaged by pocket knife several weeks ago, and the dogs have long since gnawed from the bones all but tiny shreds of flesh. Now it's magpie work.

Meanwhile, over by the cowbarn door, flies buzz in darts and circles above the manure pile. It's a nice buzzing. Friendly flies. A rush of sparrows suddenly arc in from the horse barn roof, startling the flies, which lose their friendliness and zip away. The little gray-feathered scavengers attack the refuse-pile crust with their talons, attempting to dislodge worms and bugs and whatever. As they flutter about and scratch and peck, a melodic, melancholy chime comes from the pasture. It sounds again and again and is answered from farther out, in the field. I pause a minute, cup my hands, lace my fingers, and against upright thumbs, place my lips and blow bursts of air. After several tries, I send a wheezy, whistly answer out to the doves. It satisfies me and it pleases the team, for they get a moment of peace, but the doves pay no attention.

A robin now swoops over First Creek to the manure pile gathering-place and the sparrows make a fluttery departure. At that action, a meadowlark, over in an adjoining field sends out an ear-catching song, and a red-winged blackbird, sitting on its nest in a cottonwood over the fence east in Ollie Christensen's place, sends out its spirited "o-whee, o-whee". Friendly birds. And not to leave out of this account other creatures that are hovering and skittering about, a mosquito misses my slap as it sings by my ear, and a bumble bee gets due attention as it drones too close on its unfriendly business trip. And ground squirrels waggle their tails as they chatter and chirp and scamper from mound to mound of new earth, visiting their neighbors. From far and near, their musical conversations can be heard. And a hen clucks and a rooster crows and a hound bays, far off.

As I hitch up the team, I'm aware that mine is but a minor role in a wide community of spirited activity. After the hitching ritual, I swing up to the buggy seat, settle back, and turn the team toward the First Creek crossing. The repetitive, but varied pulse of that great symphony swells from the broad amphitheater of green pastures and blooming fields. The lifting harmony reaches out, teases the ears, and swells the heart.

Crossing First Creek, our initial achievement on our way to give attention to a sagging fence in the field, shouldn't be overplayed. No swimming horses, foaming rapids, anything like that. The water does well to reach fetlock level (that's a horse's ankle); however, in the spring it may reach half way to a team's knees. The sound of horses wading in crossings is music, too, music of its own strain, a nice, hollowish clop-splash. There's just a bit of current to First Creek in June. It ripples, eddies, slides, gurgles down its course past the cowbarn and into the pasture below. I see a red flag in the stream down the creek a way. The water master has put it by a diverting dam. "Keep your hands off," I'm told the sign means. It probably has to do with a neighbor's rights to his fair share of the stream. Enjoy your water, neighbor. Friendly neighbor.

Soon, after following the wagon trail through a stretch of pasture grass, we clopped into Second Creek. It's deeper and wider, but no hazard to health or limb. The current flows darker, just about to the horses' knees. Ginger lowers his head for a drink. He isn't thirsty; he's stalling. I know his tricks. With a slap of a rein against his back, he gets the message.

Now I hear the frogs in the pasture organize their chorus. They sing out with two notes: "urr-up, urr-up." Simple. "Urr-up, urr-up." A monotone would do very well in an audition. But nice music. Friendly music. Their tune is one you can't hum particularly, but there's an anesthetic quality about it that will put most troubles out of your head if you give yourself to it.

We reach Big Creek. In the spring it snakes with powerful currents the entire length of the pasture. It branches into major and minor forks and into dead ends. It eddies into shady, deep pools. Sometimes trout can be seen darting through its dark water. The creek swells in June almost to the torrent stage, heaving and foaming at its banks, sometimes baring the underpinning roots of cottonwoods and willows, threatening their security. I slap the reins again, for the animals hesitate. They don't like the thought of cold water against their bellies.

"Come on, Homer. Ginger, get in there!" Hooves clop into the stream and we are drawn into deep water. The current might push a wading man off his feet. Big Creek is business-like, daring one to venture into it. I feel the flowing pressure against the wheels of the buggy. Unfriendly, cold water.

Now across the pasture, the buggy glides over the soft earth. We pass puddles and cottonwood trees, we wend our way over pasture grass, clover, timothy, by green-stalked and maturing Indian tobacco, and past lavender-bloomed thistles, the hollow stalks of which, with spines and thorns trimmed off, taste like tender celery. We encounter black and white milk cows, contented, munching, and lazily switching their tails at winged predators. Their tails are never quiet.

Up east in the pasture, the long, low sheep sheds slumber in silence, their work for the season finished. Let them sleep. The sheep have gone to the mountains to their summer range. No more bleating to annoy the ears. No smell of live muttons, just the pleasant odor of stale, musty, straw bedding, decaying there in the pens and corrals.

Nice smell. Friendly smell. A holstein critter seems to enjoy the aura too. She breathes deeply of the aroma, switching her tail in the shade of a big bush, just across the Wade Ditch. This yard-wide waterway was dug long enough ago by the Wade family, who reside a mile to the west, that along its banks, a pleasant willow and cottonwood hedge has grown. We dip into and cross the stream, traverse more pasture land.

Reaching the field fence, I pull the reins, dismount and open the wood-paneled portal to the cultivated acres. I feel the sun on my hands and it's warmth in my nose as I breathe in all kinds of the nice perfume that is riding in the pasture air, all mixed together and competing with the smell of the sheep sheds. Noticeable is the slightly stale, delicately pungent odor of standing water in the quiet, dead-end eddies of streams and the grassy, shaded rain-water pools. Winged insects flit about above the water and over depressions made in muddy banks by cattle and horse hooves.

Back in the buggy, we get more serious. After two or three shakes of the reins and clucks of the tongue, Ginger and Homer move into a trot along the field road. I look out at the world. For this is the world. There isn't any other. Swan Valley, Malad, New York, Mongolia, what are they? Let whoever wants those foreign places keep them. For this really is the world. I know it. I see the sleeping farm houses and sagging barns and hay derricks down west, shimmering in the spring heat waves in this nice, friendly bit of universe. Except for the Wade barn, relatively stately with its faded red paint and graying white trim, the buildings down a mile or two in quiet, rural Haden are of the uniform unpainted gray log or clapboard. Good neighbors they are down there, toward the river. Today as I write, I can't remember bad things about those humble folks. If there were less than good things, they were little things which didn't count for much, and I've forgotten them. I prefer to remember good folks, friendly, with their smiles, not their troubles and frowns.

As we trot along, the clip-clop of hooves, the jingle of harness links, the squeaks and jolts of the buggy tease the ears. We cross the field southward toward The Canal, and my optics sweep above the Haden farms, on over the three-mile-distant river, and up the valley's western incline to old Richvale. I see that community's church and its weathered schoolhouse-companion standing by themselves on the ruler-straight Richvale road, which leads the eye along its distant, lazy route toward the west mountains, officially known as the Big Holes, a name which we never use. A dust devil churns into the sky a couple of miles south of those drowsing buildings near The Flat. That's what we call our spring, sheep range, those broad reaches of sagebrush land where our shearing shed and corrals are located, graying with age in the sun.

My eyes return to the Richvale road and follow its ruler line to the base of the west mountains, where it makes a broad turn upward, losing itself in groves of aspens, distant blue-green against the grayer earth-green sage. Upward still I gaze, upward to the long, even ridgeline of those friendly west summits, which rest in the morning haze. Our Myers Place is up there and Milk Creek and Packsaddle Canyon and Dude Creek and The Cliffs and Cold Water Spring and Brubaker's. Nice names for those nice places, some of them of our own christening. Our herd grazes somewhere in those quiet, blue-green forests and pastel clearings. Those familiar heights peer down at us, reserved, maintaining their shadowy mystique, their ever-present essence of wildness, their frowning, but gentle summits.

And now, like a magnet, drawing, pulling at me, my orbs must turn eastward, high above our good neighbor, Dick Egbert's, place, far above. The Tetons dominate, demand, glower. So high, they are, so regal, so unapproachably breath-trembling. We're all serfs to the Tetons. I know that. We all know it: the west mountains, Ginger and Homer, Haden, Cedron, Chapin, the whole world. "Hello up there, Tetons, sirs! Nice day, sirs." They pay no attention, of course, keeping their glare far above and beyond us ants, who grovel at their feet. I don't know what they see, staring, forever staring, as they do. Maybe it's their own shining pavilions way off somewhere. I don't know. "Sorry up there, sirs. Keep staring. Sorry to disturb."

A jingle of tug links reminds me we've reached The Canal. Deep, eight feet wide, bush-lined, it follows an elevated crown in the field. Slow moving, it diverts water from Leigh Creek out to our 'Bench' area and down to George Pehrson's in the west. On past the Canal, we descend into The Hollow, a sixty acre strip of open field with a jack-pine rail fence guarding a haystack in its center. The Hollow is bordered on its south by a towering palisade of cottonwoods and willows, which crowd the banks of the north branch of Leigh Creek. The buggy wheels drop sharply down this creek's bank. It's belly-touching water again.

Beyond the crossing, we enter a secluded field. We call it The South End. The land suns itself between the heavily wooded north and south branches of Leigh Creek. These waterways, torrents in the spring, die to bleached stream beds by late summer, which, we often remark, have an odor of fish in their isolated pockets of standing water. Choke cherries grow in The South End, a mile from the house and barns, as do haw berries, wild currents, gooseberries, and fingernail-size, wild strawberries. Nice part of the farm. Friendly.

Now to the ailing fence, east of The South End, bordering The Johnson Place. The barbed wires, I find, are in disarray. Headstrong animals have left their trail of vandalism. Strands of the barbed wire barrier seem to be missing. So I pull the reins, tie Ginger's halter rope to a convenient tree and assemble from the buggy a claw hammer, pincers, staples, shovel, crowbar, wire stretchers, and a coil of new, galvanized, barbed fence wire. Those forty acres we call The Johnson Place are entirely wooded. A faint wagon road runs from our fence line off through the trees and bushes across stream beds and small openings in the woods to the foundation remains of a homestead. The Johnson's, I suppose. I don't know the family, don't know anyone who does. Did they settle there on the banks of Leigh Creek with high hopes and high energy and then leave with broken spirits as some Valley farmers have done? I don't know. Teton Basin's winter cold and its occasional late-summer dryness can (and has done in the past) send farmers with shallow roots packing.

The doves in The South End and over in the Johnson Place are vocal in their possessiveness of the land. So are the magpies and the squirrels. They send out their spirited protests to encroachers. But, really, all of us lowly critters very well understand that this turf belongs to none of us. The land, down to the last willow sprig is the Tetons's domain. Why argue? Paying no heed to all this feeble prattle in the woods, the giant, granite peaks keep on with their distant, heavy-browed glare. "Nice place you have, here, Sirs. Very nice. I'm not arguing."

Well, I dig and plant and splice and stretch and staple, and the sun begins to tire of the day and sink toward our sheep range in the west. The shadows reach out and quiet the bees and the squirrels. And the Tetons, now with the evening sun in their faces, look irritated by it, but keep their stare far away, maybe over to the Wind River Range, where I hear there's a high granite-crowned summit. I don't know. Maybe they just glare at each other.

I load in the tools and the left-over wire, untie from the tree the slipknot in Ginger's rope, climb to the buggy seat, cluck to the team, and head willingly toward a set table and a bed. The sun now touches the horizon out north of the Point, that pyramidal elevation which rises up at the feet of the northern slopes of the west mountains. There's a kodachrome rosiness subduing the land. In that make-believe, sinking light, you don't feel like talking or whistling. You just sort of mellow out into the surroundings. You feel like thinking, and I do it on the way along the dim wagon trail. There's a feeling of evening coolness on my bare arms - it comes with a slight current of cooler air, and then a competing current brings the warm air back again. There's a fresh smell of alfalfa blossoms and those hundred mixed-up field odors of spring. The frogs mellow out, too. They sing their doxology. I climb down from the buggy and swing the pasture gate. The last sun warms the great Teton's crown. His brooding family, down at his shoulders, now begins to sink into the dusk. I suspect they are losing sight of their distant pavilions, or whatever they see out there. But maybe now, out on their graying horizons, they see the faint, far-off lightning puffs of a storm. Maybe up in Montana's Gallatans, or down over the Sawtooths. Seeing that far must reveal a mountain storm off somewhere.

But I don't need to see that far. I know where my shining pavilions are. They're here. Here with the calming splash and gurgle of creek water, with the velvety stillness about cottonwood and willow clump silhouettes, with the sheep sheds and corrals tucked in, becoming indistinct in the growing dusk, and with the kerosene lamp, glowing warm in the kitchen window up past the barn.

5

The Black Lamb

Lambs came in the early spring on our sheep ranch, late March and early April, to be precise. During that season the long, low sheds in the pasture and the surrounding corrals and feed grounds became beehives of activity. There was daily feeding, watering, strawing, cleaning of pens and processing of the newborn lambs from pens only large enough to accomodate the ewe and her new offspring to larger pens accommodating up to six, and then to still larger pens with perhaps a dozen occupants. Finally, we moved them outside to the partially sheltered corrals, and then, at last, when the newcomers were strong enough to romp about in little bands, we merged them, with their mothers, into a herd of hundreds out on the feed grounds.

But there were always the early arrivals, those few lambs that, for reasons unknown to me, came a week or ten days before the others, which, at the peak of the lambing season, might come in numbers up to a hundred in a day. And during most years up in Teton Valley, snow still hung heavily in the pastures and fields when those first arriving lambs made their appearance. Night men would not yet have begun to make their rounds of the feeding grounds checking for possible newborns. And so these early arrivers might experience precarious beginnings if their births occurred on nights of storm or severe cold. On such nights we left our beds, taking our turns with the lantern and walking through the drowsing herd, checking for new lambs.

I was in my upper teen years on one such night when I took my shift making those nocturnal rounds. I vividly remember following the bob sleigh tracks the quarter-mile to the pasture bedding grounds. The night wind was sharp against my face and I remember, too, the tingling of my fingers inside jersey-lined mittens. Drawing my fingers into fists inside the mittens warmed them. I remember, as well, that gloves, with their individual finger compartments, were avoided during the coldest weather, for inside them, fingers soon became numb.

The complete stillness at two on a winter morning is unforgettable. There was a sensation of lonely wildness. I sensed it as I observed the narrow, communal jack rabbit trails that criss-crossing the snow surfaces and then lost themselves in the darkness. I remember weasel tracks, small ditto-like prints, leading solo off into the dark woods. A puff of irritable wind rose, as it often did on winter nights, and cold-stiffened, frost-bristling cottonwood and willow limbs swished and creaked in the darkness.

Making my way through the ankle-deep snow, which had blown across the sleigh tracks, I could see the bedded herd, but barely, as I approached, for the falling snow had mounded over them. They might have been a field of snowcapped boulders. From my distance I could not discern heads from tails, for the animals, with legs folded under them, had, most of them, turned their heads about to rest their chins against their flanks. Nearing the herd, the animals on the periphery began to look up, startled. In the lantern light I could see their eyes flash yellow. They stared at me, this human apparition approaching in the midst of a feeble globe of light. A belled ewe, startled, shook the snow from her head. A hundred white boulders suddenly rose upward to be supported on spindly legs. Their eyes, flashing yellow out of those mounds of snow, created their own apparitions in the night. As I neared, those sheep which had bolted upright began to shake the snow from their backs, stretch their limbs and then sniff about their bedding spots.

I soon saw a new lamb, wobbly upon its legs, struggling to remain upright. A dark rope of afterbirth membrane and tissues trailed from the mother's rear quarters. She nuzzled her newborn with her nose, stamped her forefeet and stared defiantly toward me. I could tell the lamb was cold. Its back was arched and as I neared I detected a pendant of birth fluid, frozen as an icicle, clinging to the little animal's underneck.

Now I could see, across the feed grounds, a second ewe lying on her side, her straining neck raised in the characteristic position of birth labor. She struggled to her feet awkwardly, turned about with mincing steps, sniffed the snow pack behind her as though expecting to find her offspring. She sank to her front knees and went down to her side again, head raised with strain. I could see the wet and steaming tissues and fluid beginning to emerge from her birth channel.

I hurried to the struggling, stiffened lamb, grasped it up and cradled it against my coat. The mother, not giving an inch, bleated anxiously, thrusting her nose against the offspring and butting her shoulder against my leg. She followed me stride for stride as I began the three-hundred yard trek along the bob sleigh tracks to the low sheds, which, though winter-cold inside, offered a dry, strawed pen and shelter from the wind and snow. Shadows of the lantern's glow danced across the drifts with the swing of my arm.

Inside the shed, the ewe followed me to the pen. Finding an empty gunny sack draped across a partition, I rubbed the lamb briskly from nose to tail and I could soon tell that its strength was returning. I helped the little animal find its mother's nipple and left it with its head burrowed into her underflank. The mother bleated attentively as though thankfully, as I closed the door and hurried back across the pasture, carrying the burlap bag with me.

Back on the feed grounds, I found that the laboring ewe had delivered her lamb and was industriously cleaning birth fluids from the little animal's back with her tongue. As I approached, this sheep stamped her forefeet with defiance, but that defiance quickly gave way to fear and she trotted a dozen yards away, bleating and circling about me and her lamb. I rubbed the small, damp coat clean and wrapped the little creature in the gunny sack, then started for the shed, but the ewe would not follow. She trotted away into the herd, arcing about me, bleating anxiously. What options I had now were all difficult. I selected the one most obvious to me, leaving the lamb inside the sack, near the lantern, and stalking the mother. I waited until her attention was focused toward her newborn, then dashed up from the rear, grasped her by the wool of her back, straddled her, and after an initial struggle, directed the squirming, struggling creature toward her offspring, and then toward the shed, leaving the lantern to blaze alone on a snow bank. Balancing the lamb, still in the bag, across the mother's shoulders with one hand and clinging tightly to the ewe's woolly back with the other, I guided her, controlling her movements with my legs, on that long strength-consuming struggle across the pasture. We labored mightily, both the ewe and I, making our progress in spurts and starts and bucks and rears, pausing often to pant, but we finally reached the low shed and I was greatly relieved, and no doubt so was the sheep, when she was deposited in the second small pen inside. I left the lamb struggling to stand in the deep straw beside its mother.

Outside I could see the distant glow of the lantern and felt the perspiration on my back as I trudged toward the herd. Now it was after three, but I was wide awake. My sweaty skin began to feel cold and clammy as I approached the flock. Occasionally a ewe would wriggle as she lay in the snow, adjusting her pregnant, distended abdomen to find greater comfort. "A thousand expectant mothers," I thought.

A black ewe caught my eye. She bleated and stamped her feet as she observed my approach. Standing near the creek willows at the outer edge of the herd, her snow-laden body gave no evidence of trailing afterbirth tissues. She couldn't have been in labor, I assured myself. But had she already given birth? My wondering was spurred by the sight of a small, white mound near her forefeet. Whatever the object was, the snow had covered it completely. As I approached, the ewe challenged me, but then backed away nervously. I scraped the snow away from the mound with my overshoed foot and discovered a small, black, woolly body. The lifeless creature was beautifully marked with white stockings, a white-tipped tail and a white skull cap on its otherwise black head. The life was gone. The limbs and neck were stiffly frozen. The mother bleated plaintively as I picked up the little form and attempted to rub its back. But there was no use. Death is sad, cruel. If I had found the black lamb first on my rounds of the herd, would it have lived? Could I have saved it? I wondered as I left the small body in the snow.

I turned toward the house. The black ewe bleated as I trudged away. Soon it would be four o'clock. I'd come back at five. And I'd sleep during the day. At six-thirty, the feed sleigh would be out and fresh hay would be spread out on the snow, perhaps covering the lifeless black body out by the creek willows.

6

We Haven't Forgotten You, Old Slim

Of all the horses that came and went on our Teton Valley farm, the one least likely to become immortalized in print (if this, indeed, be immortalization) would be Slim. Big boney head, short ears, sparse hair around his dark, protruding eyes, freckled skin showing here and there through his white-gray, rough coat; this was Slim. His spine protruded up sharply, the full length of it, even during the lush pasture seasons, when other animals became sleek and well rounded. This uncomely anatomical feature, coupled with his awkward, unsteady gait, made of a bare-back ride aboard his vertebral column a memorably unpleasant experience, as I discovered that summer day of his purchase, when I loped him the five miles home from a neighboring ranch.

"Let's get rid of the old hayburner," I can fancy the rancher saying as word must have reached him that the Hanks' were looking about for a horse to add to their stable of grays. (We maintained upwards of ten of that color, or lack of it, teamed in the harnesses.) "I'll call about ole Slim today."

So we bought Slim for forty - or twenty - dollars, I don't remember which. But I do remember as I galloped him along the soft shoulder of the gravel highway down past Harrop's river bridge on the way to the farm, adjusting my lower anatomy from one side of his spine to the other in search of more comfort, the sky darkened and lightning began to spit down from an ugly cloud overhead. The blitzing strikes of flame were close and I saw a puff of dust rise up as one brilliant streak spiked the earth a couple of hundred yards away in a plowed field. The crack of thunder caused Slim to lurch and I grabbed his sparse, white mane. Another streaking flame came down even closer and I felt a slight tingle from the metal button on the top of my cap. I turned Slim to the opposite side of the highway. I had been riding under the electrical power lines.

And so, heaving and puffing, Ole Slim made his appearance on the Hanks acres, loping through the big, paneled gate. The family came out to observe, for the acquiring of a new horse was not an everyday event.

"Well, he's big."

"Sure is." That was about the extent of the conversation as I turned the lanky horse loose to the pasture.

I don't remember that Slim ever found his nitch on the farm. Matching him in a team was a challenge. Nip, the dark-gray, home-grown gelding, stood a hand span shorter. The white-gray Star matched in color, but that great horse would pull circles around Slim. The newcomer would never tighten his tugs, matched with Star. Prince? Fritz? Bolley? Total mismatches. Ginger or Homer? Those companion grays had pulled together for fifteen years. Who could split that team? Dick and Chuck? Matching Slim with either of those oldsters would draw snickers. That left the mares. Ada? She was too squat - wouldn't match at all. Blanche? Well, Blanche was bigger, taller.

So it became Blanche, the bay mare, and poor old Slim, the misfit relegated to a nondescript, somewhat humorous anonymity.

"A short-eared ole mule," observed a hired man, with a smirk. "He's no credit to Blanche." His ungainly legs were too long to permit him to lean into the harness and with mighty bursts of power move, say, a hay derrick, as Star or Prince could do. Too sharp-backed to ride, his enthusiasm gone, past whatever prime he may have ever attained, Slim soon slips away into the backwaters of memory. How long he lived on the Hanks acres, I don't recall. Unlike Old Dick, who survived anywhere up to thirty-five years and became a revered institution on the farm, Slim just fades out of consciousness. How he died, I don't know. I still feel a pang at the thought of the gray stallion, Chief, who strangled himself one day in his halter rope, and Old Dick, again, who one winter morning couldn't lift himself to his rear legs. He got his front hooves under him, but not the rear. We watered and fed him where he lay until he couldn't lift his head, and we mourned his passing. But Slim, I don't recall that he even made the breakfast table conversation when he slipped away.

The rangy, gray animal, strange in his way, just loped in one day carrying this hard-heeled Hanks kid on his back, pulled at his tugs during those long, hot summers and shivered through the winters pawing through the deep, creek bottom snow for dried grass. I suspect he looked up plaintively with the other unneeded teams as we threw feed from the sled rack for them. I remember that sad, winter look in the field horses' eyes.

A discard, sold cheap. An old nag who came and worked and then died, all but unnoticed.

This tribute to you, quiet old friend, Slim. Long overdue.

7

The Sheepherder's Dream

The Herdsman reigned King, Sovereign, Royal Law Giver and Enforcer up in the high Big Holes, that spur of the Teton Range that forms the great west wall of Teton Valley. It was a lofty kingdom, his, with windy crags, wheezing pines and trembling aspens. On the slopes and near the cascading, sparkling streams, pithy hawberries, puckery choke cherries, and delicate huckleberries hung in profuse clusters. And there were deep, misty canyons with spooky sounds and creepy shadows and smells of last year's leaves, down and decaying, and this year's coarse-bladed pine grass, crow foot and milk weed.

This unique kingdom was inhabited by a unique citizenry forever amove on wing and hoof and claw, including some fifteen-hundred bell-rattling, bleating, woolbound muttons, with an equal number of ravenous, woolbound offspring at their sides; included also was a phalanx of the realm known not be precise numbers, but by a shadowy, illusive existance, namely, the wily bear, the slinking coyote, the mountain hen, the chipmonk, etc., etc. And finally, as a footnote to the populace above described, one must cipher into the mix three horses, two of the saddle type, more or less, and one leaning toward the more sturdy packsaddle strain, sort of. Two dogs of the readily recognizable pooch variety must also be added. At last, as a footnote to the footnote, one might factor into the equasion one entry of being, if not of content, one lackey, serf, peon, camp jack, namely me. That was the realm, the whole kit and kaboodle of it.

Now, regarding this Herdsman above mentioned ("Sheepherder"? Don't mention the lowly title in the same breath), there was something regal, royal about the said personage. Undeniably. One would readily recognize a sovereignness, as this reigning monarch perched himself on a high, windy, granite throne, giving the royal scan over his nibbling, slinking, winging, forever moving vassalage. There was manifest a brooding magesty, a somber loftiness. Undubitably. He saw farther, felt more keenly, probed the mysteries of his recognized universe more deeply by eons than all the lesser minds of his realm, which, of course, in saying doesn't say much. But let that not diminish his lofty sageness, for a prime and well recognized perquisite of his profession was the vastness of those hours during which his mind could delve undisturbed into dim channels of thought where only brave, probing minds dare venture.

"A herder ought to be listened to," he'd say, sounding his usual negative evaluation of the human family's attention to weighty matters. His neck would elongate out of his flannel collar as he spoke, signaling that his mind was rising from one of those dusky channels.

"Why's that?" I'd say. I was turning fourteen and smart.

"Only the family idiot would ask," he'd say with condescension and pretended disgust. That wisdom spoken, his neck would recede back down into his collar and the mental searching into the depths would begin again.

"Only the family idiot . . ." I'd chirp under my breath, mimicking in my private chipmunk language, which, of course, only I could understand.

It would remain quiet for a time, with only the intermittent buzzing of a white-tailed, black hornet and the lazy snort of a browsing pony giving evidence of life. And then those brooding eyes would narrow again, the royal spine would adjust itself against the white trunk of a quickum aps (that's a quaking aspen), and the neck would begin to rise; a comment was forthcoming.

"A herder's life isn't appreciated," he'd say, keeping to his theme.

"Why's that?" I'd say, yawning and whittling a stick.

"Only the family dunce would ask," he'd say.

"Only the family dunce," I'd chirp.

"And your beds give me the back ache," he'd mutter, changing the subject to another often-expounded subject. He'd readjust the regal vertebral column as he spoke. "You could at least brush away the biggest stumps and rocks before you put the tent down."

"I'll try to remember," I'd say, gazing up into the sky, where a fluffy cloud looked like a wild horse's head. "Hey, there's a horse!"

"Gives me a day-long backache, your beds," he'd say, not interested in clouds or imaginary horses.

Now, I suppose sleeping on the hard, lumpy earth was an affront to this royal entity, and the royal spine in particular. Should the King of the Big Holes be required to bed down in league with the lowest of his subjects? In his lofty words, only the family nincompoop would condone such indignity.

But in fairness to my camp jack efforts, there were occasions when I took my tent pitching job real serious. If I happened to think of it, and trees were real handy, I'd cut tender pine boughs and lay them out arch side up for a sort of rustic mattress.

But The Herdsman would routinely respond, "You always leave the sharp ends up."

"I'll try to remember," I'd say in response, then chirp under my breath, "Sharp ends, sharp ends."

Now the above gives an idea of the content of many of our days, with conversation and activity going nowhere in particular. We just lazied away the hours as the herd went about its nibbling business, our only intervention being an occasional whistle or the instrusion of a dog, if discipline was deemed necessary. They were stretch-out-on-the-grass days, campfire and riding-down-the-trail days, with the sun on the back and mountain air feeling good in the lungs.

But on an August day, a change, like a change in the weather, stirred up our lives. It wasn't all for bad; yet, it certainly wasn't all for good. It began one late afternoon as His Highness was perched on his usual rocky throne, eyes narrowed and neck receded. Heavy thinking, maybe dozing, was in process. I'd just cut a quakey limb (that's a quickum aps) and had carved a whistle. Testing my product for loudness brought the royal neck up with a thrust.

"Go check the sour dough - the sheep salt!" That was the usual royal decree, mandating that I "get lost". But no big deal. It was always more fun making a whistle than blowing it, because sap from a quickum aps stick pretty soon puckers you up, so I threw the whistle way up in a tree to scare a bird, missing it by a mile. The Herdsman's eyes followed the arcing object until at mid-flight he stared like he'd seen a vision.

He said with a start, "they'll be coming any day now." His eyes turned north toward the Milk Creek camp ground.

"Who's that?" I said.

"Only the family imbecile . . ." He stopped abruptly and changed subjects on me as one thought reminded him of another.

"You get over there tomorrow and pick a bucket full," he said.

"Pick what?" I said. Of course, I knew the talk was leading up to huckleberries, and I knew that picking a gallon syrup bucket full was a half-day job, because those little purple-blue nibbles of fruit didn't grow in easy-picking clusters.

"That'll take me all day, a whole gallon."

"Pick two gallons."

"That'll take me two days."

I teased the dog.

"They come every year and leave their messes." The Herdsman continued, consumed in his thoughts. And I was consumed in my thoughts of picking berries all alone, too.

I said, "Remember, we saw a bear over there last year."

"Take a dog - two dogs," he said, his mind reluctant to be diverted from those Valley folk, who came up the rough, canyon road each late summer, their jolting, iron-rimmed farm wagons piled with kids and supplies and aproned grandmas and bib-overalled grampas and mamas and papas in the middle somewhere trying to keep order. Invading The King's domain, they'd clean out the crop of berries and mess the whole place up in the meantime, leaving pork-and-bean cans with jagged, opened tops, and broken bottles and cumpled newspapers. At least, that was the essence of His Royalness' annual speech. He was clearly distressed.

"How about a quart?" I said, holding to my personal interest in the subject.

"Three gallons," he said. "Take your horse."

"Three gallons, three gallons," I mimicked as the royal neck began to recede into the woolen collar. But suddenly it rose with a jerk. And this was the announcement that initiated change, for a time - too long a time.

"Mattress!" His Highness almost shouted.

"Did you say mattress? Why?" Had The King blown his fuses?

"Last year one of 'em left a mattress. I saw it! Over there at Milk Creek. I remember!"

"Well. What's an old mattress?"

"You stay with the herd. I saw it there, last year. Head 'em for Sheep Basin. Set out the salt. Get 'em there by sundown."

"But it's late and spooky - where're you going?"

"Only the family dunce . . . " His words were lost as in an easy motion he swung into the saddle and in a moment he and his pony had disappeared down the aspen and pine-crowded trail toward Milk Creek, two or three miles off in the north.

The sun was only the width of my hand from the mountain horizon, those high, gloomy summits above Sheep Basin in the west. Long shadows were reaching out and I began to feel that cold gloom I always felt if I were left alone. I could never figure it. One minute, when The Herdsman was close by, scowling as he looked over his kingdom and muttering at me, for want of something more entertaining to do, those long, velvety evening shadows were peaceful and comforting. They'd give the canyons and forest a tired look, and I'd begin to think of the campfire and sitting on a log in front of the tepee eating those nice things we had brought in the saddle bags from the cook tent. But The Herdsman rides away and all at once I'd get edgy and those long shadows weren't comforting at all; they looked like creepy fingers reaching out to grab me.

Adding to my gloominess, I began to hear this little mountain bird that starts calling about sundown for somebody who's lost. "Pheeether," he kept calling in a very tired, sad little voice. "Pheee-ther". My gloominess turned to scariness. I felt lost like poor old Pheeether.

I turned my horse toward the Packsaddle Canyon rim to head the sheep toward Sheep Basin, which seemed dismal and haunted to me now. Then I heard this hollow whistly sound up in the sky and looked for one of those little night hawks with the light stripe across its dark underwings. "Whooo." The Herdsman said these birds dart around in the evening, up high, looking for bugs, and when they spot one buzzing along below they dive for it and when they open their beaks for the kill, they make that hollowish sound. "Whoooo!" I wasn't convinced of that. It seemed to me that I heard a lot more "whoos" than I saw hawks.

Once on the rim I whistled at the sheep, softly. I wasn't going to let every bear in the territory know I was up there by myself. The ewes on the edge of the herd, which was spread out over Packsaddle Flats for at least a half-mile square, looked up startled, then seeing who it was, and knowing what the whistle meant, turned about toward their feeding mates. The muttons must have sensed it was nearing sundown and I guess they were beginning to think of the salt troughs and the bedding grounds, so, nibbling as they moved along, they began to make their way toward Sheep Basin.

Feeling a scary loneliness, it was like I was the only human in the universe, up there on the rim. I could see in one glance the high Tetons standing on the far, east side of Teton Valley, the late sun in their faces. And in another glance I could see Packsaddle Lake, far down at the head of Packsaddle Canyon, two or three miles to the west. Dark shadows had made the marshy edges of the lake indistinct, but there was enough of that eerie sky glow on the water to identify where it was. I thought of those greenish, clouded depths and remembered that The King declared the bottom of the lake had never been discovered - maybe that it had no bottom. One glance at the ghostly glow was enough for me.

Turning my horse down off the rim, I suddenly heard a drumming in the forest. I felt the skin crawl and quiver along my spine. Then I remembered His Royalty saying this was only a mountain rooster drumming his wings, defending his territory. But The King didn't know everything. It sounded spookier than a rooster to me.

It took the herd most of an hour to converge upon Sheep Basin. The animals would peer into the opening, smell the salt in the troughs and trot in for their evening treat. I built a fire as the animals sniffed about for their bedding places, dropped to their foreknees, folded their rear legs under them and settled in for the night. I untied the longhandled, black, frying pan from the rear of the saddle, took from a little can in a saddle bag a bit of mutton fat and greased the pan with it, then leveling some coals on the edge of the fire, I put the pan on. After cutting off the skinned neck, legs and wings of a mountain hen and then splitting the little carcass down its backbone, I dropped the pale pieces of flesh into the pan. I always kept my hunting knife handy in its belt scabbard for just such things.

"Isn't it against the law?" I'd said when the King knocked the wild fowl off a log with a .22 rifle slug earlier in the day.

"Skin it." he'd said, with no other comment. Wasn't he The Royal Entity hereabout? Of course. Who was I to question?

"But I don't know how to skin it," I'd said.

"Only the family dunce . . . " I skinned and cleaned the bird.

"Save the liver and gizzard." he'd said.

"This?"

"That's the kidney!"

I put a kettle of water on the coals and then dropped two sourdough biscuits, halved, into the frying pan to toast beside the sizzling fowl. The chicken and the biscuits browned nicely. The smell began to reach out, but it couldn't crowd away the gloom. The dusk was deepening, even though the sky was still bright. I'd turn the chicken and biscuits then climb on my horse and wait. Pretty soon I got down and moved the pan and kettle off to the side of the fire, close enough to keep them warm. I climbed quickly onto my perch again, feeling guilty, but more comfortable. Darkness began to come down and the first stars began to blink.

Finally, The Herdsman's dog came racing out of the forest like he hadn't seen me for a year. I climbed down quickly and undid the cinch. I didn't want to be seen roosting.

"Take down the tent!" a voice came from the trail.

"What for?"

"Don't ask. Smooth a place for the mattress."

"Mattress?"

The Herdsman came into visibility like an apparition. He supported the rusted-spring remains of an ancient mattress on his shoulders and neck, balanced by his large, muscley arms. His pony was tethered to the rear of the mattress and it followed along cautiously. I could see the horse's eyes glow red with the fire light, and the mattress and the animal's flank showed crimson as the apparition neared.

We spread the tepee over the bed springs, and to celebrate, we laid out our woolen quilts on top of the tent. Tonight we'd sleep under the stars.

So, after eating we reclined, watched the heavens twinkle bright and sharp and heard coyotes wail and yap up on a nigh, lonesome ridge. The dogs drowsed near our bed. In the glow of the fire I could see their ears lift occasionally as they picked up quiet forest sounds. The deep clang of the horse bell sounded down near a little stream as the ponies browsed. And a higher-pitched sheep bell rattled as a ewe shook her head. The bed springs squeaked and The Herdsman sighed and sighed again, and again and again. And I sighed, too, for my gloom had mysteriously lifted.

"The chicken was good. Good."

"You shot it."

"You cooked it."

"Goodnight."

"Goodnight."

For a week we slept out under the sky. It took a night or two to get the hang of resting on those rusted springs, for the bed seemed unstable, too soft, after all those weeks of bedding down on the hard earth. But pretty soon I found myself smiling as I pulled up the covers. The squeak of the metal coils became comforting.

It was the moving of the mattress, though, that got a bit sticky. It was no kingly exercise. We tried balancing it on the packsaddle and lashing it down; we attempted using poles as skids; we lashed it to the packsaddle alongside the horse; we even gave a try at each of us holding a side of the mattress as we rode our ponies. But we found all methods to have serious flaws. Mountain trails were seldom wide enough, or smooth enough, to permit passage. The exercise, frankly, became a royal pain. Tepee moving got all bogged down in tree chopping and detouring. And camping on one bedground for two and even for a very illegal three nights became common.

"What if the ranger comes?"

"Don't ask."

"Well, we camped here the last two nights."

"Go check the sourdough."

In the meantime I'd gathered my gallon of huckleberries. It took two hours of furious picking. I tried to fill the bucket while sitting in my saddle, but the bushes were too low for that, so I'd get off my horse, pick like fury and then jump back into the saddle to look around and listen, expecting the worst, it staying in my mind that grizzly bears liked huckleberries very much. Notwithstanding, I got the job done, picking a few too many unripe ones and getting too many leaves and sticks in with the fruit, but I did it. And, can you believe it, just as I was riding away from Milk Creek, here came a wagon up from the Valley, loaded as earlier described. The huckleberries had come.

Now, for a long time I'd pestered The Herdsman about riding over to explore the abandoned Brown Bear Coal Mine. The word was that the still-open tunnel led through the inky blackness nearly a mile into the mountain's heart and that the old rusty mine cart could still be pushed all the way to the head of the mine, that is, if the unstable tracks were cleared occasionally of fallen rocks and dirt. There were abandoned cabins, too, a real ghost town, just waiting to be explored. Well, one day His Royalness agreed, so while the sheep were in their shade we rode over, five or more miles from our camp, up in the south fork of Horseshoe Canyon. It was an adventure, creeping along the mine tunnel until the entrance looked like a dim speck of light far in the distance. And I found some nice things in the tumble-down, log buildings, like a nicked-up butcher knife with its handle rotted away and some colored chalk in the single-room school building.

But suddenly, as I was rummaging through the classroom, The Herdsman's voice came from a nearby grove.

"Hey!"

"A bear?" I hollered.

"Buggy wheels! Right here!"

Buggy wheels. He didn't have to say more. I knew what was coming. And I knew our lives would change again with that call. I looked out the door to see the man gloating over these tall, narrow wagon wheels, still connected by their axle. The bottoms of the wheels were buried six inches in the dirt.

My exploring came to a quick end, for we must begin immediately pushing and pulling those wheels all across the mountain. How we accomplished it, I can't fully comprehend, but using halter ropes as towing lines we somehow managed the ups and downs and stumps and boulders and a hundred other obstacles, but finally we drew the wheels up beside our tepee. It had taken us two shade-up periods, two days, but at last, there it stood, and in one more day we had built a sort of a frame on top of the axle, mounted on the frame the mattress, and secured on top of the mattress the tent. The contraption had two long poles extending forward from the frame just like a one-horse shay. The pony was to stand between the poles, the ends of which were to be attached to the saddle horn by rope, and then, in theory, the driver would sit in the tent door, hold the reins and drive that monstrosity all over the mountain. In theory.

A real dream!" gloated The Herdsman. "A Sheepherder's Dream!" The name stuck. The creator walked off to the side and sized up his creation, then walked off to another side.

"How you going to move it?" I said.

"Only a dunce would ask," he said. "You'd never understand."

Well, I understood enough to know that The Sheepherder's Dream, sitting up on its wheels like another wierd apparition out of a ghost story, with no brakes and as rickety as a wired-together vehicle could be, was sure to encounter a hazardous life. And I was right. Totally right, for moving the tepee became a new and serious occupational hazard. For instance, if, in transit, a wheel collided with a rock or stump, the opposite pole (attached by rope to the saddle horn) would slap the already nervous pony a vicious whack in the ribs. So a runaway was always on the verge of happening. And if the mobile bed was pointed downhill enroute, the Dream, again, having no brakes, would ride hard on the pony's rear, to say nothing of the circumstance of The Herdsman, who, perched smartly at the door of the tent, suddenly found a horse tail in his visage. Disaster was constantly on the lurk. I knew it would be.

But not wanting to paint an altogether bleak picture, I have to say that on a nice night, if the Dream were properly achored, and leveled, back and front and side and side, it made a nice experience from dusk till dawn. But faulty anchoring and leveling, which was usually the case, was murderous. It resulted in tilting, feet high, or head high, or inclining to the side, resulting in high apprehension and no sleep. But those were relatively peaceful, non-threatening experiences. I hardly dare describe the night when, after I'd anchored our sleeping quarters to a sage bush, a storm came howling down across Packsaddle Flats. The wind and rain screamed in, converting the Dream into an absolute nightmare. It took only two or three of those gigantic wind blasts before our moorings pulled free, turning our wheeled bed loose to fly across the mountain. The Sheepherder's Dream became a bucking bronco as it gained speed through the darkness. The ghostly tent flew down the Packsaddle Flats, bounding over whatever it encountered, lurching and tilting first forward and then backward, tossing its horrified passengers about inside as rag dolls. For want of something to cling to, I grabbed a woolen quilt, and lucky it was, for when we, in due time, and it seemed like an eternity, were pitched out the door into the storm, the quilt gave me some protection from the downpour and the cold. But, to its credit, the wheeled tepee held to the Flats, more or less. It didn't fly over the Packsaddle Canyon rim. Even now, that possibility gives me the horrors.

Next morning we found the Dream, miraculously still intact, in a little forest grove, where we found the herd. The animals had left the open bedground for shelter, just as our tent had done.

"Next time, tie it down. Alright?"

"I'll try to remember."

"I'll tie it down, alright. I'll chop it down," I added in my best chipmonk talk. I'd had enough of The King's dreams. Thereafter, if there was the slightest cloud in the sky, I'd take my quilt and sleep with the dogs. Even marauding bears couldn't get me into that death trap again.

But I didn't need to chop it down. The Dream, or Nightmare, didn't need my help. It was only about a week later when The Herdsman left me with the sheep at sundown and rode off to bring in the tent. I wouldn't move that threat to life and limb for the whole mountain.

I waited, scared again, built a fire, and put on mutton steaks and pork-and-beans and some biscuits. It got dark, cloudy dark. Everywhere I looked I could see eyes glaring out of the forest at me, so I sat on my horse and listened to it thunder way off in the southwest over the Elk Flat Range. Finally I got brave, uncinched, spread the saddle blanket out for a cover and lay down, using the saddle for a pillow, like in the song The Herdsman often sang. But it wasn't the way the old ballad says. So I got up and sat on the saddle near the fire.

The thunder rumbled louder and the wind began wheezing through the pines. But before the rain came, a dog bounded into the clearing, leaping up and licking my face. The Herdsman soon appeared, leading his horse. The crimson glow of the fire showed on the white tepee, which was draped over the saddle.

"Where's the Sheepherder's Dream?"

"Don't ask."

"Went down the mountain, huh."

"Like a crazy, bucking mustang."

"I'll clear the rocks away."

We cut poles and pegs and put down the tepee.

"How did you find the tent?"

"Lucky."

The corners of the tepee, where it had been anchored to the mattress, were badly torn, but the sides and bottom were fairly intact.

So we sat in the tent door as it began to rain. We ate pork-and-beans and mutton and sourdough biscuits and drank from the canvass bag.

"The ground's not so hard as I remember," said The King as we retired. "No stumps."

"It's solid."

"Nice beans and mutton. Goodnight."

"Goodnight."

8

Rugs

It was mid-May, late afternoon, when Henry Rugsdale made his appearance, following the Clementsville highway down across the river bridge into Teton Basin. And an unusual appearance it was. He sat in the doorway of his canvass-topped sheep wagon, reins in hand, clucking encouragement to his piebald horses, which stepped along the gravel surface gingerly, for their hooves, worn and sore, bespoke of too many hours on the road. Hitched behind this readily-recognizable sheepherder's home, with its black stove pipe protruding upward from the forward quadrant of its rounded top, a small, iron rimmed, two-wheel trailer jolted along. It supported a chickenwire enclosure. Behind the trailer, two cows, haltered and tethered with ropes, followed, showing dislike, also, for the rough road. Out ahead of the horses, a sheep dog drove a dozen reluctant ewes along. The woolly animals nibbled at the clumped roadsidegrass, as the irritating intrusions of the dog permitted. And above the jolting noise of the camp and trailer, the anxious bleating of ten small lambs could be heard. The young animals, pressed uncomfortably close inside the chickenwire cage on the trailer, passionately voiced discomfort and hunger.

Each member of the traveling party was bone tired, as Rugs finally pulled the reins at sheepman Dave Harkins' high front gate. The sturdy, pole portal served as the entrance to the broad, sweeping acres that provided the base for the Harkins livestock enterprise. Anchoring the reins around a horseshoe, nailed beside the camp door for that purpose, the traveler stepped down to the wagon tongue and over the doubletrees to solid earth. His feet appeared as tender as were those of his animals. Harkins stood near a corral conversing with two men, who appeared to be ranch hands or herders.

"Rugsdale's my name," called the stranger as he opened and stepped through the gate. "Rugs, they call me."

“Dave Harkins,” was the response.

“Sheepman, I take it?”

“I am.”

“I can tell by the smell of your corral.”

“A dead give away to a man with a nose for sheep,” the rancher chuckled. “Stranger around here, aren’t you?”

“Well, I’m hoping to change that. Nice country you have. I could look at your mountains all day.” The man spoke warmly, easily.

“We do like our mountains.” Dave glanced up toward the great peaks at the head of the valley.

“I’m looking for a place to settle, and I’ll tell you, sir, it would be the best day in a year for me and my animals if you needed a herder. I’ve got my own camp and horses, as you see, even some milk cows. I’m ready for work.”

“You do come prepared. You even have your own sheep herd.” The rancher chuckled again as he nodded toward the little flock, which rested outside the gate.

“Yes, a few ewes and ten bum lambs, as you can hear, and they’re all hungry.”

“Been out on the desert, I take it.”

“Well, I have. Traveled through, out north of Idaho Falls. I picked up some bum lambs from them lambing herds out there. You know how it is with them sheepmen. They’re glad to get rid of bum lambs. . . an old ewe has two, but can only take care of one, or the ewe won’t claim her lamb. You know ‘bout that."

“Yes, we know about that. And you bring along the cows to feed them. That’s good thinking. But, the ewes. . .”

“Well, the ewes’d been left behind, one here and another there. Wandered off from the herd, you know. That desert’s a mighty big place. I sure found that out. I figured the coyotes would get ‘em, or they’d die without water. Dry as a cinder, that desert.” The voice was just a bit tentative, evasive, Dave thought. “And they’re old ewes,” the explanation went on. “Mightn’t make it through another winter.” The response didn’t seem to fully satisfy Dave Harkins.

"So you put your own brand on them, he said, looking toward the animals.

“Well, I did, yes, my Red Diamond. Didn’t ‘spect anybody’d care about it, being strays like they was. And, ‘course, the lambs was give to me.”

Not wishing to delve further into the subject, which, obviously, was a bit delicate with the stranger, and the matter not being worth more discussion, the ranch man spoke of the day's needs.

"Well, Rugsdale, it just happens that one of my men is leaving-Simons, here; he's just telling me now. Hasn't been feeling good, and I hate to see him go. Yes, I do need a herder.

"I'd do you a good job, sir. Break my neck to."

"Well, you are ready to go. Who've you herded for?"

"I just finished five years with Michaelson, up out of Butte. You wouldn't know him. Michaelson sold out. Shipped every ewe to the market and let me go with no more than a quick 'good-bye'. But that might have been my lucky day, if you'll think favorable about taking me on. Yes sir, I think I got a good deal for you here. You take me on and you get a camp and horses and a good dog. We all come together. And, course, my cows. Now, I got these ewes 'n lambs. If I could mix 'em into your herd for the summer... and wouldn't the use of my camp and horses make that a square deal? Or we could figure it all in the mix when we settle on my wages. In the fall we can cut my animals out and I'll sell 'em off. In your big herd, you'd never know mine was there."

Dave Harkins looked toward his sheep range in the west, thought a minute, thought of the man's long speech, apparently well prepared. It was a risk, making a quick decision on hired help, Dave knew that, and there was something about this man that didn't come through solid, but then, sheep herders weren't easy to come by, and good ones were of a breed all their own. Was this one so different? Maybe not. So, Harkins nodded and an agreement was struck.

Within an hour, after he had milked his cows and fed his ravenous lambs, Rags turned his caravan about and was on his way to the spring range, five miles west. There was a wry smile, bordering onto devilishness, wrinkling his weathered face, for this unusual herder had just achieved the second in a series of his well-calculated goals. He had found a job, a good one. He had a guarantee of reliable pasturage for his fledgling flock, and this little band of sheep would grow, of this he was certain. There was genuine excitement witnessing the falling into place of his well-conceived plans.

His first objective had been to travel down to the desert from the Rawlins sheep ranch up out of Challis, pick up some orphan lambs and a few stray ewes. Being forcibly ejected from the Rawlins spring range was a minor matter, for he'd planned to leave, at his own convenience, anyway. Any loss sustained in his early departure could be chalked up to the cost of education. For he had learned, over in

Challis, Idaho, learned a lot. Butte? Rugs had never set a foot in Montana. And he knew no one with the Michaelson name. That was a story. But in Challis, he had learned to be insightful, creative. . . and more cautious in applying his Red Diamond brand.

Now, here in quiet Teton Valley, the stage was set for Phase Three of the Rugsdale plan. Rugs smiled with pride and anticipation as his caravan made its way westward. His little flock of twenty-two woolly animals, had cost him nothing but a bit of time and travel. But Rugs had time and his mobile home made of travel a not unpleasant experience. He thought of his Red Diamond branding iron and the store of essential branding supplies which were kept safely stowed inside the camp. The brand was a good deal larger than most seen and it was large for a purpose, to be explained later. In addition to the brand, the supplies included a store of red, powdered, sheep paint and an ample supply of linseed oil, a liquid which, when stirred into the powder, produced branding paint. The little flock of strays and the bleating lambs bore the Red Diamond on each of their sides and a third one on their backs, between their hips. The poor lambs were hardly large enough to provide the space needed on their coats for the three brands, which, again, were unusual in size and in the number of applications, all for a well-conceived purpose.

It was a fine spring. Early, soaking rains had come, and now, under the warming sun, Rugs found forage on the range to be as high as a ewe's knees. He drew his camp up beside a bubbling stream, hobbled his horses and cows, setting them out to graze, and with a wider, wrier smile, drove his ewes toward the grazing, Harkins herd. For the protection of the tiny lambs, he constructed a corral of chicken wire beside the stream.

Heaven smiled upon the man. He saw his future clearly. Come autumn, if the Rugsdale goals continued to fall in place, the Red Diamond would identify not a mere twenty-two, but with good luck there might be fifty, even seventy-five, bearing the brand.

Now the third phase of the Ragsdale plan fell into place as if it had been planned by a genius. As the herder assumed his duties and rode about the large flock during the day and strolled through the bedding grounds in the evening, his clever eye sought out those animals bearing the Harkins red Bar V whose brands had become indistinct by the combing action of barbed wire fences and the brushing of sage and other undergrowth. Additionally, the candidates for the Red Diamond brand must not have lambs at their sides, for the Rugsdale enterprise would go down hard if a Red Diamond ewe with a Bar V lamb at her side were ever spotted by Harkins or one of his men. It would be a dead giveaway that skulduggery was afoot and would certainly precipitate the sending of Rugs off down the road again without even a 'good-bye'. And further, Rugs must not rustle a mother and her offspring, for his own ewes were strays with no lambs, and his lambs were orphans. The boss understood that peculiarity. The Challis experience pointedly forewarned him of these business hazards.

But these were only trifling inconveniences. It would not be an easy task to come up with those limited candidates for the Red Diamond brand, but Rugs was aware, as is every sheepman, that in a big herd, a number of animals would not have borne offspring, and there would be a number whose infant lambs had not survived. He would just have to take the time required to seek them out; and, of course, a herder is not without an abundance of time on his hands.

As could have been predicted, these impediments hardly turned out to be impediments at all, for not a week had passed before Rugs had swung into his saddle one evening, lasso swirling above his head, and had brought down the first of sixteen, which would soon bear the Red Diamond. He cleverly combed out the faint Bar V with a useful currycomb before applying the new brand. Rugs had discovered, and this was also learned in the Challis experience, that by applying a bit of dusty soil to the damp brand, the freshness of the marking would not be nearly so obvious. And how completely the Red Diamond covered any remaining trace of the Red Bar V! How thoughtful to design such a large brand and to apply it on both of the animals' sides. It made no difference at all that the Bar V was applied to the sheep's left ribs. Dave Harkins would have to be a magician to detect the work of the wily Rugs.

Now, Rugsdale had reasoned that, for now, his rustling should be concluded with these sixteen. If he overplayed his hand, someone, either Harkins or one of his sheep wranglers, might become suspicious of the growing number of Red Diamonds, even in a herd of two thousand. At cut-out time in the fall, with the additions to his flock, he would have to figure a way to keep the number of his ewes from suspicious eyes, but he had all summer to think of that. On the other hand, Rugs reasoned, why couldn't he just stay on with the Harkins outfit through the winter, just leave his ewes mixed with the big herd and in the spring come up with a means of quietly cutting out his animals and trailing them out to the Rexburg market? The wry smile grew even wider.

It was during the early weeks of his employment that the first unexpected bonus in Rugs' plan fell into his hands. The brand had hardly dried on the sixteenth Harkins ewe when, one morning, another sheep herd appeared on the spring range adjoining the Harkins acres. It was a smaller band, perhaps five hundred in all. A strong, netting wire fence separated the two ranges, effectively keeping the two herds separated; however, there was a gate, securely locked, but surely openable. And Rugs noted quickly that the neighboring herd often bedded near that portal, and even more notable, the herder, after settling his flock down for the night, often rode away for an hour or two. Rugs observed, too, that these animals were yearlings, had no offspring, and that their brand was a simple red dot above the hips. This thievery would be so elementary, it would hardly be interesting!

Within another week, on a moonless, late evening, after the neighboring herder had ridden away, eleven yearling ewes were eased through the gate into the Harkins range. Eleven of five hundred. Surely, the good neighbor would not miss this insignificant number. The lasso was busy the next evening and the Rugsdale woolly assets grew in number to forty-nine!

By this time the infant lambs in the chicken wire corral had matured in age and strength to a point that they could sustain themselves foraging with the herd, so Rugs turned them free. However, for several days the little animals refused to leave the camp; they were always underfoot when the herder stepped out of his door. But within a week they grew accustomed to their freedom and only pestered him at the normal evening feeding time.

In due time, about mid June, the herd was trailed to the summer reserve, high in the Big Hole Mountains, where they would remain until autumn. Rugsdale followed the sheep up into those high ridges with the heart of an entrepreneur, a man of property. He took great delight as a woolly beast, bearing the impressive Red Diamond, came within his view. And he delighted in his dozen lambs, thriving now on the abundant mountain feed. In the fall he would market them, and the lamb price, so Dave Harkins had said, was holding strong.

As summer wore on, another amazing quirk of happenstance occurred. Henry Rugsdale was bowled over again by his good fortune. Now, it had been established that the high crest of the Big Hole mountain chain would serve as the boundary between the Harkins range, which faced Teton Basin, and the Ted Willison range, which sloped from the high ridge line into Snake River Valley. It was not usual that herders from those sheep operations would ever encounter each other, for their allotted territory, covering tens of thousands of acres, did not lend to time-of-day neighborliness. But on this bright August morning, as Rugs was heading his flock on the high watershed above Horseshoe Canyon, what should he see but upward of fifty muttons, bearing the red W, the Willison brand, foraging over the crest of the mountain onto the Harkins range. The herder spurred his horse to the high ridge to permit a view down the opposite slopes. He could easily see Ashton and St. Anthony and a bit of the hazy, lonely desert over which he had traveled months before. But the Willison herder or the Willison herd? Nowhere were they to be seen. These fifty sheep, then, had strayed from their herd onto the Harkins side of the mountain.

And there was not a black sheep among them! If these had included a black sheep, Rugs would have been skittish about directing them into the Harkins herd, for which herder, on the mountain range, doesn't count the black sheep in his flock each morning as the animals leave the bedgrounds? Most sheepmen maintained a ratio of about one black sheep in ten or fifteen. Consequently, if a black turned up missing, the herder was into the saddle and riding the range, for one back sheep likely meant many white ones had strayed, too.

It was a happy day for Rugsdale, even though the straying band numbered, not fifty, as he had supposed, but eight ewes and fourteen nearly-grown lambs. And by this season, the offspring had little need for their mothers, having been weaned. Adding them to his flock would pose some risk. Of this Rugs was aware. But the Willison brand was tailor-made for changing, and up on the high, wooded range, wouldn't it be unlikely that Dave or a visiting supply man would notice the growing number of Red Diamond brands? It was obvious that the Challis experience was dimming somewhat in Rugs' mind. The glow of success and greed can dim many things.

The acquisitions were made. And Rugs was running low on paint. With a light heart, he marked in a small notebook an X for each addition to his flock. His livestock enterprise had now grown from a dozen nondescript ewes and ten 'bum' lambs to seventy-one head!

How far he had come in so few months! A year ago on the summer range up out of Challis, he had dreamed of such success. It was then that he had begun to plot the future. He had made his mistakes during those days. But not this time. After the sale of his lambs in the fall, the wool shearing in the spring, and then the sale of his herd at the Rexburg auction, Henry Rugsdale would have a bank account! He would have MONEY! And then he would head for the desert again for more bum lambs and strays!

"Now Dave," said Rugs as fall was coming on and the sheep were soon to be trailed out of the mountains to the fall range, "I'd be much obliged if I could leave my ewes with your herd through the winter. I'd like to cut out my lambs in a couple of weeks and take a few days off to sell them, then I'll come right back and go to work again. You can figure the cost of winter feed for my animals in settling my wages. I know you'll be fair, like you've been all summer." Dave Harkins accepted the deal, for Rugs, he felt, had been dependable, and the man, having some personal interest in the flock, had incentive to continue that dependability.

Then suddenly, the first dark cloud drifted across Rugs' bright sky. The herd had just been trailed down to the fall range from the Big Holes, and before Rugs could find an opportunity separate his lambs, and take his days off, Dave Harkins appeared one early morning with an Ogden, Utah buyer. The herd was corralled, the lambs cut, and as Rags was dispatched to trail the herd of ewes back to the fall range, the rancher and the Utah visitor struck a deal. The lambs were sold.

Poor Rugs, suspecting the worst, was in a state of mental exasperation when Harkins drove out to his camp to tell the news and deliver the check.

"Well, Rugs, we made a good deal," Dave said, pleased with himself. "We got top dollar for our lambs, so I sold them all. And since I was pushed to make the deal on the spot, I thought you would accept for your ten lambs the per head average weight of the whole herd. And at that sale price, you did just fine. I didn't count your animals, just figured the number you gave me when you came on last spring. I wrote the number down at the time. Ten, it was."

Ten lambs? With the Willison strays, Rugs owned twenty-four lambs. But he was cornered. There was nothing he could do about it. The rancher had remembered the number well. There could be no bargaining. The herder was beside himself as the Harkins drove away. Why had he told Dave the precise number of his bum lambs? Now Harkins would reap the profit from Rugs' work! He could not claim the Willison lambs without tipping his hand!

So, autumn and winter came on and Rugs, agitated over his loss, spent hours planning the recovery of his assets. But he did have a guarantee of bed and board for the winter for himself and his ewes. All was not lost. He settled back, endured the cold months, hauled tons of hay each day, spread the feed out on the snow-covered grounds for the animals, and in the evenings warmed his feet by the blazing fire and brooded.

Now, Dave Harkins was a rancher who didn't fix anything that wasn't broken. In other words, if a herder did his job, kept the woolly flanks well rounded with proper feed, and looked out for predators, he could be assured the boss wouldn't meddle, so winter passed and spring came without incident. However, one day, when Dave visited the feeding grounds, he startled the herder with the comment,

"I swear, Rugs," he said, "how many of those Red Diamonds are there in the herd? Everywhere I turn I see one."

"Mighty important little flock, Dave." Rugs said quickly. "A dozen of mine can look like a hundred. I wish I had that many." The jocular words headed off the conversation, and the suspicion, apparently, for Dave said no more.

Now, during those winter months, Rugs became anxious to leave the valley. With lambing season coming on, more risks would have to be run, for his ewes would bear lambs and the herd would be under closer scrutiny.

But heaven smiled. By occasional deft maneuvers, the Red Diamond ewes were kept well dispersed, and lambing days passed uneventfully. It was a great relief when the big herd was trailed out to the spring range. The early May days were pleasant and lazy, giving Rugs ample time to plan his departure from the Harkins outfit.

But how was he to separate his muttons from the herd and get out of the valley without subjecting his enlarged flock to questioning eyes? That was the subject of much pondering as he rode the sage brush hills. In time, however, a plot began to emerge. Dave Harkins let it be known that before the shearers were scheduled to come, he'd be away for a few days to look over a herd that was for sale in the Star Valley, Wyoming country. The plan was clever: Upon the boss's departure, Rugs would announce an emergency which would demand that he leave the valley for ten days. He'd quietly cut his animals from the herd, put his little caravan in motion again and head for the auction corrals in Rexburg. At ten miles a day, he could make the run in less than a week. He'd keep to the open, unfenced country, up slope from the Clementsville road. Once a member of a shearing crew, he would apply his skill in the evenings along the way and carry the shorn fleeces in wool bags, which he would bring along in the trailer. It was early to shear in the temperamental Teton spring weather, but the risk wouldn't be great. Once in Rexburg, he'd pocket his profit, and head for the desert

"A thinking sheepherder is a dangerous man" said Dave Harkins on an occasion. "Especially if his thought track is crooked. He's just got too much time to let those brain cells bubble." If Dave had only known how prophetic those words were!

It was two days after the sheep rancher left for Star Valley, that Rugs separated his little band and directed his caravan up over the northern tail of the Big Holes, above the Clementsville highway. The day before, he had announced an emergency to the busy foreman, and with the help of his replacement, a recently hired herder, he cut out his flock. There were no informed onlookers. Heaven smiled again.

The days were cloudless. The little band of sheep thrived on the fine, tender feed, and the herder found sufficient open, unfenced fields to rather leisurely make his way toward Snake River Valley and Rexburg. He honed his shears and had begun, in the evenings, to relieve the ewes of their coats. Soon, one large woolbag was filled and was lashed to the small trailer. A second was soon roped to the rear of the first. On the day when the unusual procession began to drop downward from the high hills toward Rexburg, the shearing had been completed. Another two days would find him at the auction corrals. He was on schedule.

But on the fifth day of his journey, a morning which dawned so bright and clear, all hades broke loose. After making good progress until in the afternoon, Rugs noted that the wind was picking up and mare's tail clouds began to reach out across the sky. Finding a camping site on a barren hillside, the herder pulled up, unhitched and determined to settle in for the night.

Out across Snake River Valley the sky darkened and the wind came in irritably. Over the unprotected hillside it raced, cooling and strengthening as it turned from the south to scream in from the northwest. The little flock took to the shelter offered by the camp, but with the eddying gusts the protection was inadequate.

As evening fell, a cold rain began to spike downward. The sheep huddled against one another for protection, not accustomed to the harsh cold, their coats newly removed. By sundown it was snowing. The wind had become frigid, making of the hillside a whited-out terror. Henry Rugsdale couldn't have seen a yard ahead had it been daylight. As he tethered his horses and cows on the leeward side of the camp, he found that the sheep had vanished. He trudged out a hundred yards, but afraid of losing his way, he struggled back to safety. His sheep had run with the storm to find protection. A search for them would be hopeless until the fury passed.

By morning, the clouds had cleared, leaving a foot of snow smothering the hills. Rags looked over the white expanse, but his flock could not be seen. He did observe some mounds in the snow, appearing as low, covered boulders, off in the south, where a fenceline stood as a lone barrier on the broad hillside. With apprehension, the herder rode southward. He remembered the advice of the Teton Valley men. Shearing before June was risky, they said. But Rugs wanted the wool shorn before he reached the Rexburg market. He had taken the chance, and he had paid. He knew it as he pulled the reins at the fenceline and dismounted. He kicked a mound of snow and uncovered a newly shorn, wooly back. The Red Diamond herd, the entire flock of ewes and spring lambs, eighty-three animals in all, lay lifeless in their white graves.

Rugs waited until noon, hitched and began his way down the hillside, heading for the wool market in Rexburg. The next day his caravan, sheepless, made its way toward the desert west of Idaho Falls.

9

Hereby and Wherefore

There used to be a small frame house out south and east of Driggs on the Chapin road. It resided comfortably on its lot, which lot featured the usual vegetable garden in the rear and on the sides and front of the dwelling a sort of lawn, all in harmony with the bulged screen of the front door and the peeling of paint off the eaves, which with breeze or storm became dislodged and wafted downward as large, gray snowflakes.

This humble haven was the rented residence of one Elberta Wingate, well known across Teton Valley as an individual whom a local might describe as possessing a considerable presence, which manifested itself in a prying, penetrating eye, a somewhat pronounced bulk, and a voice that cut through, rose above, and/or forced aside. One might be inclined, as some have been, to reach out with sympathy in the woman's behalf, reasoning that this bristly exterior was the natural consequence of shouldering life's burdens by one's self. Of course, in reaching out, one risks reaching too far and discovering that back in those days of yore, her spouse, Ben Wingate, bless his memory, was said to have held his ground with some quavery, living out his days, as one might say, under the threatening axe, and actually may have relished his demise.

But those speculations aren't our business and they don't matter. Our concern is only of the widow as she was at the time of our story and of the house for which she had paid monthly rental faithfully for the dozen years of her occupancy. She had not missed one of those 140, some odd, payments. Each month an envelope, bearing her check, was addressed to the faceless name of C. Smithers Smith, the thought of which had created in Elberta's mind all sorts of evil images. This entity, Smith, attorney at law, resided somewhere down in the unfathomable catacombs of Los Angeles. What business he had owning an insignificant residence clear up there in little, rural Chapin, who knows, and for that matter, who cares. But he did and that's all that concerns us.

(For those whose inclination is to dig deeper, we can let on that rumor says he picked up the real estate in a round about way for legal service rendered, that he would have preferred cash, which he understood, but rather than writing off the account as uncollectable, he took the house, which he'd had a grudge against since, keeping it at arms length and never visiting it.) He did go to the trouble, though, to dictate a form letter and instruct his secretary to send a copy out to Chapin two weeks before the rental due-date each month. The reminder was, of course, to the point, containing sufficient herebys and wherefores to get the message across that the next rent installment was upcoming and that doom awaited if response was not prompt. That monthly nudge was enough, the absent landlord reasoned, to keep communications current and open.

But Elberta greeted these routine missles with a grunt of disdain and pitched them, often unopened, into the garbage can "where they belonged". It should be added here, however, that on a quarterly schedule for the last year or two, the message from L.A. contained an addendum:

"You are hereby advised that forthwith your monthly rental will be adjusted upward in the amount of ten (10) dollars, (sic)." (Isn't rent always raised, Smithers had reasoned.)

But upon receipt of those variations from the norm, Elberta would utter a few mumbled words about "getting my hands on that lawyer" and inscribe her answer on any handy scrap of paper. The words may have varied, but the message didn't: "You say you are raising the rent. I say no. The house isn't worth a dime more than I'm paying now. It needs fixing, and lots of it, which you aren't likely to do. You ought to lower the rent, and plenty."

And so, this prolonged feud of sentiments continued, the form letters with the hereby and wherefore advisements continuing to be no match for Chapin straight-talk. Matters, therefore, went on unchanged and months trailed by.

But then, one day, one summer, a determined stranger approached the sagging screen door. His name, Wylie. He wore a shiny, green polyester suit, and to mark him of as official, not a time-of-day person, he carried a dark, vinyl case, which, to the observer, must have concealed business papers of weighty matter. Now, this Wylie was a relisher of past-dues, a pouncer upon the deadbeat, an enemy of the overdrawn account, or as one may wish, a bill collector, who on this day had foraged out to plunder some seventy miles from his home nest of Idaho Falls. Smithers Smith had found this human bird dog in an imported volume of the Yellow Pages and had struck a deal by phone. So, here was Wylie, making for Elberta's door. The man was well organized, that is to say, he had organized in his mind an efficient file system, complete with mental tabs on responses to any stall, any deft maneuver, any story glad or sad, which he may encounter during a day of work. This man's energy was inexhaustable, his conscience non-existent, his knuckles hard, and they seemed to shake the house as he thumped against Elberta's door. There was a long pause, and the humble portal was opened. They stood face to face, two protagonists, separated by a rusty screen.

"A very nice day to you," Wylie said as though impatient to get down to the business of the visit. The words came from behind a tab in that mental file labeled, "Opener for a Pushover". But Wylie had misread. The rusty screen likely had distorted his normally precise assessment of the job of work ahead. On her part, the widow read him like a book.

"What do you want?" she asked. The question shot out like a fist to the mandible. It got Wylie's attention. A huge German shepherd, curious at the exchange, appeared at the woman's side, growled and thrust its dark muzzle through a hole in a lower quadrant of the screen. The man retreated a step, an act clearly frowned upon under the tab in his file called, "Stand Your Ground". Wylie's thoughts quickly thumbed to the mental tab called "Reconnoiters" and came up with a more genteel attack, which Elberta saw through like a clean window:

"My name is Ellis Wylie, ma'am. Mr. Smither . . .

"You're here about the rent. I thought so."

"Well, yes, I have a commission from Mr. Smi..." The German shepherd growled again and thrust it's entire head through the screen. A chip of paint wafted down and clung to the visitor's green lapel as Elberta aimed with both barrels.

"Rent. You just look at this house. Look at it. And you're here to talk about rent! Look at that paint chip on your collar. Raise the rent, you say?"

"Now madam," said Wylie, keeping his cool as he flicked the chip from his person, "Mr. Smithers has authorized me to offer you a settlement of just one hundred in past overdue rent (the amount agreed upon as Wylie's commission). That's just ten dollars a month for just ten months. We could go back at least three years. You know that." The man spoke with a condescending smile. Elberta aimed the barrels again and they boomed,

"Now Wylie, or whatever your name is, you turn around and march out that gate. Or I'll sic this dog! You tell that Smithers to fix this place up. Then we'll talk rent. Not before!" With those words, the hound forced his entire body through the screen and Wylie retreated to the gate, sputtering, his mental file in disarray. (He had no tab labeled "Elberta Wingate".)

"I'll see the sheriff . . . I'll sue! A writ - I'll get a writ! You'll hear more about this. I'll . . ." Wylie was stammering. He had lost control. The gate clacked shut behind the man, barely in time to head off the hound. The collector made a quick step into his auto, gunned the motor, roared ahead, and was not heard of again.

And so, life went on in dusty little Chapin, and with it, summer wore itself out as it always does and folks said it was the shortest and the hottest they had ever seen, as they always do, and they carried on over backyard fences about what things were coming to and "it was never like this before, and that these were the last days for sure". And the Wingate rent check continued to be sent to Los Angeles with the regularity of the clock, as did the arrival of the hereby and wherefore letters.

But on one crisp, late-September day, when the trees in backyards were sending down showers of bronzed leaves with every breath of breeze, the silver speck of a small aircraft appeared in the west sky and circled over Driggs, the slumbering county seat, looking for a place to roost. In those days, the airport in this valley hamlet was much like the rural backyards, weedy and dusty, as it saw few planes. But it did boast a wind sock, faded orange and frayed at the small end. Not only did the sock identify the quirks of breezes, but it located the airstrip, if that's what it was called.

Cautiously nosing downward, the sleek, mechanical pigeon found its homing pattern and coasted in past the sock, touched rubber, and taxied to a small ditch at the edge of the field. The door opened and the pilot appeared. He fussed anxiously as though attempting to please, as he lowered steps, alit, and reached up to steady his passenger, one C. Smithers Smith, down to solid earth.

So this was the author of the herebys and wherefores, the L.A. attorney at law, flying in, mind you, "to get that infernal thing settled once and for all". Even from the distance of Elmo's Service Station, across a ditch and a block or two up the street, C. Smithers Smith would have filled most anyone's perceived description: crotchety, thin, bilious, full of gout and creaking joints. Once down to earth he shifted his weight cautiously from one hurting foot to the other and looked out over the town as though it were the unhealthy dwelling of denizens of the dark swamp. His eagle face turned toward his pilot and then he pointed instructions across the ditch toward Elmo's. The younger man trotted on his errand.

"Rent a car?" Elmo responded to the pilot's inquiry, wiping his hands on a greasy rag as his head appeared from under the hood of a stalled auto. "No rent cars around here. You can talk to Jerry over at the Ford place. He's got two new ones and some old ones that might run a bit."

The pilot spoke up with another request.

"Rent my car?" Elmo responded. "Well now, I don't know. The wife has it up to Relief Asiety. (Relief Society) No chance of gettin' it away from her right now." The garage man's head disappeared once more, then rose up again as an idea struck him.

"Maybe Wilford, here. Yes, Wilford. Hey, Wilford, want to run this feller up to Chapin in your car? Up to Mz. Wingate's?" An eighteen-year-old climbed up from the grease pit, which was hovered over by the mechanical heap know as his automobile. The machine had no muffler, no windshield, no bumpers or fenders, and it perched rather than squatted over its wheels. The hood had been painted to depict flames searing out of the engine, but that interpretation took imagination.

"How much?" the boy asked.

"Well, how about five dollars?" the pilot responded, offering a green bill.

"Good deal," chirped Elmo. "You do it Wilford."

Wilford did it. With the pilot sharing the front, open-air seat and shouting instructions, the groaning, metal monster roared into motion, leaped the ditch and rolled to a stop beside the attorney, who looked upon the conveyance and its operator as creatures emerging from a volcano crater. Smith hesitated to touch the shivering contraption, but with the vigorous aid of the pilot and with considerable muttering and grimacing, he was deposited in the rear seat. The auto promptly trembled into motion again, gurgled as it leaped the shallow ditch once more, buzzed Driggs' main street, and headed out to Chapin.

For the attorney the ride was memorable. At the journey's end, it would have been an act of mercy to have removed Smithers by stretcher, had one been available. The pilot, with Wilford's help, gently lowered the man to the earth. The duty accomplished, the youth climbed back to his seat, turned up the bop-bop volume and settled back to wait. The pilot dusted and patted and straightened his passenger, as Smith squinted along his thin nose toward his notorious bit of real estate. He grimaced as the gate creaked open for him, and then pushing the supporting hands away, walked alone toward the steps and the sagging screen door. He paused before he mounted the steps, looked over the run-down dwelling, the struggling lawn, and the unattended trees. Grimacing again, he mounted the steps, approached the door and rapped as though his knuckles pained him. He raised his hand to tap again, but the inner door was drawn open. Elberta Wingate appeared, sized up the visitor without speaking. Smith sized up Elberta without speaking. Each awaited the other's first word.

"You're Smithers Smith," the woman said to break the uneasy pause.

"I am, madam. And you are Mrs. Wingate." The German shepherd showed its head as the attorney spoke. The man shifted his weight again from one ailing foot to the other. It was obvious he suffered. He placed a hand against the door frame for support, closed his eyes and Elberta noted a tremble in his lips. Smithers looked up pitifully.

"Oh, madam," he muttered, "may I come inside. This gout is a curse." He moved toward the door. "I must sit down. Just for a minute." Elberta was caught off guard. She hesitated, then pushed the screen door open, brushed the hound aside, and C. Smithers Smith hobbled into the interior of his own real estate.

In the sitting room, Elberta directed the man to an ancient overstuffed chair, with crocheted doilies on its arms. As he sank into the cushions, he sighed. The chair seemed as a feather bed. The huge dog approached, bristling about the neck, cautiously sniffed the stranger's hand, and then, curiously, nuzzled its snout under the pale, thin palm and lifted it. Smithers responded with a pat of the willing head. Elberta didn't miss this unusual behavior.

The lawyer wriggled himself and leaned his head back. "Wonderful chair, Mrs. Wingate," he said, "wonderful chair. May I rest a bit before we talk about . . ." His words trailed off as he wriggled deeper into the soft cushions. "Ah," he said at length, "this is fine . . . fine." A bit of life seemed to come into the man. He patted the hound's head. The animal had remained attentively beside his chair. As the lawyer shifted his position once more, he lifted his nose in a sniff. The man wasn't accustomed to sniffing kitchen fare, for mealtime had long since fallen from grace in his life.

"My good woman, what is that I smell? What are you cooking?"

"Why, it's none . . ." Elberta was blurtin out, "It's none of your business," but the words stuck on her lips. They refused to be spoken. She fidgeted and then said very civily, "Why, it's only black-eyed peas and a bit of porkside. Nothing, really."

"Black-eyed peas and porkside," he muttered. "My good woman, do you know how many years it has been. . .?"

"Been? Since what?" Elberta questioned.

"A lifetime, a full lifetime it has been . . . my good woman, could I trouble you, could I impose on you? May I have just a bit . . . a cup, a bowl?" The woman was stupified; she was without words, so she uttered none. She stepped into the small kitchen, ladled into a bowl a helping of the aroma-producing recipe which simmered in a pot on a wood-burning cook stove. It was a spicy recipe handed down from her grandmother. The woman retrieved from a shelf a saucer and a Sunday napkin, cut and buttered a thick slice of new bread, arranged the food nicely on a tray and presented the delicacies to this bane of a dozen years of her life, this surprising C. Smithers Smith. The man sniffed the steaming vapors which arose from the bowl. The pleasant aroma seemed to penetrate his being. Elberta observed as the thin, bent man closed his eyes and inhaled deeply. The woman was touched. That tough exterior was being dashed asunder. At this moment she would have been a pushover for a rent increase. Smithers tasted, he sipped, ate, he slurped. He asked for a second bowl. The widow, smiling broadly, complied. She then disappeared into the kitchen, returning this time with a fancy saucer heaped with a triangle of dark cake capped high with white frosting.

"I hope you'll like it," she said, placing the saucer on the tray. It's another recipe my grandmother taught me."

"You are so kind," Smithers returned, "so very kind. I never suspected, dreamed of such a feast. You are a blessing to mankind, my good woman." He nibbled the cake, took a small bite, a huge bite. The man shut his eyes again, his countenance relaxed, the hard, hurting lines in his face softened.

At length, as his eyes opened, his attention was drawn beyond Elberta to a family picture on the wall. He studied, and with a start, straightened in the chair.

"They're my grandparents," she said as she observed his behavior. "The picture was taken many years ago. Bless their memory." The eyes of Smithers Smith lowered. They had become moist. He used the Sunday napkin to dab them.

"I called them my parents," he said at last in a struggling voice, "my adopted parents . . . so long ago . . ."

"You," Elberta gasped. "You're the boy . . . the young man! You're Charles! You came and stayed . . . back in Kansas! You helped grandpa on the farm . . . and we never heard from you again after they died . . ."

"Bertie!" he exclaimed. "You were the young girl who came for the summer. I lost track . . . so many years. What great friends we were. You, little Bertie! Oh, what a fool I've been, Bertie."

"Yes, what fools we are," she said.

The man arose from his chair. He could not feel the pain in his feet. He reached and Elberta responded. They sobbed in each other's arms.

10

A Tint of Rose

Maria Warren, single, a school teacher, and twenty-five (nearly twenty-six), was a transplant, an exile in a strange land, and she stubbornly refused foreign adoption. She lived with her mother up in Idaho's Teton Basin, in a well-insulated dwelling (for Basin winters have sharp fingers). In that alien valley the months from early November until nearly April were unbearable to Maria. They seemed a dreary, inhumane Arctic with moaning blizzards and below-zero temperatures, unfit for human habitation. (On one occasion the mercury actually plummeted down past an unbelievable fifty below.) The young woman saw no humor in a Basin sage's proclamation that "a Teton January must be very near to heaven, since it's obviously a long distance from the infernal heat of hell". Even during those unparalleled summer months, when petunias gave their dashes of color under windows and along front walks and garden hoses lay coiled as green snakes across backyard rows of peas and carrots and radishes, the teacher could not rid herself of a foreboding chill, a gnawing awareness, that off in the not-distant future another winter was edging closer.

For the Warren roots were anchored in that Louisiana soil which lay bordering the upper beaches of the gray and brooding Lake Ponchatrain. As evidence of their Southern beginnings, the watering hose in their garden coiled across rows of okra and black-eyed peas, alien life, too, struggling for survival in that foreign soil. It was natural then that the young teacher found comfort in reaching back to her early years, which, along life's thorny way, had for her taken upon itself a pleasing euphoria, a tint of rose. Even after more than ten years absence, Maria remained a captive of her past, and she was a willing prisoner. How could she feel a loyalty toward Teton Valley when she was of the blood and the ways of the bayous? In addition to her deep feelings for the old home, Maria bore the markings common in those from that land of moss-curtained oaks and white-blossomed magnolias: snapping dark eyes, a dignified carriage, and jet hair very becoming in her combed-back style.

That the teacher was not unattractive did not go unnoticed by one Clarey O'Brien, a single, good looking, local entrepreneurial man of the soil, whose acres were nurtured secondarily by the traditional and respected hands-on, swear-on-the-shirt type of farming, and primarily by the late word out of books, a calculator's unimpassioned projections of bottom-line, and a helpful tie with the State College's Ag Department, up north. Yes, the girl had attracted this farmer's attention. She had lifted his eyes above the furrow and the fellow had set upon a heart-thumping pursuit. But Maria was reluctant. Exasperatingly reluctant. Aunt Saddie Collings (everybody's aunt, next door to the Warrens) expressed that exasperation. At her eavesdropping post behind her front curtain, she stamped her foot and chirruped,

"My good lands, child, have you gone clear out of your senses? Why, every girl in this county would take that boy right straight if they could!" (Maria had just turned on her heel, leaving the crest fallen Clarey at her gate.)

The teacher was very much aware that Clarey O'Brien possessed a long list of those qualities which most thoughtful girls look for in a young man. Of course, the strapping farmer would be a good catch; in her rational thoughts this was an obvious conclusion. But her heart was another matter. A stubborn matter. Clarey simply was not a part of her tidy little package of rose-tinted memories. The poor fellow had been packaged in another of the teacher's little mental bundles, labeled "Idaho Cold". She had locked him inside her mental ice box with blizzards, sub-zero temperatures, and other winter miseries. In her mind he was a creature out of the frigid zone, the ice man. Maria would not admit it in words, but sometimes when her mind dwelt on her rose-hued past, the sound of his voice brought a chill, and on raw winter days when his cheeks and nose became just a bit unbecomingly crimson, she knew a life with Clarey O'Brien could not be for her.

But then, there were days when Maria would admit she was chasing phantoms, permitting a rose-tinted past to destroy her hope for happiness. On those occasions her feelings toward Clarey would moderate, especially when he'd drive up in his powder-blue Chrysler New Yorker, slide out the door in leather jacket and cream trousers, neat as a pin, holding his offering of a half-dozen red roses (for red roses against that jet hair were the ultimate touch of beauty in Clarey's smitten eyes). On those days the young man was permitted a momentary escape from her ice box and with that encouragement he walked on air. (And Aunt Saddie, peering raptly between her curtains, would twitter, "Now, Clarey! Ask her now!")

But these short flights into rational behavior were no match for that rose-hued flood out of the past. Rationality always died amongst the tender visions of tree-crowded lanes, the distinctively southern, rural home with its open breeze-way between kitchen and bedrooms and its stilts, supporting the dwelling above the damp earth. The gentle memory of the pulsing glow of fireflies in the dusk always triggered an overpowering nostalgia, and the sweet remembrance of the melancholy sunset warble of whippoorwills was always emotionally subduing.

And yet, even more poignant than thoughts of fireflies and whippoorwills were her memories of little David Chemeux-and Georgie. Yes, of Georgie. There may have been tree-crowded lanes and houses on stilts, but they were supporting cast only. Georgie was center stage. He was the star, the phantom knight. He was Clarey O'Brien's ghostly challenger, cavorting about in those distant rosy mists.

"Come on! Come on, Maria!" The teacher could still hear his voice from the Warren front gate as the summer sun burned up into a humid, Louisiana morning. "Maria! The ships are comin' in!" With sensitive little David Chemeux flying at the heels of the older pair, the children would race down the damp forest paths toward the narrow beaches of Ponchatrain, the great, mysterious inland sea. Diving chest to earth behind a fallen log and peering cautiously out over the restless water, Maria still caught her breath as she remembered Georgie's excited whispers,

"Don't even breathe! Don't move a finger! They're comin'!" Maria remembered her attempt to control the passage of her breath until she felt near suffocation. There was a tingling, frightening truth about Georgie's ships, "Blowin' full sail for Ne' Awlins" (New Orleans), with desperate pirates clinging to the towering masts and scanning the shores with spyglasses "that could spot a seed tick from here to Covington". And under the heavy planking of the decks, of course, there were captive princesses who ate pomegranates and blue mangos and sobbed as they tapped out desperate messages against the thick timbered walls of their prison. And who could question that there really were captured kings in an adjoining dungeon who listened helplessly to the secret code and then with a jangle of their chains turned their talk to wars and crowns and revenge? "Y'alls mean that ole wrecked-up raft?" That was David Chemeux, spoiling everything with his honesty. The eight-year-old gave total loyalty, but had no imagination.

For five wonderful summers Georgie had traveled down from northern Louisiana's "Shrezeport" (Shreveport) to spend the vacation months with his grandparents, who lived, from Maria's home, an easy walk's distance down the lane toward Covington. Each of these visits had resulted in a summer of summers, filled with the wonders and adventures and the heart-throbs which had combined to make of those growing-up years memories more precious even than the pirates' stores of jewels. During the dreary winter months of waiting, Maria lived for the spring morning when she would hear his first call from the gate. And now, after all those intervening years, she still listened for Georgie's voice. Just as she had clung to the truth of his pirate tales. In her heart she knew he would come again.

The young woman had been frank in sharing with Clarey her dreams of the past. But the Basin man was obstinate. He was determined to destroy the old illusions and this he frankly shared with Maria. He would bury those time-worn apparitions under a cascade of red roses. He would let the New Yorker spin its magic with evening and weekend drives to Jackson and Idaho Falls and the Yellowstone; he was certain the past could be bannished forever in the swing and sway of romantic ballrooms, in the subduing, mystical atmosphere of houses offering private, exquisite cuisine. Maria would not have time to look backward. Clarey O'Brien was determined to launch the most persuasive matrimonial pursuit the Valley had ever seen. His land had turned a profit, and he was determined to spend his bank account down to the last nickel in the campaign if that were required. For, he reasoned, what was a bank account without the girl he loved.

"Oh, if I was just young again," Aunt Saddie jawed, stamping her foot as she peeked between her curtains. "Maria Warren, I'd take him away from you right straight! That boy and all his land - let me see, at two hundred dollars an acre, that's . . . Mercy! Maria, you silly girl!" She watched the young man escort the teacher through the front gate to the waiting auto as the great crusade was launched. And it was an auspicious launching, one which gave Clarey some early signs of hope. But it was a capricious hope - warm October smiles before November cold. He drove her to a musical program at Ricks College in Rexburg, and as the Chrysler plied the road homeward and leaned into the curve at Canyon Creek bridge, Maria, without warning, moved closer. It had been a special evening. The young farmer had attended to every detail with meticulous care: his dress, the private, costly dinner following the show, the red roses, of course, and he had even planned the moonlit night.

"You're wonderful," she said, and impulsively her lips reached to touch his cheek. She felt the pleasing prickle of his shaved face, and she felt her car swerve, barely missing the rail, for the man had gone by his senses for a moment. That night the teacher's rational mind ruled.

But next morning when Clarey turned the New Yorker down her street and stepped out at the Warren gate, his eyes full of love and hope and his pulse thumping with anticipation, he saw in an instant as she opened the door that the uncertainty, the pall of sadness, had returned. (And Aunt Saddie's curtain trembled with her agitation as she noted Maria's reserve. "Mercy, girl. I'd like to shake you good!")

During that day the teacher found herself staring out the school windows, where gray clouds, broken and wind-driven, brushed the fields and then fragmenting, opened clearings of pale sky above the Tetons. Dark, irregular expanses of pine forests made of the high snow ridges great sleeping, pinto horses. At lunch hour Maria sat at her desk, permitting, in fact encouraging, her nostalgic mind to fly back again to that last summer with Georgie. Those final months in her beloved Louisiana had been times of mad abandon. The black-masted galleons had long since sailed away into the willing harbors of younger minds. Georgie had found new frontiers. He was now a burgeoning, undaunted, ultimately mature sixteen, and Maria had emerged as an energized, blooming, willowy and ultimately exciting fourteen.

With the arrival of those stirring emotional and physical changes, a new world had begun to drum itself onto the stage. That world, too, was mad, blowing in on dark wings, driving before it the foreboding, leaden clouds of 1941. Georgie's ingenious and tireless mind had lost itself in a new creation. He had assembled four wheels and an old automobile motor with steering column, brake and clutch pedals still intact. A seat, a gas tank, hoses, gears, and other mechanical essentials had been gleaned from back yards and refuse dumps. For weeks the boy had buried himself in a mound of books and manuals and papers. More than study them, he had devoured, consumed, poured his soul into them, emerging only to explore, in turn, every auto graveyard in the parish. That world of greasy gears and shims and couplings began to exclude Maria, but not for long. Her preoccupation with groomed nails and ringleted hair could be put aside for a time. Dressing in faded jeans and tying back her tresses, she began to win citizenship in Georgie's grimy kingdom. Of course, grease-smeared wrenches and rusty metal were repulsive to her of themselves, but she pretended to delight in them. If they were the price to be paid to permit her to be near Georgie, she would pay it gladly, grease, grime and all.

It was a notable day when the long-dead engine experienced its resurrection. At the cautious turn of a crank, there was a mysterious gurgle and wheeze. The motor shuddered into life, and from that day until the summer's end, the unusual vehicle, with its three excited passengers perched on the faded, lumpy seat, was a common and enviable sight along the parish lanes.

But as those weeks raced by, a growing emptiness began to trouble Maria. No longer could breezy rides along country lanes fully satisfy. The girl found herself gazing at Georgie through wistful eyes, which were beginning to show accents of mascara on the lashes and the maturity of plucked brows. The smell of gasoline, the tomboy ways, the Georgie-Maria-David friendship was not enough. She wanted to be the girl, Georgie's girl. The winds of change were rising across the forests and somehow Maria sensed that the old life, once so wonderfully satisfying, was rushing away. It would hever be the same.

But the changes came more painfully and abruptly than she could have dreamed. Like the ringing clang of a foundryman's hammer, a life-crumbling, numbing announcement came. Georgie's grandfather had died in his sleep. With that death, the rushing winds became hurricanes, sweeping all away. A "for-sale" sign was hung on the fence, belongings were packed, and, too soon, the boy and his grandmother stood at the bus station in Covington, bound for Shreveport. Georgie, hollow-eyed, stood silently, out of character. The prized auto had been stowed at David Chemeux's, never to quiver with life again. As Maria faced him for the last time, he stood unresponsively beside his gray-crowned and weepy-eyed grandparent. The girl's tears, held back until now, came as a wave from Ponchatrain. She gasped and impulsively grasped the boy about the neck, wetting his cheek.

"I'm coming back," Georgie muttered self-consciously, his eyes glued to the sidewalk. "I'm coming back and staying always." He followed the old women up the Greyhound steps, paused and turned toward David Chemeux. "Don't you ruin the car, David," he said. "You leave it alone 'til I get back. Don't you try to start it."

"I'll leave it," the younger boy stammered, "I won't touch it." Georgie's was not a kind remark. David, his tears near the surface, turned to Maria and awkwardly reached out to her shoulder as the older boy stepped into the interior of the bus. "I wouldn't hurt it a'toll. Maria, don't you cry. I like y'alls better than he does. All he cares about is the car."

Those churning winds, the transformers of lives, now turned their force through the breezeway of the little home on stilts, where Maria sat despondently in her lonely world. During that very week, while the hurt still pressed heavily, two young men from the little Albany church, a few miles up the road, rapped at the door. Mother Harriet Warren listened. A thirst which had troubled her since husband Tom Warren was taken, at last was satisfied, and from that day the church at Albany, crowded about with its green, creeping forest, became her refuge.

And then, within months, subject to those prevailing winds, Harriet Warren yielded to a new impulse. Another "for-sale" sign was hung on the Warren gate. Packing was done, and the mother and daughter soon stood at the familiar Covington depot, bound not for Shreveport, but to the Utah gathering grounds of those of her new Faith. It had been the week before Christmas.

In her quiet classroom, tears welled in Maria's eyes as she remembered. So far away, those wonderful scenes, but so poignant. Looking again through the schoolroom window, she saw the dark, pine forests on the mountain slopes and there came to her mind the gnarled long-straw pine which had stood in the front yard of her southern home. She remembered standing under that tree with David Chemeux on a Christmas eve.

"It's our Christmas tree," David had said reflectively, looking upward. "See the candles?" The stars, twinkling through the branches, did, indeed, appear as sparkling ornaments. "Y'alls make a wish, Maria, an' it'll come true. Y'alls wait an'see." Maria looked into the darkness of the tree. Her wish had been of the boy, Georgie. And now, after all these years, here in the lonely schoolroom, she clung to that wish. Georgie would be forever in her Christmas wishes. How could she give away that tender, first love at anyone's invitation, even Clarey O'Brien's? But then, how long since she had heard from the boy? Wouldn't such a winning, handsome young man be married long before now? Perhaps he would have children. The thought devastated her. And in his letters from Africa and England, as a soldier, hadn't his attitude bothered her? Hadn't his bit of soldier talk repulsed her? Didn't he seem to shrink back in his letters if Maria mentioned her new Faith? Would he really accept that new Faith, as Maria had assured herself he would? And now, hadn't it been a good deal more than a year since she had heard from him? Hadn't his promises to come to see her gone unfulfilled?

The weeks went by and Teton Basin's autumn faded into winter as snow began to dust back yards and fields and school grounds, and for Maria the old memories clung as tenaciously and tenderly as ever, and for Clarey O'Brien, his pursuit seemed to have reached its moment of truth. The blue car had made its turn on the Warren street each morning for a month and a red rose had been deposited in the mailbox with each trip, well insulated against the cold. ("Why, Maria Warren, what are you doing to that boy?" Aunt Saddie scolded from the seclusion of her draped window. "Why, your place looks like a hothouse with all those flowers. Now, my nephew, Charley's girl, she's real smart, and perty, too . . . Why, I've a mind to . . . ")

Frankly, Maria was becoming weary with red roses. In fact, so was Clarey O'Brien. The young man knew his campaign was going nowhere. He had become stuck, dead center, in a bed of roses. Something had to be done to revitalize his pursuit, or it was all over; his grand effort would collapse. He'd be locked in that ice box forever.

This reality jolted the farmer into a bold action. In fact, the idea had to grow on him before he could gather the courage to study it seriously. It would have been a much simpler decision if he could have fed his thoughts into the calculator, pressed the button and coldly evaluated the risks, for there would be risks. But more risks than he faced now? Probably not.

Clarey resolved that he would invite Maria to ride back to her old home over the Christmas holidays. Perhaps she would discover that her memories were only illusions. Or perhaps, in some way, Clarey could become a part of her rosy past if she could see him on those country lanes and in the old house. Perhaps he could learn to love the place and share her nostalgia. He could suggest they marry and move to the South. He could learn Louisiana's ways with the soil. But could he bring himself to sell his acres in the Basin? Could he possibly do that? He thought of the snapping eyes and the jet hair. Yes, he could sell if he must. But what if the girl should encounter this Georgie during the Christmas visit? He shuddered. Repulsive as that speculation was, it played upon him. Really, why shouldn't she confront the man? If the Georgie issue was ever to be resolved, wouldn't it have to come to a meeting with the man sometime? Even if Maria agreed to marry Clarey O'Brien, how could he manage his life if his wife kept memories of Georgie tucked conveniently away in her mind? It was a painful resolve, but Clarey concluded that he must escort Maria into "the lair of the dragon". If the hazardous venture failed, he would concede defeat. He would turn his girl back to her memories, to Georgie. "Ridiculous name," he thought, "How could she be attracted to a 'Georgie'?"

Mother Warren beamed at the invitation to go along, and Maria, after some initial reluctance, agreed that it was a good idea. And Aunt Saddie warmed quickly to the news.

"Good lands, Harriet, those were my thoughts right straight . . . I . . uh . . . I just wonder if there would be . . . would there be room? Oh heavens . . . , I'm sure not . . ?"

"That's right, Saddie, there wouldn't be." Harriet Warren was wise and forthright.

Once the agreement was achieved, enthusiasm for the trip soared, and many evenings were spent planning and anticipating. But during all the planning, Clarey did not mention his intent to arrange a meeting with Georgie.

The days passed and on schedule, one early morning, the blue charger, with its trunk bulging with baggage, raced down the highway to challenge the enemy. The trail led through Salt Lake, where the Warrens had lived until Maria's career took them to Idaho, down through Albuquerque, east to Abilene, and Dallas, and then to Shreveport. Once in that northern Louisiana town, the Chrysler drew up at a motel. Explaining that the car needed attention, Clarey went on alone, left his vehicle at a service station, walked to the near-by city library, requested a directory, and in a moment, found the name, address, and the street location of one Kendell N. Smithe. (That name had come up more than once in Maria's and Clarey's conversations.)

After the car had been pronounced fit, the Basin man drove out to the Smithe residence, which he found without difficulty. An older gentlemen, putting a golf ball on the front lawn, responded graciously as Clarey pulled up at the curb and spoke. The man's friendliness was depressing. The Idahoan had hoped, at the very least, that he might find a grouch at the address.

"O'Brien? From Idaho? Well, I'm pleased to make your acquaintance." The man's words were drawled, pleasantly southern. "Georgie? We haven't heard that name in a long time. You must have known him when he was a kid. Yes, George lives in the State, down south. He's got some land down at his granddaddy's old home, down around Covington. You'll be more likely to find him over in Baton Rouge, though. He's got an office there."

"Thank you, sir."

"You knew him in the war, perhaps? Over in Europe?"

"No, I'm inquiring for a friend of his. We're going down by Covington and we hoped we could stop and see him. Do you have his phone number?" An elderly woman, hearing the request through the open door, soon appeared and with a kindly smile stepped out on the porch to hand Clarey, who had crossed the front lawn, a slip of paper.

"An old friend? What's that name?" she asked. "You say the person lived down by Covington?"

"They moved a long time ago," hedged the young man, hoping this response would satisfy the lady's inquiry. It occurred to him now that these people would likely remember the Warrens, and may wish to see them. Bringing the girl down to see Georgie was foolhardy enough; he had no intention to subject Maria to the winning kindliness of his parents. But the woman persisted, for old adquaintances were of special interest to her.

"Who is it?" she asked, "We knew lots of folks down there. That's where I was born."

"Well . . . the Warrens," Clarey responded, feeling trapped.

"Why, Harriet! Of course! And that friend, it must be Maria! Why, we'd love to see them! You mean they're in town? Couldn't you all come by? Yes, come for dinner!"

"Well," said Clarey, fumbling, "Maybe we can drop in for a visit on the way back . . . we're sort of crowded for time today . . . That's very nice of you."

Clarey was happy to take his leave from the pair. It took some fancy verbal footwork to make a gracious departure from that winning hospitality, but he succeeded, and as he drove down the street, the man from Teton Basin took another fateful step into the fiery mouth of the dragon. Suspecting that Maria might sentence him to eternal banishment (in the ice box) for doing so, he stopped at the curb opposite a public telephone booth, and with a timorous conviction that he was doing a proper deed, his nervous fingers deposited the coins and dialed the

Baton Rouge number.

"George Smithe," he requested at a secretary's response. "I'd like to talk . . ."

"He isn't in," the girl's voice interrupted. The reply gave Clarey mixed feelings of relief and regret.

"Then could you give him a very important message?" he continued. The secretary followed with a cautiously couched explanation why this could not be done. "Then perhaps you could phone him," Clarey went on. The female agreed. "That would be very nice of you, ma'am. Please tell him an old acquaintance, Maria Warren, is down here in Louisiana and will be at her old home near Covington tomorrow evening at 4:30. Could he meet her there? The secretary responded affirmatively. "That would be very nice of you, ma'am." The nice voice responded with a question. "Well, I'm a family friend from up in Idaho. Thank you very much. Please be sure he gets the message." Clarey returned the receiver. The deed had been done. Georgie would have his chance, a much greater chance than he deserved.

Next morning, the day before Christmas, the New Yorker plied the grey ribbon of asphalt through the forested Louisiana countryside, briefly crossed the State's border to Jackson, and from that Mississippi town, raced down through Louisiana's Kentwood, and on to Hammond. Covington was just down the road. It was three o'clock as the blue car stopped at a motel.

"Mother Warren," Clarey said cautiously . . . while you're resting . . . if I took Maria down to the old home . . . would you mind? Tomorrow we can spend the entire day going anywhere you wish."

"Of course," the older woman responded quickly and understandingly to the awkward request. "I'm tired out. You go and have a good time."

"But Clarey, mama would want to be with us," Maria said with surprise.

"No," wise Harriet Warren responded firmly. "I am tired, and I'd prefer to make my visit when I'm rested. You two go on and have a good time." The woman didn't know all that was in Clarey's mind, but she did know such a request would not have been made if it had not been important to the young man.

There was little conversation as the automobile followed the highway through forests and past fields toward Lake Ponchatrain.

"Foolish man!" Clarey's brain shouted at him. "Idiot!" Why had he suggested such a trip? "Stupidity! Rank stupidity!" Challenging an opponent in his own backyard was ridiculous. What greater assurance of success could he give the man? As his thoughts tortured him, Maria was quiet, full of high emotion herself. Her eyes were glued to the window, seeking familiar landmarks as the miles to the old home passed. Trees, forever trees. She had forgotten. Beautiful, very beautiful, but she felt pressed, smothered, for the great trees often reached out over the very road itself.

"It's impressive," Clarey offered quietly.

"I don't remember it this way," Maria responded. "It is breathtaking, but I don't recognize a thing. The fields seem to have shrunken. I remember it more open, larger."

The Chrysler, slowing its speed, approached the last mile of the road home.

"Georgie's grandparents lived just . . . why, the old bridge is gone . . . it was of old weathered wood with rails, beautiful . . . now, ugly concrete. I remember . . . " Her words softened to a whisper as a faded and sagging frame house, only partially visible through the crowding growth of trees and bushes, came into view. It was vacant and the yard was deserted, appearing to have been so for many years. To the rear a collapsed, single gable of an outbuilding roof pointed askew at the sky. Standing forlornly above the tall weeds, it was the only visible remains of the shed where long ago, the teenage mechanics had reconstructed the famed automobile. The yard was overrun with the same tall weeds, impenetrable, almost. Sapling trees had sprung up all about, even very near the front door of the home. It was ultimately sad, and Maria cried.

"Let's go on, Clarey," she said. The young man had stopped the car at the front gate and was offering to lead the way to explore the grounds. "No," she repeated, "let's not. Let's go. Please." He said nothing as the motor whirred and the sedan moved on, rounding the last wooded bend before Maria's home would come into view. Clarey was apprehensive at seeing the place. He felt excluded, a stranger approaching a part of Maria's life which he could not share.

The girl's damp eyes searched about. It all seemed so different from her memories. Suddenly she gasped a startled cry. The home with the breezeway appeared through the trees. It, too, had been abandoned. The structure seemed to have shrunken downward. Gnarled, warped boards projected at unnatural angles from the roof. Windows had been broken. It appeared as if the breezeway floor had been partially torn up, for broken and displaced boards jutted upward. Clarey stopped the car at the front gate. It had been wired shut.

"Maria," he said gently, respecting her feelings, "I'll let you through the gate. I'm sure the owner won't mind. Then I'll drive down around the curve. I know you'll want to make this first visit alone. I won't be far away. Call me if you need me. Clarey's suggestion was given more from his own reluctance to meet his competitor than it was in consideration of Maria's privacy. The teacher's response was a questioning glance, but she did not object. She knew of Clarey's sensitivity to her feelings.

"Thank you," she said. As she dabbed her eyes, the Teton man glanced at his watch. It was 4:25.

The girl walked cautiously through the gate and along the weed-crowded path to the front steps. The kitchen door resisted being opened. It creaked and scraped the floor heavily as she pushed with more effort. The smell was of mice and of a stale emptiness. It was a lonely emptiness. The warmth, the spirit, that indefinable something which had given being and life to the home, was gone. The coldness caused her to shudder. It was an empty coldness, different from the physical chill of the Tetons, which can be dispelled by brisk flames in the hearth. It was a depressing and sad chill. The old kitchen stove remained. In the old days it had crackled with heat and glowed red through the vents of its damper. Now it was discolored with soot and rust. Two of its lids were missing. The cupboards sagged from the walls, split and ugly; one door hung downward from a single hinge. A bird, perhaps a rat, had gathered a nest where fancy plates and saucers once rested.

Leaving the kitchen, she found the breezeway floor precarious to step over; it was a ruin. It creaked with instability as she cautiously put her weight on the firmer appearing boards. As she peeked into a bedroom, a voice called, startling her.

"Maria, you've come home!" She turned to see a large man, handsome and kindly, entering the gate.

"Oh," she gasped."I hardly knew you!" Stepping carefully down to the earth, she ran to the fellow, threw her arms about his neck and pressed her cheek to his.

Poor Clarey O'Brien, unable to resist, had watched from the distance. A realization that he had lost the contest drained his strength. He knew the race was over. He had delivered his girl into the very arms of his undeserving competitor. He turned his back to the dreadful scene. What should he do now? Must he wait until Maria accompanied his victorious opponent to the car? That would be devastating. The man would then likely want to drive the girl away with him. Clarey shuddered at the thought of driving back to Hammond alone, defeated. And how could he bear the long miles back to Idaho without Maria. That would be some fine trip, a memorable trip, just the two, Clarey O'Brien and Mother Warren. He grimaced sardonically. The trip home could only be less endurable if the girl returned with them, outlining her future with the smug southerner as she sat hour after hour beside the noble and understanding Farmer O'Brien. His thoughts were like knife points.

The next hour was murderous. The Basin man was buffeted, pounded, devastated. He felt an impulse to charge as a wild bull and subdue this Georgie. But that would win nothing. He had presence of mind enough to know that. He could only endure, endure to the bitter end of this hour of horrors and then drift off into oblivion. He felt the emptiness and coldness that Maria had found in her old home; he was alone in an eternal void. He'd go back to Idaho, try to find meaning again in his furrows. In time, maybe a thousand years, he could put this madness out of his mind. Those furrows now seemed very bleak and comfortless, buried under the Basin's drifts.

A half-hour passed, and nearly another half-hour. He supposed the girl had forgotten him completely. But, at last, the teacher embraced the southerner once more, (and charred the farmer to the center again). The man then turned from Maria to his car, raced the motor, and sped away. That was a relief. But the fellow would be back, probably later, up in Hammond. That made sense, the Idahoan concluded. She'd want Georgie to drive away to give her an opportunity to explain, to let the jilted farmer, the jilted fool, down gently. Clarey could hardly endure this surmise. His eyes followed the teacher as she paused for a moment as though she were in deep thought. She was planning her speech to him; of that he was certain. He watched her as she turned and walked to a gnarled pine, which stood near the fence in the front yard. He wondered as he saw her pause again and look upward into the dark branches. He could not have known that she saw the early stars twinkling as Christmas ornaments through the needled limbs, and that she thought of David Chemeux' promise, given those many years ago.

She turned, facing Clarey's direction, and lowering her head, she saw him open the car door and slip inside. In the fading light she thought she saw him lower his head against the steering wheel.

Maria suddenly turned toward the gate. She hurried to the road.

"Clarey!" she called. "Clarey!" He lifted his head from the wheel. He thought he could see anxiety in her face as she approached. "Clarey!" Had she been frightened by something in the yard? Reaching the car she breathlessly flung the door open. Observing the young man's tortured face, she slid in beside him.

"Oh, Clarey," she repeated anxiously, touching her cheek to his shoulder. "I thought you might leave me. Suddenly I was afraid. You deserved to . . ."

"But, Georgie . . . that man?"

"Oh, Clarey," she purred, take me away. Fly me away from this. I found my Christmas wish. I found you, you crazy, patient farmer!"

"But that Georgie . . . what about him?" Clarey persisted. The girl smiled.

"Georgie, humph, you silly ox. Georgie at this moment happens to be eloping with his second bride. The man you saw was sweet little David Chemeux. Your phone call, my gallant, plotting sir, didn't bring the one you wanted, but he did take the time to let David know. He was good enought to do that." The dark eyes looked up tenderly. The old sadness, the tint of rose, was gone.

"Merry Christmas, my Teton knight," she whispered.

The blue New Yorker hummed contentedly back along the Hammond highway, and then, next morning, a happy Christmas morning, the car took one more circuit by the old home before it turned toward Idaho and its pleasant snow and gentle ways. And within a week, Aunt Saddie announced across the counter at the store.

"Why, do you know, they're getting married right straight!"

11

Communion

Out west of Driggs on the Bates road, Eddie Jamison's house, guarded by a low picket fence, stood as a gray, clapboard barrier at the entrance to his land. Behind that simple dwelling, a barn, small and unpainted, leaned slightly windward. It creaked when breezes played about its gables and it clattered when its insecure, corregated metal roofing became agitated with the tempests, which occasionally swept out of the west ahead of thunder and rain. Spreading beyond the barn was the Jamison plot of earth. It measured a quarter-mile on each side: forty acres. It was alternately weedy and grassy, and occasional clumps of willows gave it some variety, as did a small, muddy-edged pond and a low knoll, which lay in that order down about midway to the far Jamison border. During the spring, frogs croaked their noisy anthems from the pond, and as the weather heated up in mid-summer, dragon flies darted about above the shallow water. In the fall dark, rust-colored stalks of what the locals called Indian tobacco stood stark against the gray-green and ochre land, and impenetrable patches of Russian thistles bristled here and there along the fence lines.

Ordinary as these acres may have been, there was nothing common about them in the mind of Eddie Jamison. The quiet, unpretentious reaches of terra firma had, in a way of speaking, become an extension of his very being; they represented an inner desire for solitude, a retreat from the humdrum of life. But even more, that patch of real estate possessed a subtle ability to reach out and pluck the sensitive chords of his soul. Not that long hours of sweaty toil had endeared the acres to his heart - no, not at all. His association with the land had never been more than of the puttering, the meditating, and the feeling nature, sensitivities that were all bound up in those simple and enduring qualities which he found in his field, his very own parcel of mother earth. At a day's end, after weary hours with the county road crew, spreading asphalt along a country lane, Eddie often retreated to the rear of his barn, perched himself upon a gray and decaying stump, and communed with his land. He could sit motionlessly for an hour absorbed with the frog chorus and the softer harmonious undertones of a lapping stream, which meandered past his feet. He could lose himself in those magic nuances of change upon the field as evening slipped into dusk and then stepped down into the shadowy edges of darkness. His emotions could swell, and often did as yeast in a loaf, until sometimes he felt a lump in his throat and even a dampness in his eyes, facts he carefully kept to himself.

Now, to our story. It begins in the spring of an ordinary year and during the declining light of an ordinary evening. After eight hours in his rude and odoriforous occupation, Eddie's soul was at peace; he was seated on his stump behind the barn; he was in communion. The frogs were in full voice, croaking their hearts out down on the pond. A warm breeze, laden with the nice smells of spring, trembled the willow clumps, which were casting long shadows and sinking ito the velvety advances of dusk. A cow mooed its content over in a neighbor's farm and a bat darted as a fluttering shadow over the barn. Eddie's emotions were swelling.

But his thoughts were rudely dislodged from their reverie as a pickup truck whined through the Jamison front gate and stopped beside the house. Unseen to Eddie, a large, determined man shouldered his way out of the cab of the vehicle, walked with a heavy step to the front door of the dwelling, and thumped his fist against the paneled portal. The boisterous sounds impacted the asphalt worker as though he had been touched by an electric cattle prod. He sprang from his perch and moved, for him, with unusual agility to investigate. Before Elva Jamison had reached the door (startled by the sudden thumps, she had first peeked from a window), the big man spotted Eddie and called with a challenging voice.

"This is your land?" He thrust a hand toward the Jamison acres as he spoke.

"Ah . . . why . . . yes," Eddie stammered his response.

"I've wanted to talk to you about it. Joe Wicks is my name. I'm from out in Newdale." The man reached the corner of the barn and stepped across the stream as he spoke.

"Well . . . uh," Eddie mumbled.

"I've got a good deal I want to talk to you about," the big fellow went on, "a real good deal, as you'll see, and we'll both make some money." Jamison nodded, looked at the ground and then turned his eyes toward the barn. He found it uncomfortable to keep his focus on the demanding visitor.

"Now, I've got some equipment," the man continued, "and it doesn't pay to keep it idle. You've got some land here, good land that's not being used. The deal is, I'll plant it with spuds. We'll go fifty-fifty on the seed costs, and I'll cover the rest. My men will do the work putting in the seed, watering out of this ditch, here, and running the cultivator through 'em as needed. May take some fertilizer too. After they're picked, we'll go fifty-fifty on the sale." Eddie nodded as the man looked down on him. The nod was for want of words. No agreement was intended.

"You can call Duke Smith up in Cedron, or Ed Thomas over in Darby. I'm doing this kind of work with them - have done for three years. There's some others out in Clementsville if you want their names. They always got their money. Good money." Eddie remembered now. In his work with the road crew, he'd seen this fellow about the county with his farm machines.

"As I say, Joe Wicks is my name, lived in Newdale for twenty years. You can depend on me to treat you square." There was sincerity and firmness in the man's voice. "It's a deal, isn't it? No way you can lose." The words were not intended to be a question. They were spoken as fact, indisuputable fact. Eddie looked down at his shoe, with which he was scuffing the dirt. He mumbled and nodded. The nod was an indication that he understood; agreement was not intended.

"Now, we'll have to straighten out this ditch, here, and the brush'll have to be cleared off down there." Wicks pointed toward the willow clumps. "But that'll be no problem. The standing water down there'll have to be taken care of too, but that'll be simple to do. It'll take no time at all." The big hand jabbed the air in the direction of the little pond, and then was thrust down to Eddie for a shake to seal the agreement. Joe Wicks' agreement. The county worker mumbled in confusion. He hesitated a moment under the demanding gaze. It was obvious that the slightest objection would stir the big man's strong displeasure. Eddie lifted his hand to be crunched in the big fist. He would like to have said that he'd think the proposition over. But even if he'd found the courage to do so, he was hardly given the opportunity, for after the shake of hands, Joe Wicks stepped back across the stream.

"I knew you'd like the deal. We could clear two, maybe three thousand apiece, with no trouble." The man looked toward his truck. "Like to stay longer, but I've got to get over to Darby. My crew's there and it's getting close to quitting time. It'll be two or three days, likely, before we can get back here to your place." With that explanation, the man was gone.

As the truck motor whined its way up the road, Eddie perched himself again on the stump and leaned back against the barn. He was befuddled. His thoughts were confused. Money? Well, money had some attraction. The twice-monthly Jamison paycheck provided adequately for the couple's simple needs, but two or three thousand - that was a lot of money, and, Eddie reasoned, why shouldn't the idle land be farmed? The little man thought of his rather old car, and hadn't his wife kept the subject of a new coat in their conversation quite regularly? Two or three thousand, indeed. The appeal of money, hard cash, grew. A half-smile brightened his face.

But as the man raised his eyes, he became aware of the deepening dusk which had enveloped his land, and he saw the magic of the luminescent glow from his pond. That mystic velvet of evening shrouded his willow clumps. Eddie's real estate reached out to him. The half-smile faded. Money? Piffle. The question deserved not a second thought. What was two or three, even ten thousand dollars, as compared to that priceless communion between a man and his very own plot of earth? Root up the willows? Fill the glowing pond? Such acts would be the destruction of his own soul. The answer could not have been more clear. When Joe Wicks returned with his land-gouging machines, he would be given an emphatic "no". Eddie would instruct his wife on the answer she should give Joe Wicks, for his arrival, fortunate for Jamison, would obviously be during the road worker's absence from home. The small fellow squared his shoulders and lifted his chin resolutely, studied in his mind the instructions he would give to his spouse, and then with a look of peace, leaned back again against the barn. A bat, skittering on dark wings, crossed the glow of the pond. The peace of communion returned. And settled.

Not unusual in the Jamison custom, Eddie's wife drove him across town to the road sheds the next morning. As fence posts and telephone poles and front yards passed, the asphalt spreader felt a glow of satisfaction. He was proud of his Jamison resoluteness, for hadn't he protected his land in the very face of wealth's lure? He felt a welling affection for his plot of earth as he reviewed with his mate the firm response to be given Joe Wicks whenever the intruder's destructive machines should appear. Those groaning monsters were to be turned away. There was to be no bargaining. Elva Jamison nodded dutifully, saying nothing. Eddie repeated his instructions a last time as the car slowed and the smell of asphalt welcomed him to the day's toil. Elva nodded again as her mate stepped to the dusty roadside. Eddie closed the door firmly, squared his thin shoulders and set his jaw. He had performed his duty well, this Jamison. He watched with satisfaction as the auto muttered on its way toward the mill for a bag of chicken feed, after which errand, Elva would motor on to cousin Millie's for a pleasant hour or two of quilting. That period of time away from her watchman's post had troubled Eddie as she had announced her intent. But he conceded, agreeing that Wicks had declared his visit to the Jamison land would be in "two or three days". Eddie thrust his hands into the pockets of his bib overalls, which hung limply from his shoulders and turned to the road sheds.

"Come on, Eddie, we've been waitin' up for you!" a coarse voice sounded. The man of peace and communion, his shoulders now slumped, walked slowly toward a long, low shed.

Now, there was a twinkle of excitement and deviousness in the eye of Elva Jamison as the mill employee deposited a bag of chicken feed in the trunk of her car.

"That'll be two and a quarter, ma'am," the man said. As she clicked open the snap on her purse, Elva's mind was on her spouse. If there was one thing about Eddie that had exasperated her over the years, it was his moping and puttering over that land "that ought to be farmed or sold". She had scolded him a hundred times over the subject, but Eddie had remained firm as granite.

"Two bits, ma'am," the man corrected as Elva absently placed two bills and a nickle in his hand. Her mind was absorbed in a vision of a huge stack of bills. Money. Her eyes twinkled as she started the car and continued down the back road, her thoughts obsessed with this chance of a decade - of a lifetime. Should she call Joe Wicks and tell him to come right over with his machines? Should she contrive an emergency which would keep her away from the house on those two critical days when Wicks said he would likely be by? The little woman admitted to herself there was a meanness in this scheming, but, she justified, when the money came in after the harvest, wouldn't Eddie be pleased? Maybe at that time she could confess her deviousness to him.

But as events occurrred, Elva's scheming became unnecessary, for at the very moment when her car slowed and stopped at Millie's gate, Joe Wicks, having made adjustments in his announced schedule, stood at the Jamison door and thumped with his fist. Arousing no response, he thumped again impatiently, waited only a moment, then turned to his crew, who manned three tractors, which idled in a muttering file at the gate.

"Alright," he called, "let's get at it. Nobody's home, but we made the deal. Let's get this forty planted. You know what to do." Apparently the drivers had been well instructed, for with no further explanation, the lead tractor groaned through the gate, drawing after it a machine equipped with a broad leveling blade. The snorting behemoth rushed around to the rear of the barn and across the field toward the low knoll. The blade was lowered, and with deep gouges, the gentle rise in the earth began to disappear, leaving barren, dark swaths of new soil. The dirt was scooped along by the wide blade and spread across the shallow depression of the pond. Meanwhile a second tractor, pulling a wide, multi-disked plow, charged down a fence line leaving in its wake another swath of dark earth nearly as wide as the asphalt surface of a country lane. The third tractor was equipped with a heavy-pronged grubbing device, which it pushed toward a willow clump. Appearing as a charging, snorting rhino, it attacked the tender saplings. Torn up from the earth by their roots, the tangle of bushes was pushed to a corner of the field and stacked in a jackstraw pile. When the last clump had been deposited upon the heap, the driver doused the willows with a flamable liquid, scratched a match against his overall leg, and threw it into the pile. An orange flame leaped upward.

As that destruction progressed, a truck heaped with lumpy bags of seed potatoes drew up in the yard. Hitched to the rear of the truck was a planting machine, ready for its turn at the land. Elva Jamison and Cousin Millie had hardly finished their sweet roll and milk when the tractor pulling the leveler had scooped from the field the last vestige of the knoll and all that remained of the pond was a dampness in the soil which had been spread over it. (The weed-infested stream which had fed the pond had been dammed off at its source.) The tractor then raced about the field flattening the slightest rise and filling the least depression. This task completed, the leveler was unhitched and a ditch-making blade was attached. Cousin Millie and Elva had just relaxed to the comfort and chitchat of their needle work when the wending stream was attacked, and within a half-hour a new waterway had been gashed across the top of Eddie's land. The current, brown with the newly upturned earth, flew down the straight, ugly, steep-banked channel toward the first dark furrows of the planted potatoes, which the planter was now beginning to produce along the fenceline where the plow's disks had begun their work.

The cuckoo in Millie's mantle clock noisily thrust out its head to announce the passing of one hour after another, and the ladies had found good reasons and excuses to prolong their pleasant occupation, as the Wicks tractors groaned on to the conclusion of their project. By four o-clock (Millie had just convinced her guest that "you just as well spend the day, now"), Eddie's acres had become a furrowed wasteland, flat as Millie's new quilt on the stretcher. The county employee's beloved landscape had been erased from the planet; it had vanished under the callous, brutish power of gas and steel.

"This'll be a nice surprise for him," said Joe Wicks with satisfaction, as the tractors idled at the gate and the drivers gathered about him to look out over their work. "Nice job, there. We made something of this place, didn't we? Shaped it up good."

"Yeah," said one of the drivers, "we sure did. I burned some junk on the willow pile - an old stump out back of the barn and some other cluttery things like that."

"Nice work," Joe Wicks repeated as he turned and walked back to the pickup. The vehicle door slammed and the motor whined as the faded and soil-splotched truck led the groaning procession up the road.

"Why don't you go and get Eddie," Millie was saying. "Time you get back, Carl'll be here and you can stay with us to eat. While the men watch the ball game on TV, we can finish this."

"Alright," Elva was saying, "that's nice."

Eddie grumbled as his wife confronted him with the evening's prospects. Baseball bored him, as did the bombastic, back-slapping Carl, who saw the embodiment of evil in any team or person who had the effrontery to attack his Cubs. Eddie would much rather have gone home, for Joe Wicks had been on his mind all day and he had worried about his land. But he accepted Elva's announcement with a mumble, and he continued the muttering as his wife turned the car about and headed back toward Millie's. When she revealed to her spouse that she had spent the entire day away from home, the poor man groaned, but said nothing.

Eddie continued his silence during dinner and his boredom continued as Carl guffawed and raved inning after endless inning. But at the beginning of the seventh the Cubs came apart, went down, and Carl came apart, too, turning quiet and surly. It was a relief when the man clicked off the TV and withdrew to a back room, not appearing again, even when the Jamisons left.

Under a quarter moon, Eddie and Elva skirted the town. The stillness of the Bates road soothed the asphalt spreader's feelings and he felt a growing peace. He was anxious to spend an hour on his stump before retiring. As the familiar clapboard dwelling appeared in the beam of the headlights, Eddie's soul reached out for communion.

"I'll be in, in awhile," he said as he closed the car door and turned toward the barn.

"I'll wait up," Elva responded nicely. Although her feelings about the field were firm, she felt guilty. "Enjoy yourself," she called. It was really qite mean of her to stay away all day like that. "The moon is nice," she added. The remarks were hardly like Elva, and had Eddie given full thought to them, he may have found a clue that something was up, but his mind was occupied, reaching out to his acres and his stump and communion.

As he followed the path to the barn, the little man began to sense a troubling strangeness. There seemed to be an unusual darkness, a shadowy, eerie pall over his land, and there was the unexpected smell of newly turned earth. The sensations startled him; he stopped and stared toward his field. He became aware of the sound of fast-flowing water. Was this his land? He felt disoriented. Had he mistakenly wandered into his neighbor's farm? Impossible. But why was there no croaking of frogs? Where was the moonglow on the pond? He stared into the darkness and listened intently to comprehend this strange landscape. He looked toward the far fence line that bordered his property. Where were the velvety, shadowed willow clumps that should obstruct his view? There were no willow clumps at all! The terrible reality crashed upon him.

"Wicks," he muttered, "Wicks . . . Elva! He came!"

Under the subdued light of the quarter moon, he shuffled toward the rear of the barn where his stump had rested. Freshly cast-up soil from the new ditch was spread over the spot. He saw a distorted, rippled reflection of the moon in the flying water in the steep-banked channel. The private world of Eddie Jamison no longer existed. It had been gouged, plowed under, erased from the earth.

The poor man's mourning could not have been more pained had a near one died. His muttering and groaning continued into the night, and Elva, stricken with guilt, sobbed as she attempted to comfort him. She had no idea the man would carry on so.

"You'll feel better in the morning, dear," she attempted. "We'll feel lots better when we get the money . . . that awful Mr. Wicks . . ." But her mate only muttered in response. Elva, struggling with a conflict of emotions, dabbed her eyes as she turned to her side of the bed. She was heavy hearted, indeed, but in bare truth, the clinging vision of thousands of dollars could not help but give comfort.

The night passed and with dawn a new pain was added to the one of the night before, for barely past daylight, Joe Wicks thumped his fist on the Jamison door. "Say," said the visitor after Eddie had peeked through the window, saw the large frame of the man and then haltingly opened the door a crack. "Say, did I mention to you we'd have to cover the seed cost up front? I meant to do that. It came to three hundred, ninety-four dollars and some odd cents. You can just make it a hundred, ninety-seven for your share."

Two hundred dollars, unexpected - another devastating chapter in this unbelievable nightmare. What next? Eddie disappeared from Wicks' view, as though in a stupor. Presently a light was turned on in an adjoining room.

"We got through over at Darby earlier than I thought, so I figured we'd squeeze your place in. Glad we could get it done so soon. Been out to look over your place? Boys did a good job. You can handle the cash alright?" As the big man spoke, Eddie flipped off the light and shuffled back to the front door.

"Nice deal, isn't it?" Joe Wicks said as Jamison handed him a check. "I knew you'd like it. Thanks a lot." The visitor turned toward his truck, calling back as he hurried, "We're going to make some money. Good money."

It was after the remaining weeks of spring and on into summer before Eddie finally began to rise above his dark feelings. The slump in his shoulders and the deep furrows of his frown began to disappear, for as a matter of fact, that forty acre field was beginning to arouse the county worker's attention (and the attention of a good many others, too.) The potato crop had prospered very noticably. It actually had become a show place. The Jamison land, idle for so many years, must have built up an unusual fertility, for the field had turned a uniform green from fence line to fence line. It looked so prosperous a local merchant, who marketed fertilizers to the local farmers, gained Eddie's permission (sweetening his request with a twenty-dollar bill), to plant a sign at the field's edge to advertise his product. And the county agricultural agent visited more than once, commending the asphalt man with "what in the deuce went in that field to get a growth like that?" All the notice was stirring conflicting emotions in the little man. Eddie still grieved, especially in the evenings, when he thought of this pond and willow groves and the wending stream, but being quite human, he liked the attention he was getting, and the near certainty of making "real good money" was making its impact. He found himself swelling with importance when the boys on the road crew greeted him with, "Hey, Eddie, how's the spuds?", or, "Eddie, what'cha' goin' a do with all that tater money?"

As summer came on, he had procured a discarded arm chair and had begun to sit in the evenings at his old post behind the barn. He attempted to find the communion of tranquility by reaching out to the potato rows, but the acres of green reached back to him in a strange tongue, not of peace, but in the alluring language of hard cash. The thought of money possessed strong magic. It brought with it a sense of independence, of pride, ownership, exciting anticipation. This man Jamison had become a citizen of note, of property, prosperity. In status, hadn't he vaulted a cut above the laborers of the road crew? He was a man of substance now. Should a man of substance be relegated to the lowly role of straining his back over a shovel or a spreader on a country lane? Heaven forbid.

And the bombastic Carl, Millie's Carl, how pleasing to see his envious glances. Frankly, Eddie loved it. But then, seated on the armchair, as Eddie would look up, unconsciously expecting to enjoy the evening glow upon his pond and the velvety dusk shadowing the willow clumps, he felt a guilt, a betrayal. Was he becoming a turncoat, a traitor? Was he selling his soul at the first tinkling sound of a few silver coins?

But Joe Wicks didn't object to the thought of tinkling silver. And his mind was on the subject one October day after the nippy weather had turned the Jamison potato vines brown.

"If we had ten times this forty, we'd make a fortune!" the big man said as he and Eddie stood at the rear of the barn looking over the field. Joe pushed a shovel under one of the plants and lifted to the surface a half-dozen smooth, firm tubers. "Just look at that!" he exulted as he measured one of the potatoes against his palm. It was as long and nearly as wide as the big hand. "But we're still going to make some real good money. And soon. These spuds are just waiting to be dug. I'll have the machine here tomorrow."

Eddie watched the man hurry to his truck and stooped to gather the big potatoes which Wicks had dislodged from the furrow. He sensed relief, for the season's confusing ordeal was nearing its conclusion. An ugly field would be left after the picking machine and the trucks had finished their work, but Joe Wicks, the pushy, blustery Joe Wicks would be gone.

It was three days later that the big man stood at the Jamison door and thumped. Elva, tingling with excitement, followed her mate and peered anxiously over his shoulder as he opened the portal to face the visitor. The potatoes had been dug, loads of them, and trucked away to the market. The field was left torn and sad, strewn with tangles of potato vines. And now, the money. The good money!

"Here's your check," Joe Wicks said, displaying an I-told-you-so grin.

"Oh, thank you!" blurted Elva, her eyes rivited upon the magic slip of paper. She was quick to see the amount of the figure, the large figure, as Joe ran a big finger under it for emphasis.

"A few more sacks and we'd of made an even forty-five hundred apiece. But how does forty-four fifty sound? That's your share. Good money, just as I said."

Good money indeed. After Joe Wicks had gone, Elva, bubbling and twittering, fussed about the house, hardly able to contain herself. She closed the lid of her small, vinyl suitcase, fumbling the latches. Her sister, LaVita, had invited her to Territon for a ten-day stay and the bus was due to leave in an hour. A perfect day it was as the Jamison auto rolled toward town, purring more briskly than usual. The first stop was at the bank. After a ten minute visit, Eddie returned to the car, and smiling proudly, triumphantly dealt into his spouse's hand five crisp twenty dollar bills.

"Oh, Eddie," muttered Elva. "Eddie!" The next stop was at the clothiers. This was Elva's ten minute visit. At the cash register, Eddie wrote out without flinching a fifty-two, fifty check as the clerk removed from the lay-away hanger a dark coat with a light gray rabbit fur collar. It had been in lay-away a month, awaiting the great day of the arrival of the potato money.

"Oh, Eddie," muttered Elva as she slipped the garment on and pressed her cheek against the soft fur. "Eddie!"

The potato farmer smiled loftily as his wife waved from the window as the bus began to roll away. Her smile was rapturous. Eddie watched the vehicle pick up speed and finally disappear down the Clawson highway, and then, with a determined step, hurried to his car.

Down the street he traveled, turned a corner, and another, before stopping at a house of business. That stop consumed an hour.

A week passed. It was toward evening on a nice autumn day. Eddie had just returned from the county sheds, wearing new bib overalls. A small pickup truck, with business lettering on its doors, stirred the fallen yellow leaves as it approached and stopped at the Jamison front gate. There was a rap at the door, much milder than Joe Wicks' thump.

"Heere ees your beel," a fellow said as Eddie responded to the knock. "Thee work, hee ees all feenished." Jamison withdrew a new checkbook from the breast pocket of his overalls and dashed out a check in the amount of fifteen hundred dollars and handed it to the man. As the fellow walked to his truck and motored away, Eddie wrote a second check of the same amount as the first. This one was payable to Elva Jamison. He folded it and with a safety pin attached it to her pillow. That duty completed, he slipped on his mackinaw and walked with a light step to the old chair at the rear of the barn. The rush of swift-running ditch water could not be heard, for once again the stream meandered. And the new willow clumps and the gentle knoll, which lay in that order down toward the far fence line, graced his field. The grass seed would sprout green in the spring, and the frogs would return to the pond, which shimmered as never before with the evening glow. The landscapers had done their work well.

The county worker settled into the old chair. He adjusted his slight frame for comfort and leaned back. He and his land reached out. There was communion again.

12

Just Call Me Airball

Airball. Some name. Why not Dead Eye, or Ringer, something with some class? Yeah, or Right Stuff, like they call ole on-the-beam Joe Wheeler. Joe gets Right Stuff. I get Airball. Some deal. But I guess that's life.

This Airball thing got started in the basketball intermurals, known by some up at our high school as the bounce and blast wars. The coach, we call him The Bald Eagle, sits up there on a long-legged stool during the games like he's on a perch, and he takes aims with his beaky nose up and down the floor, and he scribbles fast notes if a dude shows a hot hand or goes on a roll with fancy dribbling or passing. Those lucky ones get a chance to try for the big time, the school team, and the rest of us go down under The Bald Eagle's quick black line. All I get out of the wars is a name. Airball. Does nothing for your social standing and your trail to the big time goes to rocks. But what can you expect when you play a wild brand of goof ball out there, dribbling watermelons and blasting up airballs that miss basket, backboard, everything?

Oh well, that's over now. I can cross it off. The ole diploma, the sheepskin-cowhide, whatever they call it, will soon take care of that. Day after tomorrow night the diplmas roll. Yes sir, ole Airball'll come scrubbing in through the smog level just under that ole sold B, as they call it. If only Miss Hensley had got up to a bettr day when she gave out the English grades, or if Figures Hardy (as he's known behind his back) hadn't been so stingy with the physics finals, big time Airball might have scrubbed in clean right on the old solid B. But what's done's done. I can cross that one off, too. The grades rolled this morning, first period, and they got attention. Everybody's. They hang big in the brain and loose on the tongue. "But what's the big deal?" I say to myself. "Diplomas say nothing about grades. The old goatskin will be quiet on the subject. And you can burn report cards, git rid of all evidence. Anyways, a B- looks like a mountain next to a C, so I say to myself just as Jim Shepard shows in the hall, stomping out of the math room. He's down.

"Miss your Frosty O's this morning?" I say to Shep.

"They gave me a C," he says.

"C is average," I say. "Just look at your report card." I open my card and show him where it says C is average. "As many above as below it," I say.

"Averages of what, the dunces?" he says. Shep's not listening. His ears are red and his questions aren't in my territorial waters, so I take a different aim as Toddy Squires now pouts by. I knew Toddy must have sailed in up in the horse latitudes.

"Miss your Aunt Jemima this morning, Toddy?"

"Isn't fair," he says, spouting.

"What isn't fair?"

"I had an A cinched. The finals brought me down to a B+."

"Big deal," I say. "Just look here." I show him my card. "Show him yours," I say to Shep. Toddy studies our finals.

"B- and C," he says and hums through his teeth. Just looking at somebody else's B- and C is sure to give a lift to a guy with a B+. Toddy looks over our grades some more, compares them with his own, then he hums through his teeth again and bounces away, still whining, but feeling better.

"See, Shep," I say, "guys with B+'s don't feel any better than you or me. Maybe even worse. So what's the big deal?" Shep nods, and now I hear Dismal Rudolph back of my shoulder. He's always there, wheezing and lowering my social standing.

"Whuh huh huh huh," he laughs. "Whuh huh huh." His name fits. It's like the kid is up out of the dismal swamp.

"What are you whuh huhing about?" I say. I don't turn to look. I know who it is.

"C-, whuh huh huh," he says.

"C-? That's terrible," Shep says.

"Terrible? It's wonderful," Diz says. "I was sure I'd flunked. Whuh huh huh."

"Well, there you go," I say to Shep. "Here a guy moles in through concrete at a C- and he's riding High Street. You got no gripe coming."

"Yeah," says Shep. That's all he says. He heads for his locker like a winner.

Well, I make for the door, giving big Knuckles Seymour plenty of space as I move up the hall. Knuckles has a female cornered there across from the econ room. He's into weights, wears tight shirts that show his biceps and tripods and whatever else. He leans with his big knuckles against the wall on each side of the girl's head. She's trapped and looks it. Mr. America. Big deal. He's all power from his toe callouses up to his neck. But the power stops there. Knuckles probably paddled in to graduation through the heavy water down in the sold D canal. That's about as solid as you can get.

"The principal's looking for you," I say, lying to the girl as I pass. Diz is surprised. I can tell by a start in his breath. His chin is an inch from my shoulder. It always is. A Smith Brothers' cough drop clicks against his teeth. I can tell by the sound and smell. The girl's name's Ann - Anet, something. Anyways, Knuckles lowers his tripods from the wall. The girl looks relieve, throws me a quick "thanks-smile" and moves out. I move out, too. I've got knuckles enough. I don't need a set on my jaw. But Mr. America doesn't know I snookered him. He walks away with his muscles and his D. He's happy.

Up the hall I have to sidestep this senior called Dennis. He uses a raised elbow like a bumper on a car. With his other hand, he's towing this girl. Top of the line. Jen - Jenfer - something. She's poured into some white pants that have creases as neat and sharp as knife blades. She's got long, red fingernails and her chin's up there in the ozone with Dennis. That's where he floats, up in that thin air where the A boys with the dollars hang out in their tight little cliques. He's the guy you always wish people would mistake you for: the right height, hair in place, to the last spear, just the way he wants it to look, and where us nerf balls pamper and wish over a scrawny patch of fuzz above our lips, Dennis has lots of dark stubble showing on his light skin. And he's already been everywhere and done everything that you've dreamed about getting done sometime during your life, and besides all that he ran on the track team for a while, sort of played with it, got as good as he wanted to be, but never getting down into the dirty, sweat level. Why should he? He's got everything he wants. Why mess up his life with unneeded grunt work? He's wearing sharp pants, too, and a shirt that's right out of the store, and his fancy shoes have neat, white soles and laces that are straight and clean.

"Hi, Dennis," I say, throwing a word up at his ozone, which a common nerf like me has no business doing.

"Hey," he says in a quick little grunt, pretending not to know me from Adam and not wanting to. He just looks at the girl, not at me. And the girl looks at him, not at me. Does nothing for my social standing.

"You lucky dog, Dennis," I say to myself. "Got your A and your dollars, your top-of-the-line girl and your fancy clothes." Dennis stoops as he passes and flicks a dot of mud from one of those shoes then looks up at the girl again. I feel flicked off like the mud. But I guess that's alright. Up in his cosmos, his ozone layer, he sure doesn't need an Airball bouncing around.

I pass the principal's office and Knuckles' girl gives me the quick run-by.

"Thanks a lot," she says.

"Principal chew you out?" I say.

"Smarty," she says. "That was nice of you."

"Anytime," I say. She hurries on up the hall. She doesn't have red fingernails or white pants, but she's got some class.

"What's nice?" Diz Rudolph says from behind. The scurffy kid's so close he'll put treads on my heels if I stop quick.

"Lots of things are nice," I say and don't explain.

Two guys slink out of the principal's office as I pass. They look like juniors straight up out of the ole D- mire.

"Miss your Post Toasties this morning?" I say.

"Humph," one of them says.

"Tough grits, huh?" I say.

"Right on," says the other and pretends to give me a high five. Then the first one grins, and I grin. Then the other one grins.

I follow the Knuckles girl outside. She holds the door open for me. I'd snooker Knuckles every day for that. It rained last night and the school grounds are all over puddles, sloshy and in some places soft with mud. But in last summer's Adidas and old Levis, it makes no difference. Let it slosh. Out the door now comes the breather of the ozone, Dennis. He's still got the girl's hand gripped, and he walks through the mud on the high spots, keeping his shoes clean. He's like he's on eggs as he leads this classy dame between two puddles, long and muddy ones. Another girl approaches them. I've seen her around; a sophomore or junior, and breathing my kind of B- air. There's no room for her to pass. She stops, not knowing which way to step. She looks out to me and the dozen or two scruffy kids that are drooping around with their hands in their pockets. But Dennis doesn't stop, and he isn't going to let those pretty shoes get dirty. He raises his elbow again to clear the way, keeping his eyes on the girl in the white pants. The sophomore kid has to step out into the muddy water. That sets something churning down inside me and as Ozone and his girl come closer I find myself saying to Diz (I don't turn to look. I know he's there; I hear a whistle in his breath).

"Push me. Quick, push me."

"What?" says Dismal. It catches him by surprise.

"Push me into the puddle."

"What . . .?"

"Quick," I say. So Diz gives me the slightest shove on the shoulder. I lunge into the muddy water Adidas first and make a good splash, a giant splash, bigger and muddier than I'd planned on. Poor Ozone and his girl catch it. Those nice white pants now look a total mess. The pretty girl flares up like a gasoline fire. She's wild.

"You repulsive idiot!" she says, squealing. She shakes the dirty water from her hands. Her long, red fingernails slash the air in the direction of my eyes. Ozone Dennis looks at his pants and his pretty shoes, but he only sputters. "You idiot!" the girl says again, squealing louder.

"It was an accident," I say, lying. Muddy water drips from the girl's blouse onto the sharp creases of her pants. It's bad. Worse. It's terrible.

"You maniac, stupid maniac!" she says, flaring up again and looking at Dennis like she's wondering why he doesn't pop off.

"I'll get you for this," Ozone finally says. He has to say something.

"You pushed the girl into the puddle," I say, stretching it a little.

"Pushed? Drown him in the puddle, Denny!" she says, flaring like a blow torch and glaring at the mumbling Ozone.

"I'll settle with you later," Dennis says. But the girl squeals again. She wants blood. Now. So Ozone lifts his dukes. But he's a Nervous Pervis. It's easy to see. He wishes the girl would shut up. That's easy to see, too.

"How about tonight at ten o'clock, behind the school. Alone," I say. I know Dennis'll like that, and I know we can work the thing out if we're by ourselves.

"Alright," he says, and he lowers his dukes. The girl accepts my offer because she thinks I'm scared. Well, with those red fingernails slashing around, I am scared of her. Anybody who likes good vision would be. But Dennis, I don't have the shakes because of him.

"You coward," the girl says. "He'll smash you, gouge you, pulverize you." She knows all the pain words. Ozone looks afraid of her, too. He's got himself a wildcat. I'm beginning to wish a lot that I'd thought about jumping into that puddle before I did the stupid thing. I'm really getting down on myself. But the B- girl and the others that saw what happened give me a "Yeah, Airball". The gasoline fire explodes again. The pretty girl is ready to take on the whole school. But Ozone leads the wild woman away toward his fancy red wheels. She slams the door and the car revs up through the mud puddles toward town.

Well, at ten I'm back of the school. I'm feeling down because of the big stir I'd caused, but still feeling that Dennis and his babe deserved everything they got. It's hard dangling between two opposite kinds of thinking. A guy doesn't know which way to turn.

It's getting quite dark and I think I'm alone, but I see Dismal and his scruffy bunch peeking around the corner. And the sophormore girl is there, too. I can't get rid of Diz and his ragtag herd. Your social standing just bottoms out if you keep that kind of a cheering section around.

"This is my fight," I say. "I promised. You got to go."

"It's our fight, too," the girl says, but they disappear.

"I'll yell if I need you," I say, calling into the dark. I'm thinking of the pretty girl. I'm not worried about Dennis.

I wait for ten minutes. Ozone is late. Fifteen minutes, and I'm ready to leave, but then he shows. He's alone and I'm relieved.

"You're late," I say. He says nothing, but fidgets taking off his jacket. He lays it on the ground. "Good idea," I say. I take off my sweater and toss it on the dirt.

"Alright," he says. His voice is shaky. He doesn't like knuckle wars. That shows even in the dark. He puts up his dukes, funny. So do I. We circle around. I wait for him to lam me. But he just circles, buzz-sawing his fists like I've never seen before. Lots of motion, but no war. So I do a little fancy footwork like I'm coming at him. I jab out a left then bring a right around. I miss by five feet. This puts more fear into Ozone and he backs off to ten feet. Some war. This goes on for a minute or two and I can see we're getting nowhere. Finally, I say,

"I've had enough. You?" He drops his dukes in a split second.

"Too much," he says and he grins. I see his white teeth in the dark.

"I'm sorry about your pants and all," I say. "I do stupid things sometimes."

"So do I," he says. That was bad of me today." So Ozone can feel sorry. I like that.

"It was worse of me," I say. "But anyways, we've settled it."

"Let's shake," he says. We shake. But then I get thinking, trying to be decent, because I'm still feeling a little guilty.

"Your girl," I say. "She's going to want blood."

"You're right," he says. "What can we do?"

"I'll tell you," I say, "let's rub a little of this mud on our faces, and let me kick a little of this water on your pants." He laughs. He knows about watery pants. "We've got to make you look like you've been in a big war," I say. "Here, you kick some on me, too."

"Good," he says. We slosh each other. But there was no blood. The girl wouldn't accept mud. I knew it when I thought about it.

"Hmmm," I say, "maybe you're going to have to pop me."

"What?"

"My nose bleeds easy, just a little tap. We'll let it drip on our shirts. Anyway, I deserve it, doing what I did to her."

"Me hit you?"

"Come on, lam me. I dirtied your pants." I stick out my nose for a good target. "Come on," I say.

"I can't," he says.

"Come on," I say. Gritting his teeth he pulls back and lets fly. He misses my nose, and I think a horse kicked me in the eye, and there's a snap.

"Ohhh," I say and he moans.

"Ohhh," he says and I moan.

"I broke my thumb," he says.

"You wiped out my eye," I say. We moan some more.

"Good," I say finally. "That'll satisfy her.

"Sure will, better than blood," he says. We walk off into the shadows.

"You're a nice guy, Oz . . Dennis," I say. I almost called him Ozone. "Glad we got acquainted."

"Same to you, Airball. You're great." We have a good laugh. It feels good having a friend up in the cosmos. My social standing zooms.

Well, its next morning and I'm in the main hall, and I pass Dennis and the pretty girl. I sort of expect a slap on the back and maybe a "Hey, hey, Airball", even though I know Ozone can't do that in front of his fiery dame. But he's back up in his cosmos. He acts like he can't remember me, just looks at the floor then up at the girl.

"I knew he'd beat you to a pulp," the babe says, giving my eye the scan. "Denny told me all about it, you coward." She's got blue fingernails today. They're slashing around and I've got my eyes on them.

"Airball let 'em do it," says Diz suddenly. He's there at my shoulder. He's upset.

"That's right, he did," says one of Diz's scruffy friends. Those guys had peeked around the corner last night. I knew they would. Ozone's chin drops to the floor. He doesn't know what to say.

"He what?" the girl says, surprised. She and her blue fingernails turn toward me. "What's he saying?"

"No, it was fair and square," I say. "He broke his finger on my eye." I don't want a war starting with her again. Dennis is relieved, and he's had too much of this conversation, so he moves out. I can't keep my eyes off him as he tows his girl up the hall, his fancy shoes, different ones today, and his hair and his dame, who's patting his sore thumb. "You lucky dog, Dennis," I say to myself. I run my finger over my sore shiner, and I hear the musical notes in Dismal's breath. I think of my social standing, down in the dirt again, and I wish now that I'd lammed the guy last night. My fists tighten up. "You fool, Airball," I say to myself, "you thought you won the war last night, and look at 'em. He knows he won." But Ozone must feel my stares and my thoughts because he turns. He looks sick, and gives me a sort of bewildered wink. I look down at my fists again and feel stupid. "You neanderthal, Airball," I say to myself as the pair disappears around the corner.

Well, anyways, tomorrow the graduation diplomas roll. The old deeplomas. I got to get a trim and pick up some new threads. Going first class to pick up the ole muleskin. Today up and down the halls there's talk about stars. Yesterday it was grades. Today it's these stars that the high fliers with the A's get by their names in the graduation program.

"Miss your Cap'n Crunch for breakfast?" I say to this guy we call Sparky as he pouts by.

"It isn't fair," Sparky says.

"Nothing's fair," I say, still thinking of Ozone. "Didn't you know that?"

"I just missed a star by one point," he says. He's down at the moan level.

"They've got to draw the line somewheres," I say. That's what I say, but inside I'm a little miffed, too, at this star business. Does nothing for your social standing if you don't get one. Everybody in town looking over the fancy graduation programs and there sits your name with no star by it. The stars lift the A boys higher and push the rest of us down lower, all of us from the B's to the D's herded and branded in the same corral.

"Means nothing," I say to Sparky, lying. "You'll have some good company and lots of it." Sparky grumps away. "Let the grades and the stars roll," I say to myself. "I'll just roll that fancy program right in the garbage can and that'll be the end of the stars. Don't need any stars around to remind me I'm an airball."

Joe Wheeler, ole Right Stuff, passes and gives me a thump on the shoulder. That feels good right now. He didn't need to do that. The social standing of a nerf like me doesn't bother Joe. Watching him circulate around, you'd think social standing belonged to another planet. I guess that's why he's called Right Stuff.

Now I feel Diz's breath on the back of my neck.

"The guys want to play a game a'rounders," he says. Come on, OK?" That's what we call a ball game without enough guys for the real thing. "Play with that bunch?" I say to myself. "A guy's social standing'd go to zilch. Got to pick your company better than that."

"Come on," Diz says. He's getting pushy. I can feel his breath stronger and I'm not in the toss and blast mood. I guess the thought of Ozone's still floating around in my head. "I've got to put a stop to this business," I say to myself. "This second rater's always scuffing my heels. He's driving me bats." Not thinking it through like I should have, I turn on him.

"Leave me alone," I say, "I'm busy now." I'm miffed. "Go on and play with the ragtags if you want." Diz looks at the floor and turns away. He's like a pup you've been nice to and thinks you like him. Then you cuff him and he doesn't know what to do. Diz's chin sags and he begins to walk away. As I watch him droop down the hall, I feel a knife between my shoulder blades and someone's twisting it. I think of Ozone and his thin air. I'm worse, a hundred times worse. I want to run after Diz. But that wouldn't be cool. But I do walk fast.

"Diz," I say. I don't need to say more. He turns like a friendly pup again. The hurt look sort of melts away into that complete trust that a friend forever shows. "Social standing go to rocks," I say to myself.

"If your guys'll have me, let's play ball," I say to Diz. "We'll celebrate the end of school.

"Deeeba, deeba doo," a scrawny, freshman-looking kid lets out in a croaky, crickety voice. He's been looking on. "Deeba deeba doo!" Now a whole scruffy bunch moves in and we head for the diamond.

The place is deserted and we begin tossing the ole pill around.

"Deeba deeba doo, come on beeby, Airball!" The kid's my rooting section. Scruffy or not, these guys know the game. They pepper the pill like a bunch of pros. Pretty soon there's a gang watching and a guy on the school baseball team says he'll get a bunch together and take us on for a game. Well, we wop 'em, the big time high-fliers. My ragtag scruffies are all over the field and that deeba doo kid knocks two homers, and the coach, who can't miss any kind of a game, talks to the freshman about the big time for next year. And I fan twice and let two gounders bounce between my legs. The Bald Eagle says nothing to me, of course, putting my social standing down the last notch.

Well, that's all over now. Gone clear back to yesterday. I'm in the school gym now. It's graduation. The diplomas roll any minute. The whole universe has crowded in. I've got one of those four-cornered hats on, and a long bathrobe, dress-looking thing. Stupid, really. But I like it. And I like the smell of my new threads. I get a whif of them even though the mothbally smell of the black bathrobe is a little strong. Up on the stand behind the mike sits the principal and Miss Hensley and Figures Hardy and The Bald Eagle and the rest. Then I see three or four guys and babes move toward the steps. Big timers, the high fliers. They'll give out with some speeches, I think. Or sing. Speeches daddys and mommys have worked over down to the last periods and commas. "Set your aim high." I can hear it now. I set my gaze high and see a cobweb handing down from a light in the ceiling.

I look over the cover of the fancy printed program they gave us as we marched in, this little army in bathrobes. Big stuff. I open the program, give it a quick skim. Real quick. The stars are there, twenty or thirty of them. I try not to look close, but my eyes insist. Hey, what is this? My eyes bug out. Knuckles Seymour a star? Knuckles? I can't believe it. Misprint! And Pow! I see right off that Ozone's name isn't with the stars. And neither is his girl's! I want to laugh. So Ozone breathes my smoggy air! Then I look up at the stand. I see ole Right Stuff walking up the steps. That figures. I like that. And pow again! The sophomore-looking girl of the mud puddle, she's up there too! She a senior and's sitting smart and pretty right by the principal. She sees me and flips me a cute wrinkle of her nose. That makes my whole night. My whole month. And no! This other kid walking up the steps, isn't he one of those scruffy pals of Diz's? Looks like his mommy's scrubbed and trimmed him all night to get him ready. This I'll never believe. The guy tosses me a grin.

Well, I can't understand myself, but as the program rolls, I'm getting into this thing. The school band thumps and then the talkers talk. I give the mud puddle girl both ears when she gives with her words. She looks up from her paper and flips me a glance and I squirm and probably red up. I keep with Right Stuff, too, and the ball player, who puts a hiss on his esses. But the others, I'm in and out, back to sniffing my threads and trying to hear what two guys are whispering about on the row behind me. Then finally, this big dude from somewhere stands up and sort of bellows out with some things, long things. I track with him a minute till he finishes this joke, but then he loses me and I'm back thinking about my dog and other stuff. When he sits, Miss Hensley makes her move toward the stacks of glossy gopherskins that are piled on a table there on a corner of the stand. Now you can hear the principal's breath in the mike. He tells everybody what to do: come up row by row and when your name is called, hoof it up the steps to the stand, pick up the ole lionskin, then move out back to your seat. I guess I can handle that. Miss Hensley flutters and fusses, neating up the piles, which they don't need, then starts,

"Abbot . . . Able . . ." She calls loud and slow with a different sound in her voice, like this is history, destiny. "Adams . . . Anderson . . ." Here and there in the big crowd there are claps and a few whistles and whoops as some kids reach the stand who have noisy families or wordy friends. And some of the high fliers get their cheering sections into it. You've got to be somebody, do some big thing to stir up the crowd like that. These thoughts turn me down on myself and I'm wondering why I wasn't born up in the horse latitudes like ole Ozone, who's sitting up a row or two in front of me. When his turn comes, his cheering section sets up its roar, and up on the stand, Dennis waves like this happens to him every day. Now his dad, in a yellow suit, comes elbowing his way down an aisle, aiming a TV camera at his kid. The black box follows Denny boy all the way back to his seat. "Well, anyway, he didn't get a star," I say to myself. But that thinking is sour grapes, I know it, and I try to get it out of my head. Ozone's girl now gets up and the dark eye of the black box begins following her and my thoughts get churned up again, "Let them have their minutes," my brain says. "Stick a star on their foreheads."

Well, finally, the kid next to me moves out and kicks over a chair as he goes down the aisle. It clatters. Let him have his minutes, too. Some people laugh and clap. Now it's me and I'm a Nervous Pervis. But I'm going to keep it cool. Up and out without a whisper. No whoops, no TV camera, just . . . I scrape my toe on a step. At least the stair squeaks for me, and I think I'm tripping on the corner of a rug up here that I didn't see. Hensley calls out my name and the principal reaches toward me with the ole coyoteskin, giving me a sort of "glad-you're-out-of-here" grin, so I think.

Then this crazy thing starts. I hear that crickety "Deeba deebba doo, bebby, Airball!" It echoes around all four walls. The principal jerks, the sound is so loud, and I'm melting in my shoes. I don't need that kind of a cheer. Then from somewhere I hear Diz, yelling louder than ever in his life, "Airball! Airball!" Then the girl on the stand jumps up, looking excited, and moves in on me, clapping. Now the whole scruffy ballteam is on their feet stomping and hollering and deeba dooing. The whole house is jiving. Then I see Right Stff and the Knuckles girl and lots of others that I don't think I even know. They're up. "Yeah, Airball, Deeba doo!" It's crazy. I catch Ozone's eye as I'm looking up from the floor. I can read him. He's fighting himself. He looks at the pretty girl, then back at me, then like he's saying, "Aw the heck with her," he's on his feet clapping. That unstrings me, finishes me, and I'm rubbing an eye to hold back a blubber.

"They love you, Airball," the principal says finally. His chin trembles. Even he's calling me Airball. I wave, like Ozone did, feeling stupid, then miss a step going down the stairs. That put's 'em in the aisles. "Airball! Get under it, Airball! Deeba doo!"

Well, its over now. But I don't think I'll cross this one off. I don't want to, and I guess I couldn't if I did. It's like high school was a big, roll of thunder that, with graduation, all at once rumbles away and dies like in the distance of a quiet night, leaving you with a kind of empty feeling, but with your head full of a thousand thoughts.

Looking back, I guess there's lot's of things I didn't have figured.

I thought the old diploma, the kangaroohide, meant you're smart, even if you did bulldoze in just under the ole solid B. I've got to think a few things through again. I don't know. I guess that's why they call me Airball.

13

You Can Smile Now, RAT Thompson

RAT Thompson grew up out north of Driggs in that Teton Valley location known in those times as "over on the Cache Road". From our casual distance, we watched the boy make a long, troubled trek through his early years. We remember him, slight of frame, running down those back roads after school, forever running, it seemed. But that gets ahead of our story. We must go back to the day when this mite of a lad, shy and anxious, first appeared at kindergarten, the day when some normally benign matters of circumstance in his life began colliding together in a cruel synergism.

First there was this sensitive boy with a sequence of initials in his name that invited abuse, then there was the emergence, in time, of two noticably prominent incisors, and finally, enter the catalyst, the unfeeling bully, who played his role well.

It's true, of course, that some kids would have popped the Pengill hellion on the nose at his first offensive act and that would have been the end of that. It wasn't to be, though, in the case of Ray Alexander Thompson. Ray was destined to bear his burden. And yet, in looking back, maybe it was best that things went the way they did. The day of victory could not have been so sweet, and the Valley would have been bereft of one of its shining hours.

But, no matter; looking back changes nothing. Things went the way they went, and the course was set during Ray's first day at school, when the insufferable rowdy, Terry Pengill, with prompting, of course, from older ones at home, announced to the world that a rat had enrolled in his class. From that hour Ray became known by his initials: RAT. RAT Thompson.

"Come on!" the bully shouted, "There's a rat over here. Come on an' see 'em!" Encouraged by the curiosity of a gathering crowd of moppets, Terry pressed the humiliation a step farther,

"Be like a rat!" he demanded as he grasped Ray's frail shoulders and forced the frightened boy to his hands and knees. "Come on, you, be like a rat!" Ray hesitated, and then out of fear, and with an innocent desire to please, he hopped about on all fours. As the children squealed their delight, the victim accommodated by emitting a convincing "squeak, squeak".

With that beginning, a pattern was set which doggedly persisted and then perpetuated itself at an even higher level of inhumanity on the notable day when Ray's new incisors were observed to be emerging a bit large for such a small lad. This observation, of course, set the stage for another proclamation by the Pengill brat, who smartly declared to the universe that Ray Thompson's teeth resembled, of all things, those - well, those of a rat. This pronouncement swept down the halls of the school like leaves on a November wind, and in the Pengill neighborhood it was greeted with twitters.

"He does, he looks just like a little rat," shrilled Mrs. Pengill. "You were so clever to think of that, Terry." Her scruffy urchin puffed his chest like a young turkey gobbler at that commendation.

RAT Thompson locked the bathroom door that evening and examined his front teeth in the mirror. Large? Yes, the incisors were a bit long and rather large. Protrude? They did, quite noticably. As the lad studied his face, he observed that his upper lip, when arched into a smile, framed the new teeth and made them appear larger than ever. He pressed his lip down against them. He was determined never to smile again.

And so, Ray became known as the boy with the sad, unsmiling face. He found his few comforts at school in being alone. When others were near, he habitually extended his lip downward, covering those offending teeth, and if a smile did begin to emerge, a shielding hand always darted upward.

"I'm not a rat! I'm not!" he blurted one day as he raced from his taunters. He ran from the school grounds, across the street, and sprinted down a back road, which took a quiet, milk-stop route through the countryside past his home. The boy sobbed and ran until his legs trembled with fatigue. Jogging into a willow grove at the roadside, he sprawled upon his back to rest. Kaleidoscopic shadow patterns of the yellowing leaves played upon his forehead, and he was aware of the damp, musty smell of autumn as he pained over the day's experience. Why did they forever torment him? There were other boys at school with large front teeth. RAT had been quick to notice them. And weren't there a dozen nicknames as offensive as his? He cried again, feeling very sorry for himself and very much alone. The realities of his life at school frightened him. How could he possibly return to those terrible halls and grounds? His mind searched desperately for an escape. Pengill and his gang glared as monsters in his thoughts; he was surrounded by monsters. He sobbed aloud as he thought of them.

As the boy gazed upward to the leaf-mottled sky, his mind probing about for relief, perhaps it was normal that he found his thoughts yielding to the enticement of daydream worlds, where the downtrodden can become king, roles can be turned about so easily. ("You be a rat, Terry! Be a rat!") He visioned himself standing over the quavering bully. The impression was strong, and it was calming. He permitted his fantasies to run free. The expressions of pain and fear began to soften. He had found his escape. His lips turned upward at the corners. RAT smiled. He raised himself to his feet, and as he brushed the dead leaves from his clothes, he giggled at the thought of the cringing Pengill. "Crybaby Pengill! Run to your mother, Terry! Run!"

The boy's musings were interrupted by the sudden appearance of a rabbit, which hopped into the grove, caught sight of the lad and bounded away. The start jarred the youngster from his daydreams and his thoughts tumbled to the cold, ungiving world of reality. As he continued his way home, the image of the rabbit played upon his impressionable mind. Was RAT Thompson to become a timid animal, forever running and hiding from the crowd, and escaping into daydreams? Was that to be his life?

Yes, that began to be his life. He became expert at avoiding his tormentors. During lunch and recess periods, he actually sensed pride in that ability. And only if cold or storm prevented it - and the elements must have been severe - he ran down the back road rather than take the school bus along its highway route to his home. As he jogged along the quiet lane, his thoughts were quick to race to his own very private world.

But there were days when his best schemed plans failed, as they did one recess when the smooth-tongued dandy, Terry Pengill, circling his arm about Rat's shoulder in pretended friendship, lured the boy into a back storage room. (The arm would have become a vice at the slightest resistance.) Terry, and his mates, who were hiding about in the room, had placed a number of heavy packing crates about to form and enclosure, a trap. Cautiously responding to the invitation, RAT obediently crawled between the boxes. Pengill responded with a whistle and the boys jumped from their hiding places, quickly pushed the crates together and tied them in place with strong cords, which were out of the reach of the surprised captive.

"We caught a rat. We caught a rat in a trap!" Terry bellowed. A chorus of cheers brought the janitor to investigate, but the school bell rang just then, setting the noisy troupe into a charge to their desks. The custodian breathed relief as the destructive wave was corraled in the classroom, and he didn't get back until a half hour later, when word reached him that the Thompson boy was missing. Remembering the commotion in the back room, he returned to find RAT huddled in his prison, face buried in his arms. Tears had left splotches on the boy's jeans. The janitor only grunted as he untied the cords and led RAT to the classroom. Despite the youngster's protests, the man opened the door and deposited him inside.

"I found 'im in the storeroom. Fenced in with boxes, he was. . . by these kids here." He nodded toward Pengill. "They done it." His duty accomplished, the fellow shuffled out the door.

With his head lowered, Rat hurried to his desk. Slumping forward, he buried his face in his arms. After a long silence, there were muffled giggles, but teacher Jenny Fry's well known frigid glare, aimed as a rifle barrel, brought an abrupt end to the outburst. The woman's eyes, accentuated in their sternness by darkrimmed spectacles, turned to the sobbing boy. There was a hint of softening in the lines of her face, but her words were tempered only the slightest bit.

"Lift up your head, Ray Thompson," she demanded. "Lift up your head this minute." RAT, humiliated, devastated, crushed to the very dirt, hesitated, then obediently lifted his head. His lips quivered, his nose needed a handkerchief, his eyes were wet and swollen.

"Don't you bow your head down to a fool again." She turned her glare toward Pengill as she went on, "I'm sorry, but the world will always have its fools. Face up to them, Ray Thompson. Don't you bow your head down to them again." The words shook Pengill, but they burned upon the Thompson boy. They burned the tears from his cheeks; the experience seared an unforgettable memory in his brain.

It would be nice, here, to say that the teacher's commands forced a quick turnabout in RAT's life. That would make a neat story. A neat, untrue story. Face up to it, indeed. Hadn't he faced enough already? But to the teacher's eternal merit, for good or ill it was not yet apparent, the experience was not forgotten. The memory burned as a new flame whenever those bitter images thrust themselves upward in his mind. And for Ray Thompson, that flame blazed often as time, the inflictor and healer of wounds, compassionately circled away.

It would be of little consequence here to labor over the troubled seasons that followed. We will let those years through adolescence rest with but a clarifying glance backward. Subject as we all are to the capricious tilts of life's balance, RAT found his way down one of many courses which his life might have taken. Perhaps because of a not-obvious tenacious reserve, or an unusually resilient spirit gently nudged along by a kindly Providence, or perhaps only because the flow of life persists in carrying one as it will, this boy did manage to survive those years.

And now he was eighteen. That moving tide had deposited him this day in early June in the front corridor of the venerable Teton High. He leaned against the ribs of a heating radiator of the kind whose valves are sometimes heard to clang as steam circulates through them in the winter. A large clock, brown-framed and venerable itself, ticked echoes down the empty corridor. The ever-present school smell of active, youthful bodies hung in the halls. Reflected in the glass doors of the trophy cabinet across the corridor, the image of RAT's slight frame could be seen. He appeared as though he were in unusual distress. (So what else was new?) The hollow, tinkling notes of a piano and the soprano of a girl's voice could be heard from the music room down the hall. A senior miss was rehearsing for the graduation program, scheduled only two days away. What kept RAT in the corridor a full half hour after the dismissal of classes? The answer would be simple if the youth had been the usual quick-blooded graduating senior. But the usual senior he was not, and so this behavior, very much out of character, requires explanation.

He waited for a girl. A pretty face had worked its miracle even in the timid heart of RAT Thompson. Simply stated, the blond soprano had found her way into the youth's private world. She had been enthroned the Princess of the Back Road. As he had jogged down that country lane - which now had become a ritual as ingrained as eating and sleeping - he always found her waiting in that daydream world, warmly responsive. What imaginings the boy's mind had conceived. Looking forward to those quiet times along the little-traveled lane had brightened his life. And not only on the lane had he found his thoughts racing to that glittery retreat; there were quick excursions during the day, and at night in his quiet room, his imaginings consumed him.

But the inevitable day came when those worlds of make-believe, which had risen up for him as though by a rub of an Aladdin's palm, began to leave in their inevitable collapse a bitter emptiness. Spurred by these frustrations, the beginnings of rational, if ill-conceived, explorations began to exert themselves. Emerging timidly in his mind at first and resulting in weeks of reaching out, shrinking, and reaching again, a daring plan, daring for Rat Thompson, had emerged. And now the moment of truth approached. RAT stood in the empty corridor determined to carry that plan out. He was determined to approach the living, breathing girl of the back road.

As the boy's eyes shifted from the trophy case to the scarred front doors and then down the corridor, he struggled between those emotional poles of brave resolve and absolute panic. An urge to bolt from the school and race down the back lane left him trembling. But courage, that capricious companion, haltingly returned and his resolve gained strength. He was determined once more to stick it out no matter what. To run would have been an unforgivable betrayal. For how could the stage have been better set? The classrooms and halls were empty of students, and she, only a few yards away, must pass him to leave the building. As he fidgited, shifting his weight from one foot to the other, the words he had rehearsed a hundred times came to his mind: "Hi there, what's the hurry? Going to the graduation dance? Mind if I drop by?" On those evenings along the back road, these questions, in his thoughts, had always brought a warm and willing response. But now the words terrorized him. Perhaps he should think more on them. . .

Suddenly the musical notes ceased. There was a rush of footsteps. In an instant she was in the hall facing him. RAT shrank backward. His hand darted to cover his lips.

"Hey! What's the hurry?" The girl's eyes danced with the question, spoken with such self-assurance. RAT's words? No. His tongue had turned to stone. The girl looked past him, where now the approach of steps from the opposite corridor could be heard.

"Where've you been?" the boy's voice continued.

"Oh, that graduation song, I've. . ."

"Hey! Hey! The big meet - this is it! You know, I'm going to run over that guy from Fremont tomorrow!" the youth blurted.

"You must be excited. . ."

"Hey, the big race, the Big One! The cross-country's a man killer, you know. Three miles. Three BIG ones. It's the State record for me. Hey, I'm going for it!"

"Hey, hey," she joined with the 'in' expletive.

Terry Pengill paused at the door, grandly clad in an orange track uniform. He turned toward the devastated youth at the radiator.

"There's a rat over there," he smirked, pointing, as the pair stepped out. "I guess they slither and ooze, from the woodwork after school." Terry's fingers performed slithery movements close to the girl's face. She squealed as the creaking door closed.

The trophy case windows reflected a frozen, agonizing image. For a long moment the figure remained motionless and then the hand fell from the face. As the silhouette moved slowly toward the entrance, another voice was heard down the hall. By the familiar bluster, RAT sensed it was the Teton coach.

"Yesterday it was Billings," the voice huffed. "Now it's Smith. Don't they know I've got a meet on?" A woman answered, but RAT could not make out her words. The voice did sound vaguely familiar, though, like one he would never forget - for an eternity. But what would Jenny Fry be doing at the high school? Likely he was mistaken.

"I'm on my way over there right now to see if the Billings kid is as sick as he says," the man's huffing went on. The woman's voice responded again with words still indistinguishable.

"You're kidding me. . .; whats that you say?" the coach went on. RAT pushed the door open and as he stepped out, the creaking hinges silenced the conversation.

He ran across the street past the track field, where the Orange Men of Teton High were going about their rounding off routines in preparation for the next day's meet. Down the back road the boy sprinted as though possessed. Perhaps on this day, as on countless evenings before, the run would work its calming miracle. For more than a half mile he ran with no lag in his pace. An automobile approached from the rear, slowed, trailed him for an uncomfortable minute, then sped past him. Rat kept his eyes to the earth, not looking up until the car, with its single occupant, was a distance ahead.

Suddenly a rabbit hopped from a thicket and, startled, bounded for cover. The memory of the frightened animal of years ago, which had scampered from the same willow grove, scurried across his mind. Rat was still running away. He was still a frightened rabbit. The boy slowed his pace, and stopped. As he agonized over his failure, that deceitful, flaky demon, courage, skittishly returned. It swelled timidly inside him, then crawled away as Rat thought of his utterly petrified behavior in the school corridor. It was stupid of him to have waited for the girl. A moment of rational thinking should have told him what the result would be. RAT Thompson should only dream of such things. Let him keep to his world of fancies. Let him find his romances there.

But out of these thoughts an anger grew and with it the traitor, courage, returned more boldly.

"Pengill. . .Pengill!" he grimaced. RAT turned and ran back toward Teton High.

But the dash was brief. As the school came into view, he could see the track team milling about on the field. In multi-colored dress, another group clumped about the bleachers. These would be the cheerleaders and the girls of the Pep Club. She would be with them. Tomorrow was their day on the field, too. Rat wavered. How could he approach her in such a crowd? He slowed his pace and with lowered head turned about and walked slowly back down the road.

That night was not gentle to RAT Thompson. For what seemed hours, he stared into the darkness, permitting his mind to take all sorts of mad flights. The raucous pulse and glitter of school life, which he longed to share, seemed beyond an impentrable wall. He felt sorry for himself as his thoughts turned to his loneliness. He was the man without the country, he mused, without a world. (The story had been a recent English assignment and he had felt a kinship.) He shuddered as he pictured himself alone, plodding hopelessly, searching over an empty earth. In its frustration his mind began taking glipses down those alluring and dangerous escape routes which he knew some young people had taken. He had seen some of these kids around, melting out their brains on the quick fixes of drugs. He thought of the far-out ones with their euphoric, strange smiles, reflecting an inner settling pall of pseudo-peace. Weren't they just seeking their own glittery, tinsel world in their own way? Perhaps some of them were. He shuddered. What violent crashes those people must experience after their drug-imposed spells lift. Rat knew something of crashes to reality. His mind paused upon the thought then turned to other kids he'd heard about whose perceived hopelessness so crowded upon them that in moments of desperation they blew themselves totally away. The thoughts of self destruction shook him and he trembled. He was not ready to look down that grisly corridor.

He stirred himself, arose, and sat on the edge of his bed, chin in his palms. But finding no relief, he stepped to the window, raised the blind, and returning to bed, propped up his pillow and gazed out into the distant sky. On the horizon two of the brighter stars blinked red.

Jupiter and the Dog Star? He wondered. Was this their season? Probably not. Higher in the sky were another two. The Gemini Twins? He had heard of them. Was this their time? The stars were so fortunate, he thought. So above it all - up where there were no walls. How nice if there were a back road up there, up to where those solar winds (Is that what they're called?) could lift one and carry him out on past the Geminis - a human satellite, floating on to the farthest limits of the mind's ability to conceive, and then, with a gigantic sonic boom, this world, this idiotic earth, could be put out of one's thoughts forever. One could just float on and on in peace. RAT grimaced. He had permitted his mind to flip out again. It was spinning its old worn-out dreams.

But the vision of peace was calming and he permitted the indulgence. He pictured himself drifting peacefully, moving into a bright, open sky.

His thoughts paused again. Drifting to where? He wondered. Any journey must lead to somewhere, to someone. Surely there was no lonliness up there. He held to the thought. To heaven? His lips shaped the word. Rat guessed there was such a place. He stared more intently as though attempting to penetrate the darkness out beyond the stars. He felt an inner reaching as he wondered, and he became as the drowning man who grasps for the illusive log. With that reaching, he sensed a warmth inside.

But that negative, iron-shod destroyer of positive thoughts came trampling through his brain. "Heaven? Sure, boy," his cynicism mocked. "Haven't you been down that back road before? You just grab your technicolor heaven. Claw till your fingernails are bloody. Yell a million years, till someone cracks the door. Say your prayers, little boy, little rat, run your back road, your starry trail to heaven. Run your guts out on it." A chill of coldness crowded away the warmth and he shuddered. For long minutes he lay motionless, staring past the sinking points of light on the horizon. The subtle warmth returned. Finally RAT lifted himself and hesitantly slipped from the bed. A pale beam from the Gemini revealed a timid boy on his knees attempting the road upward.

Morning came as all mornings come and Rat boarded the school bus for the last time in his life. He appeared to have tuned the world out as he slumped into a seat and turned to the window. Trees and fields and weedy yards slid by on the Cache Road as the laboring vehicle, rocking with last-day-of-school jostlings and animated voices, approached the faded, yellowish-tan brick high school. As the building neared, Rat observed the usual milling of students about the entrance. On the front steps a man in an orange sweat shirt was making himself obvious with a gyration of his arms. What was the coach's calamity for the day? Rat wondered. He usually seemed to have one.

Brakes squealed announcing the intended stop and the bus's excited cargo pressed toward the door, and then out onto the walk. The man in the sweat shirt quickly approached RAT. There were no preliminaries.

"Jenny Fry came over from the grade school and tells me you've been running down the back roads all your life. I passed you out there last night, flyin' like a cat out of a dog pound - on my way to see if Billings is as sick as he says. He's out cold, and now Smith calls. Both of 'em down, and I've got problems, bigger'n a dinosaur. Two dinosaurs." The man huffed as he gave his problems dimensions with a wide sweep of his arms. "Two kids sick and I've got a meet today. Now I'm the sick one - and getting sicker by the minute." Rat scuffed the dirt with his shoe as the man paused and then bore in with his noted squinty-eyed scan. "Now this is plain nuts, positive cashews, and I can't believe it's me saying it, but Randall, I mean Thomas. . .Thompson. . .RAT, yeah, RAT, I just thought I'd let you know you're on the team - with lots of notice - like a full four hours before the meet starts. Nice isn't it?" The man glanced at his watch. "But Jenny Fry - you know the old lady - she says you can do it, and I'm taking her word on it. You run like you did last night and maybe you'll put some tracks up somebody's backbone. Who knows, could even be the kid's backbone from Fremont, and he's going for the State mark today, you can bet your smelly sweat socks on that. By the way, it'll be the cross-country you'll be running. Nice little jaunt of three short miles - a mile less than out to your home. No big deal. You'll be running with Pengill."

Pengill! The name clanged in Rat's brain like a foundryman's hammer.

"I know it's just plain bongo drums, Thomas, but you'll run for us. . .won't you?" The man's eyes bore in. "Who knows, you might just win one of those nice orange "T" letters. I might even give you two of 'em." There was a softening in the man's voice and manner. "It would be an honor to run, son. You'll do it won't you?"

"Well." The man was relieved as Rat stammered and then nodded for want of words.

"Now, you be down to the locker room at twelve. I'll fit you with a uniform. And you could go down after a while an' tell Miss Twitty in the kitchen to give you a big bowl of macaroni. Don't know that it'll do any good, probably won't, but it might. High octane fuel, they say. Eat it before ten, and nothing after. Hear?"

So the door swings and Rat walks into the sun. Neat story, again. "You just call up to heaven, boy; the door swings and you walk fast. Just right. Eat your macaroni. Don't ask why."

But the crack in the door was only a sliver, as RAT found soon enough. All morning long his pulse pounded. It had begun thumping with the coach's abrupt announcement on the sidewalk, and as the old hall clock ticked off the seconds and announced each hour with a chime, his anxiety grew and the slippery imposter, courage, played its games. RAT's determination would rise up bravely, reminding him that if he could do anything at all, he could run. He had the presence of mind to know that. And hadn't he daydreamed half his life of going head to bloody head with Pengill? But with the repeated chimes of the clock, with their reminder that the meet was one hour nearer, bravery would cower and slip away and the thought of the quiet back road would rush in.

In spite of it all, RAT stayed on, and unbelievable even to himself, he ate his bowl of macaroni, and he did manage the courage to step timidly into the locker room at noon, there to be confronted immediately with Pengill's snide, underbreath comments. ("This isn't no rat race. Who let the rat in? I'm not runnin' with no rat.")

The trembling, new Orange Man was attired in a uniform which might have been reserved for a clown. ("Can you believe it? All the spare uniforms have been sent off to the cleaners, and Billings and Smith have theirs out to their houses. But it isn't like you're going to have to wear this thing all your life - and it is sort of orange.") The coach had resurrected a matching set of athletic trunks and shirt from the antiquity of a seldom-opened, odoriforous storage locker grave, last used, so the coach remembered, by one Moose Grover. Old Number Twelve, it was. Moose had washed his purple socks with the garments, so legend had it, and the uniform was discarded to the locker as unsalvagable.

Dressed for his duel in the sun, RAT Thompson stood by himself on his field of combat, a curious and unlikely warrior. He felt the gaze of the growing numbers of spectators, who were beginning to move into the bleachers from the parking areas, where bannered and graffittied busses from the visiting schools were pulling up. Each vehicle was a moving cacophony of happy, boisterous sound. The open windows were crowded with the heads of cheering, jeering, shouting teenagers. A bright June sun heralded this day of days. With the track contest as a finale, the prison doors had been swung open after nine months of hard captivity. School was out.

On the oval field the athletes were into their warm-up routines. They stretched their limbs, sprinted in quick bursts off starting blocks, bicycled their legs. More distantly on the cinder track, the great Fremont runner, on display in his school's unusual golden zebra-like markings, paced in an easy, confident stride. He was a picture of human fluidity. The youth seemed psyched into his race already, obviously a magnificent athlete. Unquestionably, the State cross-country mark would be threatened today.

And for Teton's Orange Men, this was their hour in the sun: a home team before a home crowd. Terry Pengill played his part grandly. The show-off flailed and flourished, glancing repeatedly at the crowd as he strutted. RAT observed the braggart's antics. The old animosity grew in him. He'd give his last ounce of strength, from those cheese-sprinkled curls of macaroni, to run the wind-puffer into the mud. The Fremont runner, and all the rest, whoever they were, had hardly entered his mind. They weren't even in the race. It was Pengill who kept him on the field in the clownish uniform. Pengill was his race.

"Remember what I said, Thompson." The coach, huffing up from the rear, startled him. You pace yourself, now, ya' hear? You gotta' run with your head, not your feet; your feet don't think. You don't and you'll go down like a bag of anvils out there; you'll break both knee caps against that iron wall. You'll die out on that third mile. . . maybe even the first." The man's ultimate emphasis seemed to stress the act of dying. "You'll hit that iron wall, splat, and you'll go down, dead as a doornail, and I'll have to come out an' carry you in. I get no pleasure in carrying a corpse. Remember that. Pace yourself." The man stomped away huffing and calling to his sprinter, "You remember, Schwartz. . ."

Suddenly the jiving notes of a pep band blared. There was a flourish of pom poms, cheerleaders handsprung their delirium, and the athletic teams dashed to their final huddles. A voice rose through loudspeaker static, sounding greeting and tradition. The meet was on.

The clash of gladiators began with the fleet-of-foot sprinters straining off the starting blocks; then the vaulters reached for the sky, and over in the chalk ring, the iron ball soared, a relay team slapped backs with determination as their moment for a try at glory came.

A half hour went by before the loudspeaker voice chilled RAT with a call for the cross-country men. There was a desperate inner struggle to suppress outright panic as he approached the starting line. His pale, thin legs extended downward from the too-large, purple-stained, orange trunks, which were lumpy at the waist from a tucked-in, long shirttail. The shoulder straps of his shirt hung nearly to his belt, which partially covered the numeral, Old Number Twelve. The boy's hair had somehow been skewed upward and his athletic socks, rather than cling smartly to his calves, drooped in wrinkles about his ankles.

"The State, Terry!" the girl's voice shouted. How well RAT knew that voice. Cocky Pengill thrust his fists upward in recognition as he shouldered his way to his favored position on the starting line. The world swam during those long, silent moments as RAT found space between two crowding bodies and leaned forward awkwardly, waiting for the clap of the gun. His eye caught the Fremont runner's determined face, and he saw Pengill edge his foot ahead for an inch's advantage.

Crack!

RAT Thompson jumped as though touched by a glowing ember. He ran as a frightened mustang. In a matter of seconds he was sprinting out ahead of the clump of runners.

"Slow down, RAT! Slow your pace." The Teton coach's shout could be heard above the noise of the crowd.

"RAT! Slow down, RAT!" came imitating voices and laughter from the stands. "You slow down, there, RAT!" Not to be denied a share in the fun, Pengill waved an arm as he ran and pointed jokingly at the unusual runner in the flapping, faded uniform.

Racing as though in the hundred yard dash, RAT flew down the cross-country trail, which curved away from the crowd, traversed a farmer's field, skirted a riverside pasture, arced through a wooded grove, and finally, emerging from the grove, continued arrow-straight one quarter-mile to the tape, which glittered taut across the track in front of the spectator stands. That last quarter-mile, four hundred and forty yards, had reverently been christened by runners of the past the "Trail on Fire", for the experience of leaving the cool woods and turning into the blaze of the sun, while pushing oneself to that thin outer edge of human endurance, made of the run to the tape a sprint through a blazing Sahara.

His indiscretion early in the race had assured RAT a well-earned and early appointment with that stern qualifier, the coach's iron wall, for in direct opposition to his instructions, the boy had run as that "cat from the dog pound". Perhaps he had paid too much to feed the repulsive Pengill the dust from his heels, but whatever the price paid, before the first mile had been run, Rat was sure he had destroyed the swaggering showoff, for after falling farther and farther behind, Terry now struggled in sweat and humiliation two hundred yards back on the course and no better than tenth in the file of runners. How simple that victory had seemed to Rat. How ridiculously simple. The threatening image of the abusive snob, which had hovered over his life for more than a decade, had inexplicably been reduced to a punctured hot air balloon, which now lay trampled in the dirt. The unbelievable reality startled the boy. The monstrous thought was almost beyond his mind's ability to comprehend. Could this be but one more of a thousand daydream bubbles, which after a brief effervescence would rupture and plummet RAT to the ever-waiting, cold reality? Wouldn't it be, after all, RAT Thompson who would be trampled in the mire?

But there were no daydreams in the pleasant reality of RAT's steady footfalls on the soft turf. Nor was there fancy in the exhilaration he felt in his deep, cool breaths and the easy reaching of his legs. These sensations were not daydreams.

Down over the river marshes he glimpsed flights of pintails sweeping low over their nesting grounds as he glanced back again and again to reassure himself that he was maintaining his distant lead over the steadily pacing athlete of the Golden Zebras. Now he must only hold that lead and he would win easily. RAT Thompson would break the tape. The thought frightened him. Could he handle the consequence of thrusting himself into the role of a winner? How do heroes behave? State title holders? What would his relationship with Pengill be? His mind mulled the question. He smiled. He could handle that consequence. "How do you like it, Pengill?" His mind exulted. "Like the feel of heel prints tattooed on your backbone? Hey, hey, Pengill!" RAT's thoughts grew heady. He saw himself receiving the blue ribbon - and the coveted orange "T" for his sweater. An honored Orange Man! It was impossible. Insane. The view from this pinnacle was mind boggling, frightening, wonderful. Could but all of life's problems melt away so easily. . .Perhaps they might. . .

Foolish mind. Precocious dreams. How could RAT know he was

riding on a vicious wind, carrying him to the precipitous edge of a dark pit? How could he know, for now he felt suspended, not sensing the fall of his feet on the soft earth. It was as though he were flying down the grassy path, lifted by those solar winds. The shade of the woods felt cool upon his moist skin. Foolish boy. . .

It was as he looked out from that dizzying pinnacle that he first sensed the approach of the coach's barrier of iron. He felt its onset as a troubling heaviness that grew in his legs and the first spark of a match strike in his lungs. But he put the warning impulses out of his mind. Nothing would be permitted to mar the wonder of this day. He had earned this hour. He wouldn't let it slip away.

But those sensations of tiring, once finding their place, slowly reached out their tentacles and before another half mile had passed, he found himself struggling in the coils of a python. He felt his breath being crushed from him. The match strike grew to a flaming blow torch in his lungs. Those dream bubbles of glory in whose filmy essense only minutes ago the world had been delivered to his feet, now as Pengill's balloon, had collapsed. Rat saw the iron wall, and he crashed headlong against it. The reality of his descent was more severe than he could have imagined. He struggled to put one foot before the other as the crushing, smothering weight of near total fatigue seemed to paralyse him, and there came with that paralysis an agony of mind which dwarfed the physical pain. Those gloatings over apparent victory flew away on dark wings, and with the crash of his dreams the floodgates were opened, turning free a lifetime accrued reservoir of the dirty water of doubt and fear. Out of that current, he fancied seeing Pengill pointing, his face breaking into a mocking laugh. "Who let the rat in? There's a rat over here!" Terry's accusing finger was a pointed needle. RAT's failures, as a deluge, cascaded upon him. Out of the torrent the girl of the graduation song giggled and he heard the voice, "What's your hurry. . .?" What a fool he had been. And now to have been drawn into this ridiculous race. He thought of the coach's cajoling face. It angered him. "Slow down, RAT. . ." Sure. Slow down. RAT need not have been reminded; he would always trail the pack. He was a loser. He knew it. Everybody knew it. He would quit the race. Why shouldn't he turn from the trail? He could leave this hour of horrors behind like all the others he had left in his tracks. He owed nothing to the coach. Let the clown rave - over Billings and Smith, and now over RAT Thompson, the biggest flake of all. The back road was not far away; he would leave this race of idiots, find a secluded grove, sprawl out to rest, then leave this world of lunatics in the dust. The boy's pace slowed; his eyes looked away from the trail to the inviting woods. But through the branches of the trees, a glimpse of the blue horizon grasped his attention. The light of the Gemini flashed in his mind - and the road up. If ever he needed those solar winds. . .

It was as RAT groveled in the deep pit of his agony that from somewhere out of the chaos of his thoughts there came his Moment. His Instant. Who can say more of this Moment than that it seems to await the interval after one has trudged to the end of that lowest of low roads, after the real self has finally emerged bare under the lights, stripped of its stupid facade, its ridiculous vanity, or at the other extreme, from the debilitating mire of its harbored, even savored, negatives of life. It is at this moment, there may arise an inner will, an overwhelming desire to torch this ugliness away, and with that fiery cleansing, a new threshold, seared clean, can now emerge and accommodate the genesis of a renewed soul, burned clean by the fire. And with those feelings that stubborn door swings.

RAT could not possibly have understood the complex depths of this surge of emotion. But out of those depths, his Moment did come, and he entered the Race. He saw his opponent. Pengill? Ridiculous. Pengill had strangely shrunken to the stature of an ant. RAT saw the real monster in his life. It startled him, for he looked upon his mirror image. He saw the cowering, the shrinking, the self-pity, the foolish and destructive chasing after daydreams. So Terry Pengill was not, after all, the curse of his life. Beat the buffoon? Sure. Terry deserved to feel RAT's tracks along his spine. But that was not the race. Pengill was a fool, running a race of fools. Let him sweat the marrow out of his bones for his chance at an eye-flicker in the sun. Let him and all the others run their guts out to find their fool's gold. RAT would still put them down hard, but that was not the contest. The Race was against a wasted life, a coward's existance. With victory, couldn't he put that detested past behind him forever? RAT sensed that it could be so. He could break free from those pressing walls.

With these emotions there came from somewhere out of that deep well, it would seem, of the very soul itself, a renewal. The contest now consumed the boy. He felt the simplistic resolve to die rather than fail, to be condemned to the old life forever. If by the coach's words he must be carried in, so be it. Let the coach carry the corpse. Even though the numbness now crept from his legs upward into his loins and cramps knotted his stomach, causing him to slump forward, he would not give in to them. RAT felt a nausea and he thought he would vomit. He was sure if he spat, the issue would be red with his blood. But if that was to be a part of the price paid, let his stomach spew. Let the blow torch melt out his lungs.

He ran. He drove his legs toward the last half mile and he felt suspended again. He felt the lift of the solar winds. Soon he would reach the edge of the woods and then he would turn his opponent, his own monster self, into the sun and char its bones on the coals of the "Trail On Fire".

Back on the field the coach mumbled to himself as he kept an eye on the gap in the woods.

"I was a fool to listen to Jenny Fry," he grumbled. "What does she know about a race? Runs down a back road, does he?" The man turned to the high-jumpers, where a boy reached for the sky to clear six, four. "Letting the kid run the way he did - I was a fool to do it. Today'll be his funeral, not his graduation.

"They're coming in! There's one coming!" A voice from the stands shouted its acknowledgement of the appearance of a cross-country runner on the "Trail On Fire."

"He's Teton's!" shouted another. "He's an Orange Man!" Indeed, a runner had emerged from the grove in the east. At the announcement, the coach consulted his watch, and then pretended to swoon over the runner's apparent pace. The State mark was not only threatened, it was under seige.

"How in heaven's name could the hot air puffer, Pengill, pull off a record like that?" The coach clapped a palm of disbelief to his forehead.

"The State, Terry!" rang the girl's voice. "You've got the State!"

"State! State! State!" the cheerleaders frenzied on the uptake.

Sure, Terry, take your State. Run your sweaty socks over it. Pull that straining, drained hulk out of ninth place and get your State.

As the figure on the trail neared, an uncertain murmur rose from the crowd. The laboring athlete, bent dangerously forward, in no way measured the proportions of the school braggart's thick-shouldered body. And the uniform was not of the crisp satin worn by all the Teton men - save one.

It was RAT Thompson who came down the trail, a boy being tortured in the furnace. His mouth gaped open, exposing to the world those protruding teeth. His eyes were slitted with fatigue and the sting of perspiration. His pace was unsteady, uncertain, as though at a feather's brush he would collapse. The youth heaved his breath to douse the blaze inside. His legs had turned to stone. The "Trail On Fire" was consuming him. He was offering himself up. And still, at his side, his Monster, starkly visable to him, steamed repulsive sweat, keeping pace for pace. Rat saw the finish line in the distance. The white tape taunted as though it were glittering a billion light years away. He sensed hearing his name.

"RAT! RAT!"

With that bit of distraction, a toe of stone scrubbed the earth in a stiff, spastic movement and the boy went down in a heap. His Monster's fist had dropped him. RAT flailed his arms, struggled to draw his legs under him, and in an enormous effort rose to his feet. Crimson showed through the dust on his knee and elbow. For a moment unsure which way he should go, he directed his steps toward the shouting crowd.

Now, in the wood's gap, the great Fremont runner appeared, and heartened by the leader's collapse, bore down on the flaming trail. RAT obliged again. His arms flailing, his fingers clawing the air for support, he dragged that iron toe once more and went down as a dead man. He moved convulsively in the dirt, thrashing his arms and legs, attempting to raise himself. His Monster, frothing in a last effort, reached for his throat. RAT had difficulty breathing. It was a death struggle to turn his head to prevent the dust from invading his breath-starved lungs. He was being strangled. His cramping stomach drew his knees upward to his chin.

"RAT! RAT!" the coach shouted as he ran toward the boy. "No, RAT! You've had enough!" The roar from the bleachers overwhelmed the man's voice. But the youth did not hear. The final, desperate struggle was on. He felt himself sinking under a suffocating, choking attack.

As the coach reached him, a graying woman in the stands looked on through dark-rimmed spectacles.

"Lift up your head, Ray Thompson!" she repeated the demand of many years ago. Her fingers were drawn into white-knuckled fists. "Lift up your head, Ray."

Who can say that he did not hear. He lifted his head and somehow got to his feet. He pushed, flailed himself free from the coach's grasp, and now, with that desperate effort, his Monster relaxed its grip. RAT lurched, struggled, attacking the last twenty yards.

Down at the gap, Terry Pengill made his approach on the flaming trail. Done, humiliated, languishing in the race of fools, one would hope that in his anguish he had glimpsed the face of his own Monster.

"RAT! RAT! Come on!" The roar reached his ears as the sound of distant, tumbling water as the boy went down the third time. But now, RAT's Monster, his hated self, shriveled to the stature of a groveling dwarf and groaned away. The youth clawed, he grasped, he crawled. He reached out and the eternity to the shimmering tape closed.

He came to his senses in the arms of the coach, whose face was pinched, his whole being subdued with emotion. The man said nothing. What could words have added?

In the stands, limp from that overwhelming ordeal, the teacher, Jenny Fry, who in wisdom's insight, had seen the Race, lifted her glasses to dab her eyes with a handkerchief.

"You can smile now, RAT Thompson," she muttered. "Yes, now you can smile."

Today, hanging in neat dignity in Teton's trophy cabinet across the hall from the ancient, brown-framed clock and the clucking steam radiator, Old Number Twelve rests. The purple stains, carefully retained, add to its legend, and the name, RAT, inscribed in gold, adds to its lore.

14

The Mighty Bedlam

"You're botching the works, Bedlam! There's another shipment at the dock. Move, Bedlam, move! Read my lips. It's out of here by five, or you're out! Got that?" Hardknuckled Dearmott supervisor, B.P. Park, was a mad bumble bee zooming about the receiving clerk's desk. He was Simon Legree with two whips, he was Attila the Hun on a down day. Poor Roscoe Bedlam's normally placid, plodding nature was transformed into a bungling bundle of motion. Under that heartless pressure, his mind functioned erratically; he was all thumbs.

That's the way the day ended. But it did end, and now Roscoe who, some five years before had ranged out to the big city from Teton Basin with great dreams and greater timidity, waited for the Essex Street bus on the corner across from "Benevolent Old Dearmott Supply", as Chairman Bott was given to referring to his money-generating kingdom (which kingdom, of course, bestowed its benevolence and beneficence primarily upon the Chairman). The abused Bedlam, still afflicted with starts and trembles, stepped farther backward under the entrance overhang of a printing establishment, for it rained a cold drizzle and the Essex was, as usual, overdue. Subconsciously fingering the fare coins in his trench coat pocket, his thoughts were of Ole B.P., as Parke was unaffectionately known in the Dearmott shipping satellite. The clerk stewed and grimaced, he cursed and threatened, under his breath, of course, and then, after drawing a deep breath, he shrugged a shrug of relief, for it was Friday and the eternity of a weekend lay off ahead. The prospects of that uncluttered eon of time tantalized him and the prolific Bedlam mind, being unusually creative and responsive to such stimuli as upcoming weekends, raced as a terrier chasing a stick away from that drizzly, depressing world of endless invoices, and snarling supervisors. From this moment until 8:30 AM, Monday, Roscoe Bedlam would bar the gate to his own private weekend world. The likes of B.P. Parke and the pressure kettle, Dearmott, would be refused admittance. The clerk smiled, for his mind pictured the grim Parke countenance pressing at the iron-barred Bedlam portal.

"Mr. Bedlam. Please," the supervisor was pleading, "I beg you Sir. May I come in out of the storm?" Roscoes eyes firmed (both his real and imaginary eyes), those righteous, steady eyes. They narrowed, pierced. Words were not necessary. The miserable supervisor turned, bowed low in rejection and disappeared into the threatening night.

But suddenly, this fine vision was interrupted by an unpleasant nudge in the ribs, as out of the dismal evening of reality, Dearmott dock man, Melvin Dew, his visage preceded by a huge nose, rudely intruded. Roscoe grimaced at the intervention of this lowly gate-crasher.

"You're smilin' an' squintin' like you're happy, 'n after all that Ole B.P. said?" Melvin blurted, referring to the hour of work just past. Roscoe, retaining his smile, returned the nudge. Poor Melvin Dew would never comprehend the lofty Bedlam mind, for he was cursed with that grevious ailment known as "negivitis mentalis", or in simpler, loading dock terms, he was possessed with an adverse brain wrinkle which unfailingly pictured all good things as bad and bad things as a good deal worse.

"Gonna' git canned, Rosc?"

"Canned? Why, no, Melv."

"Thin, you gittin' a pay cut?"

". . .why,. . . why, of course not." Melvin's affliction was catching. Roscoe began to feel the old Dearmott gloom again.

"I thought Ole B.P. was gonna'. . .Hey! There he is! It's Ole B.P!" Melvin's proboscis was suddenly thrust up to touch Roscoe's ear. "Don't you look at 'em, Rosc," he whispered, "don't give 'em another chance to can ya." Against the glare of the wet street and traffic lights, the unmistakable profile of the Dearmott foreman passed. It was a hard face even in its silhouette.

"You're safe now 'til Monday, Rosc." Melvin whispered. "He's gone. He can't fire ya' 'til Monday, 'nless he calls ya' on the phone. That's the way he canned Billy, on the phone, ya' know. Don't answer it, Rosc. Whatever you do, Rosc, don't. Let it ring. Well, see ya' now, Rosc. Have a nice weekend. Call me if ya' need cheerin' up. I'm good at it, ya' know." With that, Melvin turned his beak toward the approaching Haver Scranton, whose front tire swirled a spray of moisture across the dock man's ankles as it pulled up to the curb. The bus door opened and Melvin disappeared. Good riddance. Roscoe shrugged once more. The likes of Melvin Dew must be barred at the Bedlam gate, too. There must be no dark clouds hovering over Roscoe's private horizons.

So, Bedlam's mental portal closed down once more. Peace returned as his eyes followed the departing bus, which shouldered its way into the traffic flow. With that visual stimulus, his creative brain fancied the conveyance as a ravenous sea monster, which had stopped momentarily to devour the dock man and then like a great whale jostled with a school of lesser motorized, aquatic life for moving space down the channel. The thought produced a fine mental image and Roscoe's mind was quick to advance the scenario:

"Man the scuppers, there, Dew! This is the Captain!"

"Aye, aye, sir, the scuppers are manned!" The prominent nosed swabby cocked his arm in salute as the Great Bedlam, facing the storm, tugged at the gold-clustered bill of his sea cap. The sharp spray nipped at his bronzed face and his lips tasted of brine.

"Lay for the Straits, Parke! You, there, B.P., read my lips!"

"But there's sharks and whales, sir, and we're wallowing!"

"Damned the minnows, man! One third sta'board ahead, or it's the plank for you, Parke!" With the command, the ship shuddered and the towering masts strained as though they would crash to the deck, but then the creaking frigate relaxed as it knifed head on into the giant swells off Tierra de Fuego.

"Secure the rat lines, bo'sun. . .!" Drawing vague innaccuracies from Hornblower, the Bedlam mind was in fine form.

But, interruption again. As his ship plowed off into the heavy sea, the dismal, earthly form of the Essex Street bus sailed down the whale channel and stopped at the curb. The vision faded and Captain Bedlam, pulling at the brim of his gray felt hat, stepped up, jingled his coins into the glass-sided fare box and finding a seat, settled back. As the passengers boarded, he reached back for the scuppers and the ratlines, but the frigate, now dipping the distant seas, was reluctant to return. Roscoe had found, though, that sometimes the essence of those vivid mental images, once gone, were difficult to recapture, and likely as not, if returned, came with an unpleasant twist:

"You blithering idiot, Captain! Sta'board put us into the reef!" So Roscoe let the sea adventure go.

As coins continued to jingle into the box, an odious appearing, unkempt man turned into the bus aisle. He was coarse and loud, brutish. He scanned the bus interior, selected with his eye a vacant seat beside a young woman, across the aisle from Roscoe, and strode arrogantly toward it. Observing his intent, the lady quickly arose and slipped to the vacant seat next to Bedlam. Innocently drawn into the little drama, the Dearmott clerk figited under the ruffian's glare, and was relieved when the glare turned as a leer back toward the woman. The man sat and leaned back with an unlit cigarette in his lips. Roscoe turned furtive glances toward the brute and he sensed the closeness of the female beside him, but frankly, the Mighty Bedlam behaved in the finest milk toast form. The thought did cross his mind that he might ask the lady if she would like to take his seat, that he would trade with her, but as the thought came he felt the threatening glares again from across the aisle and the notion raced away very quickly.

But the offending hooligan, after a short ride, left the bus and peace reigned. Roscoe wanted to say something like, "Lots of strange people around," or, "I was just about to knock his block off," but before his mind could put the right words together, the woman slipped back across the aisle to her original seat. The clerk felt guilty and let down, sitting as a stump as he had done. That would have been a fine opportunity to have risen up in true Bedlam spirit and defended a desperate soul in need. He glanced across the aisle, uneasy with his guilt, but the female stared straight ahead, her hands folded in her lap. So Roscoe shrugged again, leaned back, closed the mental gate.

The subdued interior lights of the bus and the mesmerizing drone of its engine created an atmosphere normally conducive to a nice nap, but the Bedlam mind, stimulated by the events just passed, and observing the blinking sign of a Mexican restaurant, rather than relax, raced away from that mundane setting:

"It was nothing." The great Bedlam's words were deep and melodious as rolling water, barely audible as befit the rider from the Tetons. The firm, narrowed eyes looked away, seeing that which one of common vision will never view.

"You saved me - you saved my family. Yes and you saved the whole village." The young woman across the aisle was now a lovely senorita, who looked up dewy eyed. The bus interior became the broad vista of the Rio Mesa spread. The hard Bedlam arm was extended to assist the beautiful creature as she stepped across the prone body of the brute who had offended her, one of many bodies which were strewn across the board walk. She touched the knuckles of his fisted hand. They were bloody. It was a feather's caress.

"Let me soothe them. . .horrible wounds." She touched her cheek to the hand.

"The scars will remind me of you," he said, looking down upon her.

"My father will want to reward you. Please come." But Bedlam, the stranger, his work done, with a distance in his eye and an upward tilt of his chin, swung effortlessly into the saddle and. . .

But the heroic vision was jarred from Roscoe's thoughts as the bus lurched and his head thumped backward against the metal hand bar at the top of his seat. The spacious acres became the darkened bus interior again and the senorita sat quietly as before, across the aisle. Roscoe pressed a fingernail against the skin of that wounded knuckle, making a white indentation. That was such a nice vision. He would just have to resurrect it again sometime. What a noble cause. And what would the father's reward have been?

But, reality again. The bus stopped at Essex Street and Roscoe made his way up the aisle, stepped out into the drizzle and turned down the concrete walk toward a small, gray shake home and a smaller, gray shake garage, two humble structures which stood closely tucked together under the pale glow of a bare, forty-watt porch globe. The front window revealed Elva Bedlam's rounded profile as she passed between a floor lamp and the curtained window. Roscoe recognized the silhouette of a frying pan in her hand. The sight of the pan reminded him that he was hungry. His steps quickened toward the door.

"We need a sack of potatoes, Roscoe," Elva spoke as she watched him fork up the final gravy-smeared whip of tuber from his plate at the supper table. "Fifty pounds will do us 'til Christmas."

"Lots of spud eating," the clerk muttered unintelligibly, swallowed, then spoke more clearly. "I'll drive out tomorrow, dove."

Roscoe clung to every hour of this precious, uncluttered time. The TV featured the Mauling Monster and Butcher Butler alternately stalking and bruising each other on the 'rassling' mat, and there followed a vintage 'oater' with heavy gun play about a threatened corral. The Rio Mesa relived. Nice. He reluctantly retired past midnight and was up at eight for his hashbrowns and eggs, and then he dropped Elva off at the mall for her weekly rejuvenation of 'shopping around'. After his run out into the country for the bag of spuds, he'd meet her at McDonald's, and then to the movie, where a noted mega-thriller was on its second week's run. Very nice.

From the mall Roscoe motored out on Route 13, where, five miles into the countryside, a number of rural people sold bags of potatoes from their front yards. It was a fine, stimulating ride. The smell of burning weeds on ditch banks and the inspiration of the clear, open sky and the fall fields combined to touch and enlarge the Bedlam spirit - and his mind:

"Yes, I operate ten thousand acres, give or take a thousand." The steady, narrowed eyes of the Teton man swept across his private landscape. "Yes, I hire fifty men - two hundred in the peak seasons." His listeners were a foreign delegation on their high-level mission to observe the world-famed Bedlam operation. Yesterday's troupe came from Mongolia, today it was the Queen, her escorts, and a large company from Katmandu: "My nation would like this gold medal upon you pinned," her highness purred in a pleasant, broken tongue, "and honor will be ours, you come our land, guest. . ." The Bedlam acknowledgement was appropriately reserved. Of course he would accept, and he was conveying his message when a boisterous clutch of clucking intruders shouldered their way through the crowds, demanding an audience. Their leader bore the hard profile of B.P. Park. But at the piercing glance of the famed Bedlam eye, the clucking was stilled and the strange visitors, wearing curious monkeyskin turbans, stepped quietly to the display table and passed the famous Bedlam potato strain from hand to hand. They sniffed the tubers and one of them, in absorbed curiosity, pressed a fingernail into a delicate potato skin, but sensing the glare of the all-seeing Bedlam eye, he bowed apologetically and, continuing to bow, stepped back, giving way to the Russian team of agro-scientists, just out of the Steppes. They, too, palmed the fabled produce, whispering in unintelligible, but obviously envious words. They examined a potato eye with a magnifying glass, which one produced from a briefcase.

"They'll never find the secret. . ."

But suddenly, Roscoe's well-assured response was interrupted when, from out of reality, there appeared in his rear-view mirror, on the brink of the hill behind him, a black sedan, closing its distance with high speed. He could hear its engine roar as it approached, swerved and passed him. The occupants were desperate, angry appearing men. The black car careened on down the road and then, the instant before disappearing around a wooded bend, Roscoe observed what appeared to be a black carrying case thrown from the auto's window into the heavy foliage at the roadside. And more startling still, there as suddenly appeared in the rear-view mirror a second and then a third vehicle, which had joined the chase, but these bore the ominous, car-top flashing lights of the police. Roscoe screeched his brakes, swerved from the road onto a convenient two-track lane, which led off into the trees near the very spot where the dark object thrown from the car appeared to have touched the earth. The Dearmott clerk brought his auto to a stop as the police cars, sirens wailing, flew by. Relieved, but perspiring, the innocent onlooker's eyes trailed the official vehicles until they, too, disappeared around the wooded bend.

Unsure whether to continue ahead, or to turn about and race away, Roscoe started the motor, which had killed with the abrupt stop, and looking over his shoulder to back the vehicle onto the asphalt road, he found his eyes suddenly focusing upon a black object not a dozen feet from the car, partially hidden by the thick undergrowth. The sirens now fading into the distance, the far distance, and Route 13 being for the moment deserted, Bedlam squirmed and gulped as though B.P. Parke were present. There was a strong magnitism about the dark object in the bushes. It held his gaze. He absently slid the zipper tab up and down on his coat, let out the clutch too fast and killed the motor again. He fidgeted, gulped, and then in an impulsive, uncharacteristic movement, flung the door open, hurried to the object, grasped it and in five seconds had thrown it in the back seat and was gunning the motor in reverse. He turned the auto about and sped back toward town. Poor Roscoe was all fidgets and starts again. What had he done? What was in the bag? Was the case full of money? Drugs? Was there a time-bomb concealed inside? The car lurched at that thought. He listened for a tell-tale clicking of a time clock, which obviously would have been used to time the blast. But his car roared too loudly to permit hearing such things. Sensing unusual speed, he glanced at the speedometer. The needle pointed past eighty, faster than he had ever driven! He pushed the brake pedal too hard, and almost lost control of the car as he was thrust forward against the steering wheel. Not only did the speed unnerve him, but the alarming thought that a roving patrolman might be clocking him with a radar gun and pull him over terrified him. Wouldn't an alert officer demand that the suspicious appearing valise on the back seat be opened?

But, as the car slowed, and Roscoe reached out desperately to control his senses, the thought occured that the bag likely contained only a dirty shirt and a change of socks. Why get so excited over a little suitcase? But, then again, why would anyone throw his shirt and socks out the window if the police were on his tail? An overpowering fear returned with the thought that the bag might be full of heroin, cocaine or crack! It would be jail for sure if he were caught! At this alarming thought, the clerk slammed the brakes again and the car careened as it slowed to fifteen. The mighty Bedlam, frankly, had lost control. The lofty smile and steady eye, where had they gone?

Up ahead, Route 13 intersected an unnamed country lane. Struggling with indicision, Roscoe turned the last instant onto the quiet gravel-topped avenue and motored a full five miles into the tranquil countryside, clearly advertising his escape by leaving a very evident trail of dust. He felt relieved to observe a secluded roadside rest area ahead and resolved to pull over, collect himself and check the contents of the mysterious bag. If it contained guns or drugs or dirty socks, he'd ditch the thing post haste. Stopping beside a leaf-covered picnic table, Bedlam eased out of the car, scanned his surroundings carefully and listened intently. The bronzed leaves rustled above him and a crow called hoarsely from a treetop. He heard his heart thump. Trembling, he looked about again, and satisfied that he was alone, he opened the rear door, quaking as though he were opening a tiger's cage. He eyed the case suspiciously. It appeared to be of leather, about as long as his arm and as thick as a brick's length. Two heavy straps were buckled securely at the top. He reached out a nervous finger and very gingerly touched the valise as though he expected it to be hot. Pausing again, he reached a hand toward the grip, but before his fingers made contact, the rather distant shot of a gun shook him to his shoes. The police! He was caught! All fidgets and starts again, he rushed to the car trunk, raised the lid, hustled back for the black bag, and shielding it with his body (and thereby making a much greater suspicious spectacle of himself), rushed to the trunk again and dropped the bag inside. Covering it with the spare tire and the empty gunny sack, which he had brought for the potato purchase, he slammed the lid, flew into the car, reved the motor and letting the clutch out too fast again, the car jerked and lurched ahead onto the gravel road. He reversed his direction and, leaving the long trail of dust again, motored back toward town. Across the field he saw a lone bird hunter and his dog following a weedy ditchbank. Roscoe sighed.

The Bedlam auto, behaving as a homing pigeon, found the shortest route back to Essex Street, stopping enroute, dutifully, at a farm house where a hand written sign advertised potatoes for sale.

"In the trunk?" the rural man asked as he carried the bulging bag toward the car,

"No. . .no!" Roscoe stammered. "No! Not room. . .not enough!" The farmer shrugged at the over-reaction, hoisted the dusty bag through the rear door and onto the seat, giving his customer a quick "well,-it's-your-car" glance.

At last, the Dearmott clerk breathed easier as he steered his auto into the gray shake garage and pulled down the door. Taking the case from the auto, he left the building through a rear portal and then attempting to shield the valise again with his body, hurried to the back porch, fumbled his keys, entered the kitchen and placed the bag on the table. He then hurridly pulled down all the window blinds in the house, returned to the kitchen and faced the black case as though it were a breathing monster. Now he would solve the great mystery, once and for all. With every caution, he reached out his trembling fingers, unbuckled the straps and clicked the brass latch open. He lifted the lid a crack, paused, then jerked it fully open. Roscoe Bedlam grasped the table to keep himself upright. There before his transfixed eyes, stacks of green legal tender stared up at him. A fortune it was! There were crisp fifties, twenties and tens, stacks of them. Roscoe was required to lean back in a chair to collect himself. It was a full two minutes before he stood again, faced the case, reached out a trembling finger, touched a pile of fifties and pressed. The stack gave slightly with the contact as a pile of greenbacks ought to. There was no cocaine, no bombs, just stacks and stacks of hypnotizing, green wealth! He lifted a pile of fifties from the valise by the broad rubber band which bound it. He thumbed a corner of the stack. The alluring, mesmerizing corners whisked by. How many were in the stack? Two. . .three hundred bills? Fifty times three hundred? How much was that? His mind attempted to comprehend the mathematics of wealth, but it bogged down into a stupor.

After a pause, Roscoe lifted the band slightly and slipped out of the stack a number of bills. The green came free. He counted. Ten bills, there were. Five hundred dollars! Roscoe reached for his wallet, unbuttoned the rear pocket tab, opened the leather purse and beside the five and the four ones inside, he slipped in the ten new bills. Folding the wallet, he held it up for inspection. It appeared hardly thicker than before, really. But it looked different just the same. A wallet with four ones and a five inside gets no attention, but deposit ten fifties in there and it's a different matter. It'll feel like a hot rock in your rear pocket, as Roscoe found, and he became aware, too, that his hand just automatically reached back, ever so often, to touch the folded fortune and to reassure himself that the pocket flap button was secure.

The erratic Bedlam mind finally got around to Elva and how he should drop this bombshell on her. However, he dropped it, it would be a bombshell. He knew that. What if he just nonchalantly lifted out of his wallet a fifty, just like it was small change, there at McDonald's. The Bedlam mind took the bait:

"You, there, Mac, how about two of your Big Ones and make it two more to go. Toss in a triple order of fries and a gallon of your dark-shaded diet, heavy with the ice. Hop to it, Mac." While the help was busy pouring and frying, he'd hold a fifty between finger and thumb and give his wallet a clean-out, tucking all ten fifties, one at a time, in his shirt pocket, visable to all.

"Here, keep the loose change, Mac."

"But there's forty dollars."

"Forty doesn't buy much nowadays, Mac. Spend it on your mother." As Bedlam tucked the other nine bills in his wallet, the clerk would gasp, "You're wonderful, sir. Thank you, thank you. . ." But the vivid picture faded as the white-powdered image of Elva's nose emerged. She'd wait until they had reached the car, he knew that, and then she'd let him have it:

"Roscoe! You've drawn out all our savings! Roscoe! All those fifty-dollar bills in your pocket! You gone crazy, Roscoe? I think I'm going to faint!" Those would be her words, right to the letter. He knew it, and she'd faint, too.

"Well," he thought, "maybe I ought to wait until after the movie and drop the nuclear devise at the super market." (They always went to the supermarket after the show.) The Bedlam mind flew to this challenge. The image was clear: Just like it was pork and beans, he'd drop a dozen cans of salmon in the shopping cart, salmon, mind you, the fancy brand, big, top-of-the-line cans. Elva's eyes would glaze over. In the past she'd bought this Bedlam delicacy only once or twice a year and the small, inexpensive can at that. The Dearmott clerk's mind charged on: Then, what if he tossed in a half-dozen frozen pizzas, heavy on the cheese and pepperoni, Elva's favorite, and then drop a two-gallon bucket of Rocky Road ice cream in, with a quart of chocolate topping and one of marshmallow, and to go with that, he'd toss in a dozen of those exotic guava fruits that had always sat there on their private shelves, arrogant and untouched. And why not two orders of spareribs at the deli? Roscoe drooled; his mind was gaining momentum.

"And while you're at it, drop in a couple of those browned chickens, Mac, there on the spit. . .make it three."

" Three?"

"Three, Mac, and now as I think of it, make it four."

"Why do I carry these fifties in my shirt pocket? Easier to reach, Mac."

But the Bedlam mind had trouble holding course. Reality kept intruding. It was Elva's pestery, powdery nose again, there in the car:

"Roscoe! What on earth have you done? You spent your whole paycheck in there! Take me home , Roscoe! Home to mother's." Those would be her words. He knew it. And she'd go home to mother's, too. For a week.

Well, what if he should just slip a twenty occasionally in Elva's purse. The idea sounded good at first, but as he thought about it, he knew what she'd do:

"Roscoe, I was sure I paid the clerk for your black socks and my broom and the jelly beans. But here's the money, still in my purse. Roscoe, you've got to take me right back, now." That's what she'd say. He knew it, and he'd have to take her right back.

That left just going to the mall, picking up Elva, escorting her to the kitchen and confronting her face on with the whole valise of cash, then be prepared to catch her, for the sight of those bills would do her in. He knew it. The Bedlam mind refused to expand on that scenario. It had had enough. Roscoe stared again at his fortune. He felt confused. One would think the sight of a stack of fifties, as high as a brick, would clear any frustration from even the most reluctant mind, put it at peace. But to the clerk, it brought only confusion. Roscoe, in his wild fantasies, had dreamed a hundred times that he had come across a fortune and while under those wonderful spells had always viewed his wealth with that steady, unshakable control. Of all people, Roscoe Bedlam should have taken this day's events in full stride.

A sudden knock at the door shook him. The blood drained from his face. It was the FBI! He knew it. He thrust the stack of fifties back in the case, closed the lid, and nervous to the point of collapse, he forced the bag behind the refrigerator.

"You feeling alright, Roscoe? Your face is pale." It was Mabel and her clutch of scruffy kids from next door, forgetting again that Elva was always away at the mall on Saturday mornings. As she spoke, one of her hellions pulled free and made for the kitchen, but Bedlam caught his shirt tail and eased him and the whole brood back out the door.

"She's. . . at the mall. . .mall. Yes, fine. . .I'm fine." Roscoe was muttering and blubbering as he closed the door. He turned to the frig. The bag protruded very obviously. He had to get it out of the kitchen. On an impulse he grasped the valise, stumbled down the basement steps, looked about for a hiding spot and settling on the spare bedroom, pushed the case under the bed. It was a risky place, he knew it, for Elva would ferret it out in a matter of hours, for 'under the bed' was crowded with her treasures. But that had to do for now, for Roscoe was a half an hour past the appointed meeting at McDonalds, where he found Elva, fifteen minutes later, glancing at her watch and turning her powdered nose sharply at him.

"You're late. You sick?" she said in one breath as she observed her mate's unusual behavior.

"No, dove."

"You meet B.P. Parke, Roscoe?"

"No, Dove."

The clerk only nibbled at his Big Mac, staring past his wife out into the street. It was the same at the movie. Even two clawing, warty monsters emerging from a smoking volcano did not raise a gasp from him, for his mind was on the fifties in his pocket and the black case under the bed. But Elva came under the cinema's spell.

"Oh, Roscoe," she wailed softly, "Roscoe, hold my hand!" He dutifully clutched her reaching fingers, but his mind was probing possible hiding places for his fortune. He simply couldn't leave the valise under the bed, or anywhere in the house, for aren't houses of the wealthy robbed, and don't houses have fires? A hideous screech from the movie screen and a desperate gripping of Elva's fingers reaffirmed his conclusion that the leather bag must be removed from the premises. But where? The back yard? Of course. He could bury the bills in gallon jars, glass jars, for glass doesn't rust. He felt a bit relieved. There were a half a dozen empty cider jars in the garage, dusty and cobwebby. He'd bury the money tonight. But then a face on the movie screen, very closely resembling the Bedlam's nosey neighbor, shook Roscoe.

"What cha' doin', Roscoe, ole boy? You diggin' for oil, or maybe a grave, hea, hea, hea?" Or, "Now Roscoe, you're all mixed up, here. We dig in the garden in the spring, don't we?" A snow scene flashed on the screen, a dismal, cold scene, and Roscoe observed himself in the backyard digging into a snow bank every time he needed a bill. And would his neighbor miss that? Bury the treasure in the back yard? Never!

The film finally came to a snarling, crashing climax and Elva's wail snatched his thoughts from the bank across from Dearmott Supply, where he had visioned himself at the teller's window with a huge stack of greenbacks being counted out by the young woman who usually cashed his pay check. He saw himself turn toward a buzzing sound and saw the inhouse TV security camera flashing warning signals as it clicked away, its ominous lens focused toward him. Roscoe moaned. The T-men, wouldn't they swoop in on him before he could get out the door?

"There, there, Roscoe, it's just a movie." Elva comforted. "There, there."

There was no dropping in the shopping cart the dozen top-of-the-line cans of salmon. There were no browned chickens or guava. There was only silence between the two as Elva followed her usual shopping route, her pale, powdery nose sniffing out sale items and the free samples in the aisles:

"Here, Roscoe, taste this. Nice. And there's a nice lady giving hot beans on tacos in the next aisle, and she doesn't mind if you take two. Hurry, Roscoe."

The six, fifty-dollar bills remained untouched and secure in the buttoned-down rear pocket as Elva paid the bill.

"We overdrawn, Roscoe?" she muttered as she observed her mate.

"No, dove."

"A check didn't bounce?"

"No, dove," he repeated absently. His mind was preoccupied with another thought. Wasn't it highly likely that the cash in the basement was stolen? And wouldn't those T-men be out like bloodhounds, alerting every business in town? Surely by now they would have the men in the speeding car in custody, and don't T-Men, of all people, have ways of drawing out confessions? Roscoe's wallet felt like that hot brick in his pocket. He was carrying hot bills. He muttered quietly.

"Roscoe, you got gas?"

Evening came and even Crusher Candice and Buttress Beatrice on the 'rassling' mat, and not even the mid-night Voodoos could relieve his mind. The case in the basement had taken the form of a monster. Roscoe was very depressed. Every avenue he pursued, every conceivable approach to spending that mountain of wealth, met with a frightening roadblock. The money was surely stolen. He was certain of it. Else why the police chase? And wouldn't the serial numbers on each bill be recorded in every law office in the state? In the nation? Stolen! Of course, it was stolen!

Roscoe's mind then turned to a Dearmott scenario, sure to happen.

"New car, Rosc? On your pay?"

"New boat, Roscoe?"

"Quiting your job just like that? Rob a bank, Roscoe?"

The Great Bedlam had contracted Melvin Dew's mental ailment. Negivitis mentalis was destroying his mind. Where had those uplifting, wonderful dreams gone? The private Bedlam world had been destroyed. Wealth had destroyed it.

"There, there, Roscoe," came Elva's voice during the night as her mate pitched and tossed.

The tormented clerk had no heart for church next morning.

"You stay at home in bed, Roscoe."

But as Elva motored away to worship with Mabel and her brood, the mighty Bedlam had come to a conclusion. The steady mind was returning. He bounced out of bed, dressed, dashed to the basement, grabbed the detested bag, dropped it on the floor and kicked it, then rushed out the back door to the garage, threw the valise in by the spare tire again, turned the car onto the street and headed for Route 13, missing stop signs and turnoffs, but greatly pleased with himself. He'd had enough of riches. Let the wealthy keep their miseries.

He slowed and turned onto the familiar two-track lane into the bushes and stopped. It was a pleasure and a relief to open the trunk, grab the hated case and throw it right back where he had found it. Roscoe actually whistled a little tune as he took a final look at the dark shape in the bushes, opened the car door, backed out onto the asphalt and moved off toward town. But his whistling stopped abruptly as in his rear view mirror a car approached around the wooded bend, suddenly screeched its brakes and turned onto the two-track road Roscoe had just left. The auto stopped and a tallish man got out, quickly hurried to the black bag, grabbed it with both hands and threw it in the back seat. Roscoe was astounded. As his car opened a distance from the one just stopped, the clerk yelped with surprise. It was Ole B.P.! Ole B.P. had seen the bag, and now it was in his back seat! Roscoe yelped again.

"Let 'em have it! Ole B.P.! Serves him right!"

Monday came and the receiving clerk approached his desk at Dearmott with mixed feelings. Today there was excitement, but he also felt the old Monday gloom.

"You sad, 'n ole B.P. not comin' in, Roscoe?" It was Melvin Dew.

"B. P?"

"You haven't heard?"

"Hey!" Roscoe chirped. He smiled, he chortled. He danced a little jig around his scarred desk.

"Won't git fired today, Rosc!"

B.P. didn't come in. And he missed the next day, too. And the next. That was the morning the local news people broke the story that the police had swooped down on this couterfeiting gang, nailing the ring leaders after a high speed chase out on Route 13. The crooks had confessed to throwing a bag containing samples of their product into the bushes at the bottom of Milburn Hill, but a search had failed to turn up the case. . . however, a fifty and four twenties had showed up on a line, first at a suburan 7-11, then farther out, at Joe's Eats, and then still farther, at Sam's Easy Company, seventy miles on.

"The ring's closing," the report concluded. "We'll have the crook who's passing this stuff by sundown." The police Chief was certain.

An eon of peace trailed off ahead in the receiving clerk's mind. Roscoe, smiling, looked down upon a friendly stack of invoices. The Great Bedlam ruled again:

"You have the mind of a calculator, my good man." The Chairman was speaking. "Give this genius a raise. Triple Bedlam's salary!"

"Why you so happy, Rosc?" Melvin Dew interrupted. "Don't you know it's snowin' outside?"

But suddenly, the smile paled. Roscoe felt the wallet in his pocket as he sat down. It still contained ten hot fifties.

15

Thanks, Harkness, a Lot

So this is Trimington, whatever Harkness called it. Can you believe the guy was so puffed up about the place? Skink. This has to be it - the four-way stop with the gas pumps and the eat shop on the right, just like he said - then to the left. Good thing it's to the left. Nothing ahead but corn and squash and tomatoes. Piles of it for sale in front yards - shekel a dozen, six bucks a bushel, four coppers a pound. Whoever'd want a dozen shucks of corn, whatever they call 'em, or a lug 'a tomatoes? Lug? What's this lug, some local dude? A carrot picker skink? Hey, there's a local peon out by his squash pile waving his sign: four cents a pound. Mega bucks in this enterprise.

"Hey there, mate," I call. This narrow spot in the road labeled Trimington?"

"Tremonton."

"Know a local skink lizard, moved down from the Teton country to this squash patch, called Harkness?" I pour the smarts on heavy.

"Administer hari kari," he mouths off. No humor, the guy. Probably's been chained there to a stake by his ever lovin' pappy.

"I'll take mine with salt and pepper and a brew, mate." I give him a put-down grin with that final verbal needle then wheel left into the sun.

Let's see, now... from the four-way stop, proceed to Frosty's, then it's four west and six north. I guess I can handle that. Hey, there's ole Frosty's. Right on, Hark. Looks like the gathering place for all local squash pickers. The joint must be dead center of this berg, so it's four into the sun, then six toward the north pole. Slick. Alright . . . here's . . . one, and . . . now . . . number two . . ., three coming up . . . and four, the last one. Hey, I'm out of town headed for the corn. Can you believe it? Four squirrely blocks and I'm headed for the squash patch. Well, back to Frosty's.

"Hey, watch it, dude. Car here. Nice car, see it, squash eater?" As

I'm cruising along this goat path called a street, this skink aims his wheels at me, misses by a corn whisker then pulls up his trash heap at Frosty's and stops. Well, he's the only life I see, if you can call him life. Guess I'll give him a try.

"Hey mate," I say, pushing the brakes. "You piloting the wheels." ("Yes, you, I say under my breath. Who else am I looking at right in the phisog?") "You got a squash eater around this metropolis known as Harkness? Charley Harkness? A new dude here with that Idaho broque?"

"No."

"Got any Harknesses at all stumbling through these corn stalks?"

"Some."

"A young skink? Lizard skink."

"Yah, I guess." He gives with an uncertain grin.

"What's he answer to at dinner time?"

"Chuck."

"Chuck?" (Chuck, yes, Charley, no. What's eating this peach picker?) "Where's this Chuck live?"

"Fourth north and sixth west."

"Man, that's where I been and I'm out in the corn. He live in a corn field?"

"Humph."

"Listen, mate, hows about bird-doggin' me up to this four north. Guide me 'round the turnip piles, OK."

"Come on," he says.

"Thanks, mate," I say. The dude backs his heap of bolts into the street and heads out. Man, this skink's wheels can't be for real. Trash can. But there's motion, so I follow him up the asphalt to the roost of the great Harkness. From Hark's talk, I expected another Chicago, but . . . hey, the dude's pulling over. Here, I'll parallel him.

"Take a low five, mate," I say out the window. "This is the place, huh? Like Brigham Young? The prairie schooner with the cucumber pile and the babe in front?" I nod toward the nearest house.

"No. Up there." He points.

"With the peaches?"

"Yeah, the peaches." (Well, dude, why did we stop here? Skink.)

"Know this Harkness, huh?" I ask.

"Yeah."

"Some dude, huh?"

"Humph."

"Not your best friend, huh?"

"Humph." (Man, this kid hasn't discovered there's nice little noises called words.)

"Well, thanks, bud. Guess I'll go stir up Harkness."

"No, you won't."

"What'd you mean?"

"Isn't home." (Now you tell me. Man, you got real style.)

"Where is ole Harkness?" I say.

"Don't know."

"Sure, but like in the territory, or in outer space? Did he head back to his Tetonia digs?"

"Don't know." (This dude's no answering service.)

"When's he coming back?" (Why ask? I know his answers by heart. Skink.) I change the subject as I look toward the babe down the street by the cucumber pile.

"You a Mormon," I say with a heavy shade of putdown. He mumbles. "I thought all you pickle pickers up here were Mormons."

"I hate 'em all - can't stand 'em."

"That's a lot of hating," I say.

"Well, I do."

"Yeah, I can see you're puffed up about it. Hey, that babe over by the cucumbers, five dollars she's a Mormon and goes to that church." I point to a white spire that shows above the trees down the street.

"Go ask her," he says.

"Hey, mate, I will. Thanks, bud." (This skink must have been lost too long as a kid out in the squash patch.)

As the bucket 'a bolts clunks back down the street toward Frosty's, I make for the cucumbers and the babe. She's tallish, got her hair tied back and's wearing Levis, and her eyes miss nothing.

"Hows about a dime's worth of that big pickle," I smart off. She breaks a cucumber and gives me the short half. She's quick, I can see it. I give out with a dime. She dips in a pocket of a funny little apron-type she's wearing, gives me a nickle and four cents change.

"There," she says, "what else?"

"What is all this?" I say, giving the eye to the bulging boxes and baskets, "Peaches and corn and . . ."

"Acorn squash," she helps out.

". . . potatoes and tomatoes and watermelons . . . " I tick off the stuff heaped up behind the cucumbers. "How come you're up to your apron in this alphabet soup business?"

"It's a family project," she says as this big dude in bib overalls interrupts, driving up in his pickup. He steps out, looks from box to pile to basket, then begins pointing.

"A sack 'a corn and a box 'a tomatoes," he says, scratches his head and thumbs his suspenders, "three watermelons, dozen cucumbers and five boxes 'a peaches." He gives her a twenty. It goes in the apron pocket. She calls him 'brother' something as she thanks him. He likes it. I can see it. He'll be back, he says, and drives off.

"This brother of yours head an army?" I say.

"Yes, his family," she grins. Her eyes call me an idiot.

"Mormon, huh?"

"Of course." There's no hedging in her come-back.

"Your church, there?" I point at the white spire.

"Of course." This bob-tailed style with words on this plantation doesn't lend to conversation. I'm being kept at arm's length, and I'm grabbing for ideas to keep the talk going, which is new territory for a dude with my kind of ready tongue.

"Well," I say, "I'll take a nickel's worth of squash." I give back the nine cents and tell her to keep the change. She points to a greenish-yellow discard with a chink out of its side. It's a monster.

"It's all yours," she says. "Every bit." Those eyes still call me an imbicile. I change the subject, and sit on my squash.

"You know a Harkness dude, skink type, lives down the goat trail, there?" I point.

Those eyes put like a railroad spike through my visual orbits. I must have trampled sacred territory. Then she repeats her usual, "Of course." The dark peepers tell me there's lot's more to that subject than she's saying.

"Out of town, huh?"

"Well, yes."

"He go to church there, too?"

"Of course . . . yes, he does."

"Know when he's due back to his skink burrow?" I look over at his house.

My words aren't fitting with her. She turns on me, her eyes saying like, "who-is-this-wacko?"

"I think he'll be here on Sunday, maybe," she says a bit protectively. She knows more than she's saying. Those eyes tell me.

"Some dude, this Harkness," I say.

"Great dude," she answers, giving with a little laugh as she picks up some corn shucks that have spilled from a sack.

"Well, save me a watermelon," I say, "I'll be back."

"Don't forget your squash," she says, then tosses me a big apple.

So I load up and head out. Harkness. Skink. Wheel clear up here through the corn patches to see 'em and 'es gone. Oh well, an OK drive, and the babe's alright. Next Sunday it is.

Once out cruising on I-15, I manage to unload the squash through the window. It bounces once, then paints the road yellow and a big chunk hits the bumper of this pickup that's following. Oh-oh. The navigator's the big dude who loaded up at the babe's cucumber pile. His truck shudders and slows. I push the gas pedal, putting distance between us. Oh well, squash is biodegradable, my mind says. It almost biodegraded his truck.

The autumn days click by and it's Sunday and I'm back in this one-horse town, which is closed down, all five blocks of it - except the squash-picker's den of iniquity, Frosty's. Right off I spot this dude of scanty words sitting in his trash heap. He's slurpin'. I parallel him and jab the needle,

"Haven't skipped town yet?" He responds with a grunt.

"Seen Harkness?"

"No," he grunts again. A cop car flashes down the street toward the white spire.

"I hate 'em," he says, his eyes following the revolving light.

"Big hate you got, mate. Guess I'll follow the Smokey," I say and head out toward Hark's white spire. It's an OK day. Crisp. Leaves coming down and rasping across the road. I pull up in front of the church, nervous. I'm not my best around synagogues. Juveniles are chasing each other across the lawn. I wonder what the celebration's about. I get out and slink up to the front door like a thief, pull it open a crack and see her right off. I slip in.

"Who's manning the acorns?" I say, not knowing whether to whisper or not. She's leading a moppet set down the hall, turns surprised at me. Those eyes drill me.

"Oh, you. You're here." She looks nice, all fluffied up.

"I said I'd come. Save me a watermelon? Where's Harkness?"

"Oh, I'm sorry. He's gone again. I think he still might be over at Honeyville." She glances at her watch.

"Beehives, ten cents a pound?" I smart off.

"Silly," she doesn't need to say it. Her eyes tell me.

"At church over there?"

"Well, maybe. I don't really know."

"Say, hows about you piloting me over to this Honeyberg when you're through with the diaper brigade, here?"

"I don't know you."

"You've met me a whole week, almost."

"That isn't enough," she says quick. She's too fast for me. I'm grabbing for words again, a malady I seem to get when I'm around her.

"We could check out the price 'a cucumbers. Gotta' keep ahead of the competition." Her eyes nail me. My smarts fall like a pancake.

"Go to your class," she says, "I'll be through in forty-five minutes. I'll say 'no' properly then."

"My class?" I say. "It's you that's got class." Her eyes call me an idiot.

"Down the hall, and left," she directs, then disappears.

Figuring she's worth the wait, I go down the hall, and left, and see an open door. Inside, a dude's into it with chalk at the blackboard. He's putting out an oration. I slink into a back seat, making like a thief again. Ten or twelve high school-college types seem to be doing their best to tune the poor dude out. I lay low. The talk's about Mormon, of course, all about 'em and their books, then it swings into this stuff they call their 'Wisdom', 'Wisdom Words', something. They're deep into this 'Wisdom'. They even bring smokes and good ole brew into it, and, believe it, even beef steak, if I'm hearing it right. Well, it's their church. Got to chant and pray about something.

"Oh, just down I-15," I say when they try to pin a 'brother' and a location on me. I think I'm getting set up for the 'saving' process that I've heard of in churches, but a buzzer sounds, saving me from being saved. I'm pushed to the wall in the rush and I wonder if there's refreshments being served in the hall. The chalk dude wants to shake on it and pass some words. I don't object, but side-step 'em when I see her up the hall. The paritioners have her cornered. I'll have to stand in line. But then she spots me and moves up.

"It's just down the freeway," she says, pointing. "Not more than ten minutes away. Even you couldn't miss it."

"Thanks, ma'am, a whole lot," I smart off. "But that two east and five north doesn't mean what it says here in ole Trimington. Ask me. I know all about it. All directions lead to the corn. Listen, I need you more'n that runny nosed set does. How about it?"

She twitters and says, "Just a minute," and heads down the hall toward this noisy clutch. The babe's no pushover. I hear some distant buzzing, then she's back with two.

"Alright, we'll come."

"We?" I don't need a regiment.

That was some cruise down through the countryside under some mountain peaks she called "The Apostles". In ten miutes, beside The Apostles, I knew about every dude in the territory and BYU and these missions everybody seems to go to. But in ole Molassesberg, whatever they call it, just as I expected, no Harkness. So we head back, passing this Shorty's Brew joint and I'm for going in for some burgers.

"There?" she says like the place was akin to a haunted house, "Of course not. And besides," she says, "it's fast Sunday." So I'm down on two counts that I don't understand. But I'm saved a ten, and I get a strong shot of Mormon, which she can administer with no effort.

So, after being assured Harkness was "sure to be at the church next week", I leave her on the sidewalk and head for I-15, but seeing the mad dude pulled up at Frosty's, I remember I need a burger, so I pull in.

"What's with the babe of the cucumbers?" I say, "Hey, hop, make it two burgers." The car hop heads out for the two B's and I pry on the hate man.

"Tell me, what's with her?"

"Ask her," he says.

"She's got eyes."

"Two of 'em," he grins. He opens up a little, but not about the babe. He's mixed up, that's all - a good enough dude.

"You into this fast Sunday?" I say as the burgers come.

"I hate it." He actually gives out with a little laugh, "and I hate mustard."

"Listen," I say, "I'm back here next Sunday to corner Harkness, and I want to keep words going with the chick of the cucumbers, but she says church is the only place she'll see me. It's like she's locked in a fortress, man. Hows about you hittin' the synagogue with me?"

"I don't know. I hate 'em."

"Well, that's alright. You can keep the hate going. That makes no difference. I need a mate, man."

"Well . . . I don't know."

"Couple a cokes, there," I bark. The hop hustles.

"OK?" I press.

"I don't know." The dude's like budging granite, so I pull back as we finish off the B's, and then I burn rubber down the pike to the Great

Salt City, the Mormon beehive.

The days spin by and when I pull up at Frosty's next Sunday at ten-to, like I'd said, the junk man still doesn't know. But he's out of his Levis and when I turn the wheels toward the white spire, his bucket 'a bolts rattles after me and he follows me inside.

The babe's there in the hall again, wiping noses, and she almost drops her handkerchief at the sight of my partner. Seeing him, obviously was like a rocket blast to her. Then she turns on me with something like a "oh-oh, here's-that-wacko-again" look. The diaper regiment pulls her toward the corner. I'm feeling pushed off like one of those bible lepers and I guess I'm showing it. I blubber,

"Hey, I got a runny nose, too". Those eyes nail me, then just before she's pulled around the corner she holds back. Those eyes can keep no secrets. She gives her head a little "what's-a-girl-to-do" shake and she says, "I'm sorry. I'm glad you came, really." That was enough. I slip out of the leper colony and walk down the hall and left with a little bounce.

This time the back row's full and I'm forced to front and center with the trash heap kid slumped beside me. More "can't-believe-it" eyes nail the hate man. I'm like a lost friend, though, now knowing the two chicks of the Honeyberg trip, and the chalk dude having passed words with me last week. So pretty soon I'm chirping up as they begin nailing me with Mormon. It's a blast.

"Where doest it say that?" I say, warming up in the language of the hour. "Prove it, man." I'm getting into the debate. It's one against a dozen. The trash can driver straightens from his slump. He's mad at nobody. Now he's laughing and spouting off. I don't know who's side he's on. Neither does he. As a matter of fact, neither do I. But that doesn't matter. I'll take either side.

Well, I survive, I think, and after a half hour with her on the steps and then chauffeuring her on a quick buzz through the five blocks of Trimington, I'm outa' there. (Getting her on the tour was like pulling a double molar, because, I find, 'joy riding', as she called it, on church time does not meet with big smiles in the Mormons' Wisdom.) Some wisdom. Course she reached way out for that excuse; those eyes spoke clear enough. So she got in, "but not for more than five minutes". It was clear enough that I wasn't all the way out the leper's gate yet.

So, I leave her on the steps and head out, but not before I'm asking if I can cruise in for more chalk talk next week. Course, it's the babe I want to involve in talk. She says 'sure' and even says I can come over for dinner afterward if I behave.

"Squash and acorns?" I'm heavy with the smarts. "I'll take mine with salt. Shall I bring my own brew?"

That, I shouldn't have said. The leper's gate slams again. Those eyes call me a double wacko and I think I see just a flicker of hurt in her quick glance.

Feeling like a jerk I said, "Sorry, leave off the brew." I guess that didn't come off as the world's smartest comment, either, but I meant it right. Around this babe my foot's always up to the knee cap in my mouth.

As I roll on I-15, a bit down on myself, it strikes me that I didn't get around to mentioning Harkness this time. "What are you heading into?" I say out loud. Then I notice, partly hidden under my coat on the seat beside me, she's forgotten her book. It's fancy leather, with her name in gold, no less, on a corner. Now I've got to go back. She'll miss it. Hey, maybe I'll hit the asphalt even before Sunday. I like that. I'm up riding the high horse again.

I glance at the book a hundred times as I cruise, imagining her fingers flipping the pages and those eyes drilling the words. The babe's getting to me. I squirm.

Well, I give it till Wednesday, then it's up I-15 and I'm at the cucumber pile again. And just as I'm swinging the door open, this big dude with the pickup pulls alongside. The man's on my schedule.

"Hey, you know," he says, "I was nearly done in by this Hubbard squash out on the highway. Biggest monster I ever saw. Like a bull, it was, right there. Must 'a fell outta this car ahead, but I don't know how." I say nothing, but choke from laughing inside. He loads up, drops another twenty. He doesn't recognize me.

The babe is busy, slipping ones and fives into that apron as the citizens drop by. I'm impressed. I hold out a quarter. She gives me a turnip.

"Your book," I say, "you left it on the seat. I'll get it."

"I left it on purpose. You read, don't you?"

"Not me."

"Keep it till Sunday. You're coming, aren't you?"

"Sure it isn't one of those quick Sundays?"

"Quick? Oh, fast Sunday. Yes, I'm sure." She laughs a nice laugh.

Now I'm laying out on the grass and we're talking a full hour, then I'm into counting turnips and corn husks and heaving squash and peaches. I play it up. But those eyes tell me when I'm edging out too far, which is often.

The sun goes down and business buttons up, and reminding her I'll be back, I head out. As I roll I squint at the book, glance at the name. There's a magic in it laying there in the subdued light. It has a way of jumping out at me. Not the book, of course, it's those talking eyes that reach out and grab. "You read, don't you?" Dude woman. Course I can read what I want to read, but holy librarys? I'm not into holiness. Leave that to dumber dudes than me.

Later, on the sack, I'm rubbing my finger over the name again, and thinking. I flip through the pages. She's handy with the red pencil. Half the book's marked. That's worth a laugh. She's serious about this thing. Not only are the lines marked in red, but she's written little notes to herself in the margins, shorthand stuff that I can't track with. I take a run through some of the stuff she's marked. An hour later I'm still wading through the red; I'm feeling like Moses in the Red Sea. Red everywhere, coloring names like Almon and Lephi, and I see this Mormon name popping up out of the print. But the thing just isn't in my lingo. It's a foreign tongue, like this two north and six west language in Trimington. I'm way out in the corn.

Well, I cross off the days and on Sunday I hit the trail early. She'd put on a mite of pressure, in her way, that I come at sunup and sit in with the Priesthoods. I wondered about that, but decided to drop by. Show time, you know. It turned out to be just a bunch of local dudes, squash pickers, doing more chalk talk, turning up their religion jets. And I found out that some of their jets were flaming like blow torches, too hot for me. There weren't any backward collars, or anything like that, though. The pickup guy was there. He turns out to be some kind of a bigwig. They call him something like the 'higher counsel'.

"You should 'a seen that Hubbard," I hear him pass on to one of the Mel-kez-a-dicks, whatever they call each other.

Then it was down the hall and left again and more chalk talk. I'm getting hit heavy with Mormon. I still have her book, but keep my finger over her name. No need to advertise. Pretty soon it's buzzer time and I'm out the door with the stampede and pushing the diaper set aside that's following her.

"We eat now?" I say, showboating starvation.

"After Sacrament Meeting," she says.

"Sacraments? I'm just outta Priesthoods! My collapse is eminent!"

"Silly." She doesn't need to say it. Her eyes do. She gives a dude no chance.

So I'm with the Sacraments, an hour of 'em, stationed on the hard bench between the babe and the mama. For looks I narrow my eyes, pretending to soak it all up. But my hungry stomach grumbles and I'd like to take a spin around the building, but I'm penned. Three hours of Mormon in one day, and that's a dose.

And even that wasn't all. There was more at dinner. I didn't complain, though, with that nice creamy gravy over peas and carrots and little potatoes, and a side order of beef steak. The mama can whip up a storm in the kitchen.

"What's with this beef and your 'Wisdom Words'?" I ask with a mouthful.

"You're learning," she says and I think there's just a trace of apology in those eyes. Wrong thing for me to say? My foot's in there again, with the potatoes and carrots.

Well, maybe I'm learning, but I'm surprised when the junk dealer, my mate, slinks in and takes an empty seat by me. I learn again. The kid's a part of the brood, a renigade part. Well, that's alright.

I'm really into the peach pie and ice cream. I groan after two pieces and scoops and pretend to slip under the table, but recover, and to keep up show time, I make for the kitchen and the dishes. That puts me right on the mama's team. She fusses and makes sure the dish towels are clean and says I really don't have to do this. But I don't listen.

The papa slips out to another meeting, making four today if I've got the count right. Talk about flaming jets. The hate man's in the kitchen now, too. It's the gathering spot. He's snapping the dish towel around in good humor. He's on my side, for reasons unknown. I hear, too, about this George brother, who's missionarying down in South America with those Lame - Manites, raking in new Mormons by the truck loads. And I hear about the cucumber pile family project that's paying his fare.

"Here," she says after the kitchen is closed down. "Now you have one of your own." She reaches out with a book. It's the Mormon book, of course, but this time it has a blue cover with a gold dude and his horn on the front. "Now, what do I do with this foreign language course," I'm thinking. I'm not the kind that's made a habit of cozying up to a book, and I already know all I want about this Nehi and all the Zizromites. What more does she want? But I'm in no spot to say 'no' and remembering that unneeded baggage like squash and books can be turned loose out on I-15, I say,

"Thanks a hundred. Just what I always wanted." I toss the book on the table. But the babe's on to me almost before I'm thinking the thoughts.

"Read it," she says, "won't you?"

"Sure," I say, but those eyes don't believe me.

"Promise?"

"Hows about a red pencil to go with it . . . and, say, let me have the fancy leather one for another week. I'll need help marking in the red sea." That'll throw her off track, I think. She leaves it at that, hands me the leather one and gives me that "what's-really-with-this-guy" look.

As I'm spreading rubber over I-15, loaded down with books and heavy thinking, those eyes keep nailing me and I do the squirm again. Seems like she's always reading me like this newspaper with its thimble full of good news, but mostly bad. Sometimes I'm the comic section. Dumb things I do like to turn her upside down and she laughs up a storm and I feel like a king. Then I guess I get ranging out too far with the cool word and then its like hitting a spot of black ice; those eyes let me have it and I come flopping down, wondering what went wrong. I'ts back with the lepers again. "You don't need to be like that," she says like it's her theme. "Be yourself." Sure. But what is 'myself'? Crazy, man. It's like she's got me dangling on a string.

But despite taking shifts at playing the Yo-Yo, I'm gone on the babe. I feel this thing coming on like an avalanche and I can't see anything else. I'm like out of control. "Man," I say out loud, "you're sinkin', man." These little ways of hers can be smoothed out along the way," I tell myself. Give her time. Give me time. I glance at the Mormon library there on the seat. Course, it isn't just the way she looks at me sometimes, but its this religion thing. She's filled up with it, to the ears, jets singing. Well, so what? I'll bury the books and the priesthoods and the higher councils. She'll never need to know. I'm smart enough to turn on with religion when I'm cornered, and dust it out of my mind fast when I'm out of range of the disciples. She'll get the stuff out of her system, too, in time. Her jets are bound to burn out. It's only the girl I want - with no clutter attached. She'll see through this synagogue thing. No problem. Give her time.

Well, Sundays get to be millions of miles apart, so mid-week I'm burning rubber, and then it gets to be two voyages on weekends. I'm on a roll, man. Things are good, I say, real good. To keep up the needed image, I'm doing regular pentance with the Mormons in their synagogue, grinning a bit inside, and I'm a regular customer at the family gravy table. Ole Trimington is taking on a new citizen. Good. Yeah,

I'm really on a roll. Harkness? Who is that guy anyway?

Yeah, on a roll alright. You bet, as they say in this corn patch called a town. If I'd 'a been smart, kept both eyes open, I could've seen it coming, rolling at me like the Hubbard on the freeway. But I wasn't looking, just flappin' along up in the clouds like a blind bat. Then she nails me right across the frontal lobes. Zap.

"Some dude's slid in home ahead of me, huh?"

"I didn't say that."

"Harkness, huh? I've known him for a long time."

"He's doing the victory chant, huh?"

"Silly."

"Harkness."

"You don't understand."

Well, I understand enough to know that with me everything has changed. I'm the tom cat hit by the truck. I'm floppin' around feeling sorry for myself and down on everything. I reach out for something to stick the whole mess on - why not the Mormons? They're handy. So I'm teed off at 'em and their sacraments and books. I ditch the gold dude with the horn into the garbage and I toss the leather one out of my sight in the car trunk next to the spare and jack. Aren't the Mormons just a bunch a sheep packed tight in their corral? Get interested in one and she pulls back into the middle of the herd, ringed in by all those higher councils and turnip piles - and Harkness. Harkness. My friend. "You're fenced out, boy," I hear him say in my head. "Trimington's outa' your territory. You're outside the wall, man." The thought scalds me.

I think of the mad dude at Frosty's. I'm on his track, in his territory. I need a mate. I'll join him, then we can cuss and fume and hate together. Hate likes company, I found that out, and it spreads. And I find out pretty soon, too, that hate gets to be a tiger inside that strikes out everywhere with its knife-claws, not caring who it slashes. I start off hating I-15 and the corn patches and the whole direction north. Then my acid feelings make the big circle, stabbing out everywhere. Finally they get back to me and I'm hating myself.

So, for a couple of weeks I miss I-15 and brood and burn. I take a flier down at Sundance and hit the glacier. Big deal. Then I'm bird-doggin' RV tracks out in this baked up desert, chummin' up to the horny toads, that want no chums. Now I'm paddlin' in the briny lake and telling myself it's cool, but I can't keep my eyes from taking quick, hurting squints north, where the refinery smog hazes over I-15 and mists up the far - off squash patches of Tremonton. I watch the salty, lake ripples jiggle my stupid reflection, bob my head up and down - swell - shrink - widen - narrow. "You're a bobbin' clown," my mind says. I stretch out into a beanpole giant, a starved Gulliver, and then the ripples contract and I'm a fat-bellied dwarf. It does nothing for my already blasted ego. No wonder she greased the skids, I think, watching the reflection. Who wouldn't? I keep my eye on the shimmery surf as it distorts, exaggerates.

Well, it's right here, floating on the brine, that I'm unloaded on. It's like the higher council dude's truck dumps a ton of onions on my head. And then I get knifed in the spine by this cold fall wind. I get the shakes. I'm like in Siberia looking out of my igloo at the yaks. Rotten life, trailin' these yaks across the tundra. It's the 'cool dude' show, of course, that's bouncing off my head like the smelly onions. The big talk. Show time. I feel the Arctic storm again and shudder and sit on this big ice cube trying to think.

But then, funny thing. All at once I see, looking up at me out of that cloudy water, those eyes. Suddenly its like the breeze feels warm, and all at once I'm switched from my ice cube to toenailing it up these palm trees. It's like those honest eyes are looking through me again, but it's different now. They're gentle like the warm breeze and palms. All at once a thought comes into my mixed-up brain that I should have been thinking all along. Dumb dude. Wasn't she trying to say it in her nice way, not wanting to tear me all apart. "You don't need to be that way." Sometimes, I guess, ears get too smart to hear. The babe was on to my phoney act at the first squint. But, maybe—I hope—tucked in between the smarts, she saw something worth salvaging.

The sharp wind bites me again. From day one I've been bobbin' and swellin' and shrinkin' right in front of her. Big act. Fluff. Making big talk of things important to her. She could see through me like I was window glass. The 'cool dude' show, all the smarts, the gorilla chest-beating, I can see now I've put it on heavy. Half my life I've been spreading it thick, like it was my armour. What are you hiding, dude? my brain says. You afraid of yourself? Down on yourself? I don't know. Maybe I am.

But didn't the cool ways get laughs, open gates to the "in" dudes? Maybe. I don't know what it really got me that I want right now. It got me big troubles. That I know.

But again its my thing, man. It's me. Take it away and what's left? Talk it big. Play it cool. Show time. Man, I don't know.

I head back for the pad, but the pictures I saw in the shiny surf won't let me alone. I try sackin' out, but my head's too bombed, so I stare at the white ceiling. A little spider dude churns his legs across the plaster. I wonder if he knows there's a million miles of white desert ahead. He stops, and then churns off again. Dumb dude.

Well, I've never heard that spiders can crawl in and spin sense into a guy's gray-matter, but I have to say, sacked out there, I could see myself running like mad alongside this little dumb, black speck of life, heading out over my own millions of miles of plaster, and it shook me. "Sense, man," I'm saying to myself. "Get some sense even if it's only a peanut shell full." I grin a sick grin and then my mind takes a trip down to the car trunk and the leather book. I'd made up my mind to mail it back, cut the whole thing off clean. While I'm jabbering at myself the spider still windmills across the plaster, but now I've had enough of his race. I take the stairs down to the wheels in three jumps. The book is still there by the jack. I flip through the pages and think, then I'm looking north. Where else? The car door slams and I'm cremating rubber toward the turnip piles. Big decisions, man, things are goin' to get turned around, man.

"Hey, mate! I've got to talk, mate." I'm at Frosty's paralleling the junk heap.

"Where you been? Talk? 'Bout what?" he says.

"Get in. We'll cruise the corn, man." He does and we do. We're up I-15.

"What else is new," he says when I tell him I want to talk about his sister. Then we're cruising down I-15.

"Harkness? Harkness doesn't have as much to do with it as you think," he's saying. Now we're all the way out on Dog Path 23.

"You just can't fly in here and expect that." He nails me hard. We head down Cow Trail 35.

"Sure, your not being a Mormon's big to her. It's like one of those mountains." He points up to the Apostles. Now we're getting into this biggest load of onions, this religion thing. The guy pops from the hip. Now we're cruisin' the lake shore.

"Listen, you get dunked for that reason, and you're out in the corn." The guy's into my lingo.

"What do you mean, man," I say, "why else would I sign in. That reason is big enough. Why would anyone else sign in?"

"You're not thinking."

"You're wrong, mate, I am. That's all I been doing. What do I lose if I just up and go for the plunge to get her?"

"Her."

"Her? You crazy, man? You mean I'm out if I'm out and out if I'm in? What do I do, mate?"

Well, even in my thick head things begin to spark. I don't need to ask. I know what I have to do, if I do anything. I'm playing the phoney again. Can't seem to keep those quick fixes out of my head. Can't I dump these phoney moves? No more Gullivers or dwarves, no hitting the baptism water for show.

Some man, this mad dude. Cool. Knows more than you think. He didn't have to talk about all this. Maybe he shouldn't have. The big sister would come at him with a bucket of turnips if she knew.

Well, anyway, finally I get the picture, a little squint of the lay of the land. It's just what those eyes were trying to tell me all along. But it was a foreign language, all that church talk about whispering spirits and books talking out to a guy. And me, I was just that blind, flappin' bat, living it up like I'd always lived. But anyway, now it's coming in clear. Now I know. Harkness? Sure, he's running hard. Who can blame 'em? Maybe every dude in the territory is on the chase. But Hark hasn't won. Didn't she try to tell me that? "Idiot," I say out loud to myself.

Knowing isn't winning, though, by a hundred miles. That thought comes on me like another big acorn squash. Even with knowing, I'm a light year out of her world. Like the junk man said, a guy can't roll in through the corn rows and expect a girl like this one to flip somersaults. Man, I'm feeling like a Moses, sloshing through that Red Sea. That girl's got me underlined in red.

Well, if this Trimington venture's going to go on, somebody's got to change, I can see that. And I'm smart enough to know it isn't going to be her. And thinking about it, I guess I don't want her to. It's the way she is that's got me hooked, blows me away. Those eyes, how could they change? "It's very simple, mate," I say to myself, "before you can even get in the race with Harkness, you've got to shape up, or it's ship out, man", as the saying goes. And one more thing sinks into my thick skull: This book, and in fact, the whole Mormon thing, it's got to float in its own Red Sea. No strings attached. Course she's part of it. I know that. She stands up in it as big as old Nephi, but I can't be tied into it by her funny little apron strings.

So, I try to stand off to one side and look ahead and then back. Both ways are scary. I don't know if I can hack it ahead. Can I handle all that church business? Brother this, Elder that? I don't know if my jets can handle it. It'll be a burn out. But back? Go back? That looks even worse. I won't go back. What's a dude to do?

Well, I could tell lots of things about the months between then and now. Some things I can explain and some I can't; some things just finally settled with me and I lose it if I try to put the reasons in words. I'll just say that snow made an adventure out of I-15, and spring and summer came, and another fall. And my life was an adventure, a high adventure, as they say. It was like I'd read those eyes and take one mouse step forward (I guessed it was forward), then I'd get the shakes and take a camel's step back. I even copped out to L.A. one day and tried to find the old life again, tried putting this Tremonton thing out of existence. But it wasn't any use. My universe had changed. One little cruise up country to visit a pal whose digs are in the squash patches and my roots are pulled up like a ripe turnip. So, I hot-footed it back across the sage and the salt flats, hardly able to wait until the cucumber piles came into view. As those millions of miles of asphalt came at me as I put-putted over the endless Nevada hills, I'd see those eyes and that hand that always seemed to be there reaching out to pull me over the next hurdle. And, man, sometimes, I have to say, that reaching hand almost did me in. It was always out ahead. There was no compromise, no stopping here or there, saying this was far enough. Some of those steps were more than giant steps; they seemed to reach up to the moon, such unbelievable stuff as giving the chalk talk 'down the hall and left' on Sundays. For me, that exercise was more than breaking the world record, it was high-jumping nine feet-two. Believe me, hitting turns at the cucumber pile, where she's standing long hours again, because the family project has got to go on, was duck soup compared to the chalk and blackboard.

Well, it happened one day that this George, he came home, and after she had hammered on me until I couldn't recognize myself anymore, old George comes in and tosses me on the truck with all those South Americans, and while he was at it, he tossed my mate, the trash kid, on, too. I needed my mate. He made it easier.

So, today it's I-15 again, cruising south like mad. The junkman sits on one side of me, in the rear seat of the family wheels. He's got less to say than usual. And she sits on the other side. I can feel her shoulder. She's not talking now, either. She doesn't need to. I know what she's thinking. And what is there for me to say, except how else was I to prove that she wasn't great big in the formula, at least wasn't the whole formula, that brought me in? If this venture won't prove it, nothing will. And I guess I ought to say that before I went for the plunge, I thought I ought to let on to this High Councilor that it was me that turned the Hubbard loose on him out on the freeway. You'd have thought he was the sinner. He put a bear hug on me that nearly cracked a rib. I found out that repenting has some pain. I have to say, too, that I've still got the Red Sea book, the one in leather. I picked up another for her, leather, too, and name in gold, no less. The worn one just seems to light my jets best. Sort of like those eyes are following along when I'm trying to get a handle on all those 'came to passes', and, of course, the volume keeps a little tie there, which is important, with Harkness still prowling the territory. Can you believe I'm giving the guy two years free run, and he's living almost next door? That's the thought that hits me the hardest. I try not to think of it, at least not every five minutes. But it's too late to turn back now.

So the bucket 'a bolts kid and I cruise through the big doors and they pin those Elder's badges on us. Before we disappear forever from this universe, though, we've got to turn back, just for a minute.

"Thanks, Harkness, yeah, thanks a lot," I say down inside as I take that long, last look north. "I guess I owe something to you." It's the only way I can say anything. I can't talk. "And to you, ole Tremonton, you wonderful ole berg. . .with the best dudes in this universe. . . the thought puts a turnip in my throat.

Now I turn to those misty, wonderful eyes, and this isn't easy for my kind of fluffy dude to say, but it's like they're these big windows opening right into the feelings of her . . . well, I'll say it . . . right into her heart. It's like those teary eyes are whispering at me, and they finish wiping me out. "Go. Go," they're sobbing, "race hard. I'm so proud of you . . . And come back. Come back to Tremonton. . . and come back to me."

16

The Tetonia Bandit

A cold, pale sky arched over the great snow fields that swept west and north from the community of 211 souls who populated little Tetonia (In East Idaho's Teton Valley). The countryside lay frigidly sullen, appearing as white waves of an endless sea that had been snapped by a camera in the brutal act of crashing across the earth. At noon the day before, the second day after Christmas, a sharp, nervous wind had begun an ominous moaning out of the northwest,whiplashing the loose surface powder into darting rivulets and sudden churning plumes, which leaped upward as ghostly apparitions and chased themselves over the open fields. All afternoon the squalls had snarled and swelled, and by the bitter, four-thirty twilight they had worked themselves into rage, driving a torrent of new snow out of the thick, gray sky and beating the powder on the surface into a frenzy. The horizons were lost, the buildings had vanished, there were no trees. Any evidence of an existing universe was lost in the leaden turbulence.

By five o'clock of the morning that followed, the blizzard had worn itself out, leaving in its wake a quiet countryside under a gelid, open sky. Three hours later, at eight, Wilt Haskins paused briefly at a light pole near his drug store door, rubbed the frost from a thermometer with a mittened hand and shook his head. The reading was an unbearable forty-two below.

Near the town's south limits, where the hidden highway asphalt curved eastward to begin its seven-mile course to the valley communities of Clawson and Driggs, the massive snow cover had obliterated any evidence of a roadway. A country truck, with a steaming engine and a fringed display of icicles, had begun butting its six-foot-high snow blade into those mountainous tons of white.

But the greater challenge lay in the opposite direction, where a second plow had begun its attack on the highway north. For this snowbound artery, a mile out, turned westward to the river bridge at Harrop's ranch and then inclined upward into the Clementsville hills. It was more than thirty miles over that high, rolling, wind-tortured terrain to Snake River Valley and the hub town of Rexburg.

Except for the drug store and the general mercantile, Main Street, Tetonia was iced up, closed down. Over at the depot, on the hamlet's west limits, the telegraph clacked messages of long delays. A rotary plow, pushed by two or three engines, was on its way, but the time of the train's arrival in the Valley was a hazardous guess.

And across the Valley, from Alta to Richvale, from Cedron to Felt, out along the country lanes, rural men would soon be at their labor of breaking new roads to town with their lunging horses and light, covered sleighs.

By eight-thirty, windrows of snow appeared along the highway in the wake of the plows, towering higher than a man's head. The lengthening segment of opened road became, in effect, a precarious trench, barely wide enough to accommodate a single auto's width, let alone two passing cars. The north plow, after a half hour of struggle, had reached the barely visible roadside sign, "Tetonia, Population 211, Elevation 6,011", which marked the village's outer bounds.

On beyond the sign a few rods stood three outlying dwellings, separated by the high, white banks and each huddled windowsill-deep in the snow. In the first home, a rust-colored bungalow, the widow, Anna Wyzanski, stood at her window observing the laboring plow. There were worry-furrows in her brow. She gazed thoughtfully for a moment, returned to the kitchen to fuss over the stove for another minute, and then returned to the window to peer westward toward the Clementsville hills. After a brief hesitation, she hurried to the telephone and dialed Haskins' Drug, which doubled as the town's Greyhound station.

"Hallo, Meestar Haskin? Da bus, oder zeug-train, is coming, no? Haf du . . . you harrd?"

"No, Anna," Wilt responded, "we haven't heard yet. We're having trouble getting through on the phone to Rexburg. I think the line must be down."

"Ya . . . "

"But don't worry, Anna. These Greyhound people know how to deal with the snow. I'm sure the bus didn't leave the lower valley last night, with that storm. Your boy probably stayed in Rexburg. He might even come in on the train, you know, if the bus was held up. The train, you can count on its getting through. I'll call the minute we get any word." The druggist's comments were reassuring, but as he hung up the ear piece, his thoughts were less so, for the bus, he well knew, might at that moment be a prisoner of the snow out in those notoriously hazardous hills. Everyone in town, Mormon and non-Mormon alike, was well aware that John Wyzanski's two-year church mission was over, that he was bearing homeward and that his bus was long overdue.

The widow, preoccupied with her anxieties, returned to the window and observed again the pulsing exhaust from the plow truck's vertical pipe. The filmy haze partially obscured the faded blue stucco home of Sam and Lydia Blaine, which appeared rippled through the frozen glass, seeming to be sinking under its heavily drifted roof. Anna's attention was drawn momentarily to a billowing column of wood smoke, which rose from a stovepipe that protruded upward from the high-gabled roof of the neighbor's large, backyard shed. Could it be the Blaine boy so early, she wondered, and on such a morning? "Mercy."

The Blaine boy it was, and if Anna could have heard, there were emanating from that shed the incredulous staccato thuds of a cold basketball bouncing off a frigid concrete floor. Explanation? Well, only that obsessions of this sort have and will continue to reveal a focus in some kids lives that prompts the thought that a bouncing, air-filled sphere can become life itself. For on such a morning as this one, whatever else could compel a kid to build a fire in a pot-bellied stove out back and before the heat could do more than warm the stove itself begin bouncing a cold melon around the place? Why shouldn't Anna Wyzanski seek for mercy? But there he was, Powell Blaine, in 3-D reality, peering from a parka hood with those intense, glistening eyes, pounding this basketball. Explanation again: This was THE day. The Big one. It should have been the day before, but for sure before the sun went down on this ice chest called a day, Ole Jumpin' John would sail in on the Greyhound.

"Watch your ears, Wyzanski! I'm ready! I got 'em right here!" That would be his salutation and he'd dangle a chain of safety pins so Johnny wouldn't miss the message. "I'm pinning your ears, Wyzanski!" Pow grinned. Hadn't those sentiments been Johnny's good-bye to the Blaine kid as the new missionary had stepped into the bus those two eternities, called years, ago?

"I'm gonna pin your ears back, Pow," he had called as he stepped into the bus. "Grow a foot and I'll bring the safety pins!"

So, here the kid was, throttling around the cold cement floor in the high-roofed shed, feinting, darting, careening between five large barrels, his slow-heeled, carefully-placed defense. The kid had antelope's feet — a cold antelope's. "Hold up, square away!" his instincts commanded. "Let 'er go!" The ball arced, "Swish!" He paused a moment, for his glance had swept over the sleek, new cross-country skis hanging from their rack down the wall from the stove, and the up-to- the-minute poles, blue with red trim. In the afternoon, after the bus had sailed in and after he'd pinned Ole Johnny Wyz to the wall, he'd take a run on those skis, hit the open fields west of town. Ole Santa had out-done himself this year with this gift. Pow could hardly wait to get his hands on the fancy slats, give them their chance to show their stuff. What a day this would be. "Pow! Pow!" he yelped his name as he turned to the ball and swept it up again into those magician's fingers, digits that had their own eyes. The ball was on a string. It was a Yo-Yo. The boy's breath, like a human con trail, billowed out from the parka hood. He skirted, feinted, drove again and at that intuitive signal, the sphere arced upward again and swished the strings, "Pow!" He was ready. Bring on ole Jumpin' John and his heavy artillery. Powell Blaine would roll out his own big guns and there'd be war. Basketball's one-on-one contest may come across as inane, straight up out of adolescence, but let it be said here, the duel can be a clash of titans. It can determine the fate of worlds, galaxies.

Pow's mind darted back again those two years, as it had done a thousand times since John Wyzanski had shipped out. He remembered walking down the snowy highway from Haskins' Drug that morning. Big times it was for him that year, turning thirteen. Big hard times, really, seeing your grown-up pal, your jostling, kidding mentor, your Mr. Everything just up and walk out of your life. Real hard times. It was like this mission trip was to Pluto and back, forever. He remembered watching the bus as it rounded the highway curve, gaining speed and distance, and then disappearing toward Harrop's bridge. He remembered, too, that he had followed at a safe distance sixteen-year-old Maryanne Howard on that lonesome walk. Thirteen and sixteen they were. No social bridges between those ages, even if their houses faced each other on opposite sides of the road. It was infancy and old age. The Bandit, that was her best-known name, a sobriquet she couldn't miss with that prominent mask of freckles strewn across her well-assured nose. But now she was eighteen, a month from nineteen, and she stood at her window on this frozen-down December morning carrying her own little mad-cat bag of anxieties. She gazed first to the north, where the self-made blizzard of the train's rotary plow would eventually appear, and then to the westward, where the overdue bus would make its approach. Her glances were pensive, troubled, even exasperated, for to her the train and the bus, representing horribly conflicting emotions, were cruising in, dead on, on a collision course.

"Just tell me, please," the girl sang out in frustration, "why everything always works out like this. It's insane! Pure insanity!" Well, insanity or not, there she was, packed and ready to go. Los Angeles, no less, the great, the fabled L. A. And this earth-shaking trip, this chance to skip out of old frozen-up Tetonia town in dead winter, comes all of a sudden, right on top of the arrival of that long-gone Tetonia dream boat, John Wyzanski. After those two eternities, called years, of dreaming and scheming, as only The Bandit could dream and scheme, over all conceivable means of corraling this long-gone Don Juan, here comes this letter from the Darbys, Valley people six months in California, announcing a nice job with that astronomical West Coast pay and a room available with the old best friend. And naturally, the job wouldn't wait. "Be here by the first. For sure." Of course. For sure. Even if it means chugging out of town on the very day ole lover boy is due to chug in. Talk about collision courses.

Johnny had been due in at 6 P.M. the evening before; that was bad enough — The Bandit had figured the time available for a fast-forward romance to the minute. From six Tuesday until three, Wednesday, when the smoke-puffing engine was due at the depot to transport her to The Golden Coast, equaled twenty-one hours. Twenty-one hours to throw out the bait and land ole sonny boy, the slippery fish, who had never given one perceptible romantic flicker of an eye toward the freckled girl. Bring on the magician, please. And now the bus goes and gets itself entombed out in the Clementsville refrigerator and fifteen of those twenty-one hours have slipped by unused. Bring on two magicians. Make it Houdini.

Well anyway, what right did The Bandit have to take aim on this innocent, untouchable Romeo? Some audacity. Like drawing bead on a flying bumble bee. And she'd told herself of this audacity upwards of a thousand times. Get ready for the crash, girl. Bring on the plaster and crutches.

But, on the other hand, someone, sometime, somewhere, had to spring the trap. Why not The Bandit? Of course, she had mulled over this hope-filled thought upward of a thousand times, too, even though, as said, this particular romance, to date, was as one-sided as a paid-off umpire's call, its high points having reached only such amorous declarations as: "Hey, Bandito, ole girl, how about we scrub off those freckles here in this snow drift?", or, "Atta kid, toss the ole apple right down the pipe, right over the bag!" Some romance. Especially when you were born with two left arms, couldn't hit the broad side of a barn with the 'ole apple' or anything else.

Then, again, a lot can happen to a girl in two years. The Bandit had mulled through this thought a thousand times, too. Weren't those freckles fading just the slightest bit, especially under the subtle tints and pastes and powders that teenagers apply with enduring patience before mirrors? And weren't the all-arms-and-legs look of sixteen and the horrible tendency toward knock knees, mostly imagined, sort of maturing into some semblance of inconspicuity? Well, maybe. But five hours to land him? Bring on a cart load of Houdinis. It was just like the nice, big welcome-home banner The Bandit had strung from her front porch to the Wyzanski's, next door, complete with a believable Santa's sleigh and one big package labeled, "Johnny Wyz". A couple of days late for Christmas, but clever, Bandit clever. Of course, blizzards care nothing for cleverness. After the terror of the night just past, all that remained of the fancy sign was a fragment of paper fluttering at the end of a broken, icy cord. Shredded. So, what else was new?

That, then, was The Bandit, standing at her window wishing she could get her hands on one over-due, unsuspecting dude, who was messing up her life. She felt like throttling the poor innocent guy, and herself, and L. A. Insanity!

She observed the sun, which moved inexorably through those last precious hours, edging upward toward its zenith, cold and distant and reflecting a glare off the drug store window, where, inside, a small crowd had gathered. A phone call had just come through from the outer valley and the worst had been confirmed. The Greyhound bus had, indeed, left Rexburg the night before and it had made its scheduled stops at Sugar City and Newdale. Better judgment would have dictated the cancelling of the Teton Valley run, for a rising blizzard, so hindsight soon affirmed, was giving ominous signs of things to come. But with human nature being what it is ("Why, it's only thirty miles into the Valley and we've got to get home . . . "), the bus rolled eastward into the Clementsville hills and had hardly made the first mile when the big storm came hammering in.

"The Rexburg station called," said Wilt as Rock Ebert, sheepman and Mormon bishop, stomped in through the door brushing the snow from his coat and pants. He had just made the quarter-mile trek from his ranch headquarters, his face ruddy and a fringe of frost clinging to his eyebrows. "I hate to do it," the druggist went on, "but I've got to call Mrs. Wyzanski and let her know that her boy is somewhere out in the hills. That bus pulled out of Newdale last night at six and hasn't been heard of since, and her boy's on it."

"That isn't good," said the bishop, frowning. "You know, almost all the Clementsville folks move into the lower valley (Snake River Valley) when snow comes. There probably isn't a stove burning over that whole country, and the houses and buildings are locked tight. It would be hard to find shelter out there."

"It is bad," reaffirmed the druggist.

"It's worse than bad. Say it like it is, Wilt, it's holy hell," spoke up Joel Roundtree, one of Rollie Christensen's free wheeling sheepherders.

"They said they're talking about a caravan of dog teams out there taking in blankets and food. They have racing teams in that country, race over at Ashton every winter, you know," Haskins went on. "And they think on our end we ought to do something."

"Dogs? Good hell. What chance would dogs have?" Joel chirped, blotting a drip from his nose with a gloved hand, "I wouldn't take dogs in there on a bet."

"You're probably right, Joel," agreed Wilt. "They're thinking, too, that they might even try flying in with supplies, dropping them by the bus. That's a long shot, of course, you know.

"Long as hell."

"Yes, you're both right," said the bishop. There's a snow cloud rising up over the hills right now. I suspect the wind is beginning to pick up out there."

"And you know that's a blindin' ground blizzard," Joel chirped again. "I've been in 'em. I know. On a day like this that wind would freeze a man in his tracks in fifteen minutes. "Planes and dogs? Good hell."

"Do you know who all was on the bus, Wilt?" asked the churchman.

"Well, there's young Wyzanski for one, we know that, and I think one of the Braxtons was due in."

"Weren't the Harris girls from Cache coming home from school," young William Brien spoke up. "I think so."

"There are likely others," the bishop continued.

"Likely as hell."

"How come you know so much about hell, Joel?" William asked with a wink.

"I just know trouble when I see it, Willie, and this is the most low-down, cussin' kind." A swirling burst of surface snow flew by the store window as a wind gust creaked the front door, accentuating the sheep wrangler's language. Joel stepped to the window and looked north up the highway, where streaming surface snow was beginning to sweep across and into the trench opened by the plow.

"Hell's bells," he muttered.

Out of Joel's vision, over at the Howard home, The Bandit had tuned in KID, Idaho Falls radio.

"Listen, mother," the girl was calling. "he said the wind over the hills is rising again and blowing into the highway where the plows have been. And the Valley bus left Newdale last night for Tetonia . . ." Her face paled. "Mother . . ." she hesitated. Frustrated, confused and now alarmed, her churning emotions turned on those tender spigots and damp, mascara-tinted trails edged downward over the freckled cheeks. Tough as nails? Humph. The Bandit had met her match. There was a sob.

"Maryanne . . ."

"Oh, I'm so confused."

"Now daughter, you brighten up. I know it's hard to leave this frozen-up nest, but mushing out of this Tetonia igloo would make a dead man laugh. Believe me, kido, you just ask me to trade you places and I'd mush a dog team through Siberia, if good ole Californ-I-A was at the end of the line. You know I spent a bit of time in that heavenly State, like my first twenty years, and don't ask me what I'm doing in this Idaho deep-freeze. You should be shouting hallelujah, not sniffing."

"Well . . . It's more than that."

"More than what? What could be more than that?"

"Well . . . the bus . . . and . . . "

"Hmm . . . the bus . . . Now, just who's on that bus . . . let me see. Well, there's old Ed Bellows, the driver. And Santa Claus. . . course, he already came; can't be ole S. C. John Wyzanski? Say, you're not sniveling over John Wyzanski?"

"So now you know. Stupid, aren't I? It was so stupid I'd decided not to tell anyone."

"Well. . . Now, before we call you stupid, let's run that message by one more time, slow. Johnny, the great J. W. . . . the big drip next door. Well, well, it's me that's stupid. You keep secrets like a Mormon bishop, daughter. Well, well."

"Don't look at me like that, mother . . . sob. I know I don't have a chance, but I can't help it. And going to California. . . it's terrible! It's all stupid. The train's coming, and I'm going . . . and he's out there. . . " The mascara was floating away and a mother's Kleenex came to the rescue. Mae Howard reached and the normally self-assured Bandit melted as a ten-year-old. Mother and daughter used the Kleenex alternately and mascara smears appeared on the younger and the older cheeks indiscriminately. The mother, having kept her emotions in check over the maternal tragedy of another chick leaving the nest until this moment, wilted and the flood gates were opened.

After considerable tear-letting, Mae Howard choked.

"Well, now that we've had our howl . . ." she wiped her nose, "what was that Shakespeare tragedy all about? Oh, yes, California. . . and the poor, lost chump next door. Well, first off, don't you worry about old Romeo. He'll be alright. He'll survive."

"It isn't just that."

"Isn't just what?"

"Well, I've only got until three o'clock, and he isn't here yet."

"And you could miss him, of course. Hmm. Well, this isn't the end of the world, kido." Mae Howard, back to her zany ways, lifted her arms with a chant, "Stay away, oh train, Alacazam! Stay out in the Judkins drift. Stay!"

"Oh mother," the girl chided. "If there's no train, there's no job in L. A."

"No job? No L. A." The arms rose again. "Alacazam! Come train, come!"

"Then no Johnny." They both spoke the words and laughed a laugh of irony.

"Well, there's always romance by pony express, you know," the mother said, dabbing her eyes again. "But which all-American girl is going to trust a mule with her love letters? Poor animal would die of heart throbs."

"The mule hasn't done any good the last two years. I've learned that."

"You have? The big lug didn't go for love letters, huh?"

"Well, a Christmas card last week signed, Sincerely, Elder Wyzanski."

"Sincerely, huh? Well, don't forget that lots can be tied up in that little word, 'sincerely'. That's the way your pop used to sign off, Sincerely, P. H., and look at me now. At least you got a word instead of initials, even if it was just 'Elder'.

"Oh, Mother," the girl chided again. "I thought I'd have a few hours anyway, before the train leaves. I thought maybe in a few hours I could tell . . ."

"A few hours to turn up the charm and nail ole Prince Charming. Daughter, I know you've got a knockout punch, but . . ." Up went the arms again. "Alacazam! Train, stay. She needs more time! Stay out in your Felt icehouse!"

"Oh, mother."

"Well now, Maryanne Howard. . . and now as I think of it, maybe that fancy drip is worth putting up a cat fight over. I like your taste." She kissed her daughter and continued, "Now, you and I aren't going anywhere for a while, sitting here in this Tetonia igloo, and for that matter, neither is the train. Maybe we're never going anywhere. So why not put our tootsies up to the fire and let's get these two airy, women's heads together. Two scheming, female brains against one wet-behind-the-ears neighborhood kid? It'll be no contest at all, even with the iceman and California against us. And who can tell, maybe those two villains are really on our side."

The Bandit and her mother walked arm in arm to the window and observed, as at the moment, Anna Wyzanski was making her way up the steps to the home of Sam and Lydia Blaine. Lydia opened the door and assisted the widow inside. Anna was speaking.

"Oh, Lydia! Lydia, da bus, she — he ferloren — loss in Clementsville, unt ma' Chon, Chonny, he in da bus — unt der more bleezart, heute — t'day, yetz — now!"

"Oh, Anna," her neighbor's voice rose, "you're sure?"

"Herr Haskin, he say — yust now he call."

Through the open doorway into the kitchen, Powell Blaine, back from his cold-storage workout, could hear the anxious conversation as he burrowed his reddened fingers into the frig. He produced peanut butter, jam, baloney, vienna sausages and mayonnaise. Hearing Mrs. Wyzanski's sobs, he paused.

"Ma Chonny," she wailed again, "he tote — die, sehr kalt — freeze!"

Preoccupied, Pow layed out a clean slice of white bread on the white table and knifed on its top a quarter-inch layer of peanut butter.

"Oh, Anna," Lydia Blaine's voice came, "you mustn't talk like that! John's going to be fine. You wait and see."

Powell placed a second white slice on the dark mound and pressed. The brown paste squished into view at the crusted edges.

"Anna, the bus people are prepared, they have to be. I've heard they are." Lydia continued. "They take along emergency blankets."

Pow poured atop the second slice a huge blob of red jam and pressed over the mass a third slice of bread. The reddish goo appeared at the edges and a drip escaped to the table. A finger wiped the errant drip, leaving a crimson trail. The finger was wiped clean between clucking lips.

"Anna," Lydia continued, "why don't we go over to the drug store? That's where any news of the bus will come, and Bishop Ebert is over there. I called his wife, Ellen this morning and she said he was worried and left for the store earlier. Here Anna, let me get my coat."

The peanut butter and jam swallowed hard. From a quart jar, Pow took huge gulps of icy milk, but even the liquid seemed reluctant. He munched and gulped again and wiped his lips across a parka sleeve as the front door opened and the ladies stepped out. The hinges creaked with the cold and the Arctic blast reached even into the kitchen as Powell pushed back the half-eaten sandwich, spreading another sticky smear of red across the table top. The usual delicacy clung as paste to his palate. The wailing of Mrs. Wyzanski had rendered his taste buds inoperative. The great Johnny Wyz in trouble? Inconceivable. Anyone else, believable. But Ole Jumpin' John? Impossible. The teenager absently dropped a limp disc of baloney on a new white slice of bread, shook out a mound of red paste from the ketchup bottle and with a finger wiped across the bottle top, then smoothed out the mound across the baloney with the same digit. As his clucking lips licked the finger clean, his thoughts turned critical. Here he sat, Ole Big Deal, Pow Blaine, ingesting (was that the word?) baloney, while out in the hills the truly great one froze and starved. The boy's brain pictured an immobile bus, window-deep in a drift. A sweep of wind from outside the Blaine house dashed a volley of frozen white against the frosted kitchen window. Powell shuddered as he pressed on top of the ketchup a second slice of bread and fingered the vienna sausages out of the can and mounded them on the bread. One left in the small tin found a quick exit to his lips, where it clung cigarette-like until at a coordinated puckering and sucking, it disappeared.

If it were Pow Blaine out there in the bus, the boy's thoughts continued, or anyone else, would Johnny Wyz be feeding his face here in the kitchen? You know he wouldn't. There'd be action, you know there would be. John'd be ahead of a pack doing something, probably out at the bus right now, building a fire, boiling soup. Pow topped on the third slice of bread after spreading a layer of mayo on a surface. He pressed the double-decker and a sausage squirted free from captivity to the floor. He retrieved the slippery cylinder and stuffed it back between the upper slices.

So here sat Pow Blaine with his baloney and safety pins. The big dude. Ole Dead Eye. He licked his fingers again and pulled the silly pin-chain from his pocket. The kid's brain threw the barbs. "Big getter, no giver," he said to himself as his glance turned to the fancy Christmas tree, visible in the front room. He felt its sharp needles in his conscience. A guy, an old pal, gets in trouble . . . What kind of a friend is this Pow Blaine, anyway? Big talker, no doer . . .

The baloney and sausages clung to his gullet like the peanut butter. Hard swallowing. Two bites - half a sandwich - was enough. He pushed the uneaten half back across the jam smear, coloring the jam red with ketchup red. He drained the fruit jar in big gulps, wiped the white froth from his lips on a mitten as he pulled the handwear on. In a moment he was out the door bee-lining it for the drug store. He saw The Bandit, ole Bandito, looking over Tetonia's frozen wastes from her window. Pow flapped to the top of the highway windrow like a wounded turkey, and then as an Olympic luge, tobogganed down the other side to the snowy asphalt on his chest. On his feet, he gave a two-arm, two-leg wave. Maryanne managed a grin and a two-hand "aw-get-out-of-here" motion.

At the drug store gathering place, the talk was subdued and ominous. Joel Roundtree and William Brien had just agreed to make a run at the Clementsville hills with a team and covered sleigh. Attempting to drive a car or truck along the narrow highway trench was considered too hazardous, with the wind still on the rise and the surface snow streaming across the countryside as a shallow, broad river. In the immortal words of the free-speaking sheep wrangler, it was "a hell of a risk".

"I'd bet a mutton herd we don't get out farther than Harrop's bridge." Joel was saying. "Just look at that wind." As he spoke, a swirling cyclone of snow rushed past the store window. "Bishop, you sure as hell better get to your prayin' an' right now."

"That we will," answered the sheepman, "and I know you'll join us, Joel, but first, I've got a strong team and a light sleigh with a good stove. It'll take me a half-hour to hitch up and get back here. You and William make sure you're dressed for the ride. I'll blanket the horses. How would you like to come along with me, Brother Rob?" Older brother, Rob Brien, readily agreed. "Ellen will see that we have blankets and food supplies aboard. Lydia, would you call some of the nearby sisters for some extra coats and whatever else you think might help the folks out there?"

"I'll put in some supplies," volunteered grocer, E. C. Milner. "Just drive the sleigh up in front of the store."

"Thanks, Brother E. C.," the bishop said, then went on. "Now, you folks, Joel talks about the infernal lower regions a good deal, as we know, but he's got his best eye up above, we know that, too. Let's all bend the knee and as your bishop, most of you, I'll say a prayer. Come on, Joel, your knees bend, too."

"Knee caps to the floor, Joel," sang out William Brien. "I want to go on this sleigh ride with a prayin' man."

"You do your prayin', Willie, and I'll do the cussin'. It'll take the best of both to get this job done."

Powell Blaine entered the door as the little crowd set their knees to the damp floor.

"Join with us, Powell," the bishop said and the boy self-consciously knelt.

As the church-sheepman supplicated heaven's powers, the boy's mind tracked with them, then departed from the words of appeal. He heard his stomach groan as it attacked the baloney and peanut butter, and he became aware of the slow tick of the old, brown-framed wall clock. The bishop prayed with strong emotion and as Pow stole a glance, he saw a bead of moisture on the ruddy cheek. Closing his eyes again, his mind raced away once more. He saw the defensive barrels in the backyard shed and he thought of the safety pins in his pocket. His mind then pictured those slender cross-country skis, sleek, comfortable in their rack. He sensed the elation of skimming over a frozen surface, the sharpness of the frigid air on his face. How great to skim over the drifts, alone. Feeling a twinge of guilt at his errant thoughts, Pow, sensing that the bishop was drawing near his close, turned his thoughts again to the solemn words, uttered a barely audible 'amen' with the others and then rose to his feet.

As Rock Ebert and Rob Brien stepped out the door on their frosty errand, Pow's thoughts were of the team and sleigh and the streaming snow over the treacherous highway trench. What chance would Willie and Joel have? Say they caught up with the plow; what then? Battle the drifts, some as high as the horses' backs? Would the two men be required to leave the team and walk on alone? Up to their belts in the snow? Maybe they'd take snow shoes. But even so, what then? With his thoughts, the barbs of guilt returned. At least Willie and Joel were doing something. Pow thought of his skis, and quietly, he, too, stepped out the door.

In ten minutes the cross-country skis and the blue and red poles leaned ready near the Blaine's back door. Inside the kitchen the boy pulled on a heavy wool sweater, slipped a goggles strap over his head, slipped off his Levis and pulled on heavy, white underdrawers. Replacing the denim jeans, he hurried to the kitchen and stuffed the half-eaten sandwiches in a paper bag and stuffed the bag in his parka pocket. He filled the other pocket with a half-package of Fig Newtons, a handful of dried apples, a pack of matches.

Once outside he crossed the highway trench, walked down the plowed street to the depot, crossed the snow-drifted steel rails, buckled on the skis and stepping over the visible top barbed wire of the fence, turned west toward the river bridge. He kept to the fields. On the highway there would be questions. He wanted no questions. He lowered his head into the piercing wind, feeling the frozen snow pelt his clothing and collide with the lenses of his goggles. The streaming currents of white swept across his skis as they skimmed easily ahead, and sang. He turned for a moment and saw behind him the towering summits of the somber Tetons with giant wind-blown snow plumes clinging to their frigid crags and pinnacles. The peaks appeared as gigantic tombstones of ice, glaring across a white, frozen valley, quiet as a cemetery.

And he saw the snow-burdened bungalow, where The Bandit and her mother sat together, feet to the blazing wood-burning heater. The heat radiated outward pleasantly. Mae Howard was speaking between sobs, but still her zany self,

"This part of blessed old Tetonia I can endure, Maryanne Howard. About the only part. Burn oh ye fires burn! Someone ought to write a hymn, "Burn oh ye winter fires burn." Sing it every week in Sacrament Meeting.

"Mother, please don't cry. I can't stand it . . ." The two reached for the Kleenex box again.

"Maryanne."

"Mother."

Suddenly a plaintive and distant steam whistle was heard!

"The ole ding-a-ling! It's coming! Man the bags, daughter!"

"Mother, let's go!"

"No holdup. Let's slow down and think a bit. Don't panic. That chug-a-lug's got to plow its way to poor ole Tetonia, then hit the drifts up to the Victor turn around. It'll take hours to get back here for you. What say we go on down to Wilt's store and see what they know that we don't? Could be the train won't make a run for good ole CAL until tomorrow. Pray, girl, pray the engineer is done in. Give the Reluctant Lover time to come in!"

The wind, sweeping unobstructed over the Felt country, was overpowering the huffing steam engines. The whistle came from up to two miles away, reaching Tetonia ears a few moments after the whistle steam rose from the black pipe, for sound travels slowly in frigid cold. The train was still hours from the Tetonia depot.

And as the whistle sounded, Rock Ebert's team was drawing the covered sleigh around the highway curve westward toward those torturous Clementsville hills. Joel, urging the blanketed team on, saw the swirling blizzard of the train's rotary plow far out north, and far westward, he thought he could see a wisp of the plow truck's exhaust. But he did not notice a small, dark object moving across the snow field on his left, the distant image of a parka coat and faded Levis, too distant to reveal an easy glide of skis.

"Well," said Haskins back at the store as afternoon deepened, "at least we've got a train coming in." He peered out the door to the light pole, rubbed the steam from the glass to get a clearer view. "Looks like the thermometer's going down," he said, "Right at ten below, now." As he spoke, the door opened and the Howard ladies entered, shuddering.

"Stoke the fire, Wilt. Women here. Frozen women! What's the news, Wilt?"

On the up slopes of the Clementsville hills, the sun, its cold fire hanging low in the sky, had about it a yellow glow. Long ago, it seemed, Pow had heard the straining engine of the highway plow. He had kept to the fields, the smothered dry-farm fields, until a safe distance ahead and then followed the drifted highway. If too far from the road, he could miss the stalled bus.

As the hours passed, the slide of skis was no longer a song. The sleek slats had become heavy slabs nailed to his feet. The never-ending drifts and the hills, forever reaching upward, had drawn out their payment. The twin enemies of fatigue and numbing cold had exacted their price. He was tired and the cold knifed to the marrow.

At last he reached the highest of the elevations. The hills rolled off ahead, gradually losing stature for fifteen miles, and then opened into Snake River Valley. The sun had gone, leaving a pale haze, turning to yellow-rose the distant, sharp ridges of what Pow thought were the Sawtooths, an eternity away. As he paused to rest, he thought of the Fig Newtons and the now frozen half-sandwiches.

He ate, mingling cold saliva with frozen bread. It swallowed hard, as before. He scooped a mound of snow on his mitten and moistened his mouth with the harsh crystals.

As he paused he felt the first onset of panic. With the frightening sensation, he thrust the skis ahead and struggled to the crest of the next hill. He thought of the warm fire in the drug store heater, he fancied warming himself by the enameled heating panels. He should never have left. The great hero, Pow Blaine. Dumb hero, Dumb nothing. A weary, anxious mind can hurl stinging barbs.

What was happening now at the store? Had his parents discovered yet that he was gone? Would they suspect he had skied into the hills? He pictured his father shaking his head in despair, as he often did over his son's antics. Was his mother shedding tears with Widow Wyzanski? Was another covered sleigh out after Pow Blaine?

His mind now pictured Joel and Willie in their warm sled. Where were they? Were they just over the dark elevation behind him? He listened for the creaking of the sleigh and the jingling of tug links on single trees. He thought again of the blazing stove and as he searched the indistinct swell of the hill, he was sure he saw a billowing of wood smoke. His heart thumped excitedly and he turned his skis about, shouting,

"I'm here! Over here!" His voice sounded strange in the emptiness and his throat felt dry and tight. There was no response. He shouted again; it was a desperate, hopeless cry, a cry of panic.

It was then he remembered the matches in his pocket, and he looked about for wood, but he saw only the sodden heads of the fence posts rising above the snow. A quarter mile to the north, he detected the dark shadow of a willow hedge, which bordered a field. Green willows would not burn; he knew that. What value were matches, then, in a world of snow? As he struggled with his thoughts, he heard the sound of his breath, drawn and exhaled through the woolen scarf which covered his mouth and nose. Thumping heart sounds pulsed in his ears. He thought of his bed and its warm covers, but his thoughts startled him and a swell of panic thrust the vision from his mind. He pushed the skis ahead desperately. Was he going to die? Didn't freezing people think of warm fires and covers, have visions of nonexistent, sheltered coves and warm dens in the snow? He forced his legs stride after stride. They felt numb with fatigue and cold. He heard the slow slide of the skis, but their movement now was a desperate cry.

"The wind has stopped," said the bishop, back at the drug store, as he looked into the street. "That's a blessing."

"Ve vait forever," muttered Widow Wyzanski. "Da day so lang."

"It does seem like forever, Sister Wyzanski," responded Maryanne Howard, who had found a place at her side.

"You haf to go avay, Maryanne? I vas hoping . . . maybe you unt my Chonny . . ."

"Now, that's the most sense I've heard all day," spoke up Mae Howard. "Anna, I just wonder what you and I could do about that little idea." The crowd chuckled.

"Mother!" scolded The Bandit.

"I can think of lots of worse things," responded the bishop. "A lot of things."

"I think Johnny will have something to say about that," the girl said, her cheeks flushed.

But the sensitive conversation was interrupted by the whistle of the train, as it approached the Tetonia station, not visible from the store window.

"The bags, daughter! Where's Daddy Howard? This girl's going to miss that train, with all this gabbing! The old chug-a-lug will be up to Victor and back in no time. Man the bags - and the Kleenexs!"

Back on those hills of despair, Powell Blaine's mind was obsessed with a vision of a blazing fire in a warm, glowing cave in the snow where he could rest and warm himself. He fell to his knees at the base of a towering drift, but being beside the highway, as he attempted to dig into the white bank with his mittened hands, he soon encountered a solid, icy obstacle, a chunk of frozen, water-soaked snow which had been thrown out by the plow on an earlier run. It was useless to attempt to dig a cave. That reality came over him as a numbing terror, driving him to rise to his feet and struggle to the top of the huge mound.

It was then, in the smothered road ahead, that he thought he discerned a large, long, lifeless mound, and he thought he saw a brighter glow on the horizon ahead. The Rexburg lights?

Back in the Valley, the train had left the Tetonia depot, spiritedly opening the road over the fifteen-mile run to Driggs and finally, to little Victor, the tiny hamlet which huddled at the Idaho base point of Teton Pass, that high, precarious, snowbound road which linked Teton Basin with its neighboring mountain valley, Jackson Hole. At the line's end, the train would turn about for the return run to Tetonia and those distant points beyond. As The Bandit, at the depot now, waited on into the late evening for her transportation, her emotions reached the upper limits of endurance, and she let the tears flow.

"I must look hideous," she sobbed, searching a dry corner of her Kleenex.

"You look your gorgeous best," said the mother, wiping her own nose. The two sat close, sharing despair and comfort, and a slow hour went by. Then out of the darkness, southward, toward the Spring Creek woods, a blazing light beamed toward the station and a throaty, steam whistle was heard.

"It's here, daughter." The two stood and stepped anxiously out into the cold night. "More Kleenex? I've used two boxes."

Through their tears the two sobbing females glanced toward the Clementsville hills in the northwest as the train approached and both gasped as they saw the startling, but unmistakable lights of an automobile appearing out on the highway, heading for Harrop's bridge and old Tetonia!

"The bus!" exclaimed The Bandit. "It's coming!"

The train huffed and puffed to a stop, streaked with snow and frost and trimmed with a haphazard fringing of icicles. There was a sound of live, escaping steam as indefatigable Mae Howard ran to the engine. Her voice sounded above the hissing vapor.

"Open your window, there, engineer! Woman here! Open up!" A cab window slid open.

"Coffee and sandwiches!" she shouted. "It's only a block up to the drug store. Good, stout Mormon coffee. You need it after today!"

"Sounds good. Thanks lady, I'll take about a gallon of it. Thanks. You, Henry?" There were words of agreement from deeper into the cab as the fireman responded. "We'll bring George, our conductor, too. We're all about finished with this run."

"Daughter!" Mae turned to the girl. "Run and tell Bishop Ebert to get the coffee pot on. Tell him to read on the coffee bag, it'll tell him what to do. Make it strong. You know, black. You help him if you have to. Run, girl. A big pot, now! We're not finished yet!"

As The Bandit reached the store and gave the happy bishop her message, the highway plow was nearing the town's outer limits, repeatedly sounding its horn. Maryanne's knees trembled. She found the widow, assuring herself that standing at the woman's side, she would share the first glimpse of him, and she'd be there, handy, when he reached his mother. She heard the truck's brakes growl, the vehicle creaked to a stop, and the Harris girls leaped out of the cab door.

"Where's Johnny?" someone called.

"Oh, he and the Blaine kid wanted to ride back in the sleigh," the driver responded. "Nice way to end his mission, young Wyzanski said. They'll be along. And, say, that kid who skied all the way over from town, here, it was him that likely saved 'em all. 'Least he helped get to 'em a lot quicker. He spotted this spud cellar, way off the road, that the rest of us missed. They were all holed up there. There with fifty tons of spuds. Plenty to eat, and not so cold, but mighty glad to see us."

"Well," said the engineer, wiping his chin. "Looks like everything's turning out good, just like your coffee, here. But we got to get on down the line. Real good coffee you brew, here, Bishop Ebert. I'll sit down with you anytime." The crowd laughed. "And you, young lady," he turned to Maryanne, "let's get your bags loaded. I think you'll be warm enough in the passenger car. If not, you can ride up with Henry and me." The crowd laughed again. "Ready to go?"

So, before Joel and Willie and Johnny and Pow drew the blanketed horses up at the drug store an hour later, the poor Bandit was wiping the last remains of mascara from her cheeks, way out on the Judkins line.

Now, the story could end here. Of course, we'd all have mascara streaks and Mae Howard would have missed out on her most shining hour, but, as they say, that's life. We'd all get over it in time. But let's not do that. Let's keep going and say that after the train rolled off into the dark toward iced-down Felt and Judkins, carrying away her 'chick', the 'zany' mother hurried away to the telephone.

And next morning as she knocked on the Wyzanski door to welcome home the "illusive drip", he greeted her with,

"Hey, I hear The Bandit's gone to L. A. Ole Bandito. And, you know what? I got a call from the Darbys this morning. Can you believe they have a job for me down there, and a place to stay? I hope I can find where ole Bandito's staying. Got her address?"

Well, this would be a better place to end the story, but let's take it just one more paragraph and let it be known that after two weeks, the Golden Coast couldn't compete at all with little old iceberg, Tetonia. The first paychecks were anxiously spent for return tickets, and today, this frigid January day, from across the lot there comes a call,

"Hey, Bandito! Now that I've pinned Pow's ears to the shed wall again, how about we wash off those freckles in this drift? Got to get you ready for the big dance tonight! Remember? Eight-thirty. I'll be around!"

17

A Vain of Harse Scients

Now, there's lots of scients talked about and written of in books, a whole lot of it. But none of it gets you down as deep as harse scients, and especially that fork of the curriculum known as hornesses, of the harse variety, of course. I can tell right off that some of you who have never been out and about the rural acres and have never learned to scrape off the soles of your shoes without thinking every time you open the kitchen door, will llikely sniff and pipe up with something like, "Aw, come on, a horness is a horness, just a bunch of straps and buckles that amount to nothing." You can say that. But you wait. Presently I'm going to get into some of the simpler horness and hornessing principles. That will set your minds straight.

Now I know, too, that some of you will fade off into lighter trains of thought when we get into deep water. But that's alright. Scients isn't for everybody. So, with that bit of erudition and luminosity, let's go on up to the barn and get started. As you can see right off, I'm given to words of length and thickness. But this is a thick subject and the words are needed, as you'll see.

Alright. Now, as we reach the stable door, here, I want you to take a nice deep breath. Smell it? Sort of nudges the back of your palate, doesn't it? As anybody into the deeper scientses knows, a harse barn has its own smell. It isn't the same as a pig sty, or a cow stable, or a sheep corral, not at all. Not to put those other smells down or anything, but a harse barn stands alone in redolence or effluvium, as the case may be. Now, redolence and effluvium are heavy words, again, out of books, thick books, but they're needed on this subject, so ponder them. Regular words of speech can't get you very far into the smell scients, you understand. Of course, I could get way deep into smells and smelling, but that scients is off in another direction, and anyway, as I say, it's deep. You wouldn't get it. . .

What's that you're saying? You, over there in the orange shirt . . .

You say you can't stand the effluvium and you're leaving? Well, how do you like that? I'm not even getting into the subject, and you're finished. Go on, then. I could tell from the start you were light on scients. Go.

Alright. Now, as I open the stable door, here, you can see the hornesses hanging on those wooden pegs on the wall opposite the harse stalls. As you will note, I am now walking to Ginger's stall and untying the end of his halter rope from this hole in the top plank of the manger. . . and I lead Ginger across the stable over here to the hornesses, as you see, and tie his rope to this two-by-four. Tight. Got that? Ponder it. You see now, with the harse over here by the horness, we can get on with the hornessing procedure, because harses and hornesses go together; one's no good without the other, never have been and never will be. Ponder that. It's a principle.

Alright. Now, of course, all I've said 'til now is just preliminaries, just getting us down into the subject, you understand. From here on it's serious business, deep water and heavy thinking. I'll do my best, mind you, to keep this as simple as the subject permits, but, you understand, that won't always be possible. . .

Hay, over there. You, over there in the brown shirt. Where're you headed? . . . You're just leaving. Well, why's that? . . . You don't like heavy water 'cause you can't swim? Good night. A harse stable's no place for dog paddlers. Go.

Alright. Now, first we deal with the harse collar. Remember that. Ponder it. You see, it's hanging right there on its peg like a big cushioned donut of leather. That's what I say to keep it simple. Donut. Of course, it really looks like the radiator on the Edsel car. Edsel. Remember that. The collar, you understand, made the car famous. Of course, the collar came first. Before the car came in, you understand, there were no words that really described the collar, so 'donut' was used, and still is by some. But, donuts can't really get you far into the subject. So thank the car. I do.

Now, of course, I could get way into the branches and vains of car scients, but it's high knowledge and you wouldn't get it. So, I'll keep to the horness subject by saying that the collar fits around the harse's neck. . . like this . . .

Whoa, there, Ginger.

... and it fastens by a strap and buckle at the top, up here by this long hair, known in harse circles as the mane. Remember that. Now, you note that the collar doesn't fit up by the ears, here. . . like this, but back at the thick end of the neck, here against the shoulders. . . like this. . .

Whoa, there, Ginger. I'm just making a point. Whoa. . . settle down, there.

Alright. Now, make a note of this, all of you. In hornessing scients, the collar comes first every time. That's a principle. Ponder it. Deep. You horness a harse and forget the collar and I'll tell you, you've got trouble. And while you're pondering, add the word "top". "Top", got it? If you ever horness a harse with the collar buckled down at the bottom of the neck, here, you just as well take the rest of the day off. You're going nowhere. You've got the collar on upside down.

Hey there, you over there. Where're you going? You in the red shirt. . . . You decided to take the day off? Well, how do you like that? And I'm just getting started. Go on, then. Go.

Alright. Now, with the collar buckled in place, we're ready for the horness, so I lift it off its pegs, here, you see, and sort of swing all these straps across the animal's back like this. . . uh- oh - wheeew. . . The belly strap dinged my nose! . . . When the smarting stops we'll proceed. Wheew. . .

Alright. Now, done right, as you see, the horness just sort of falls in place with half of it on each side of the hairy spine. . . which runs along the top of the harse, right here, you see. . .

Whoa, Ginger - whoa, there. Easy, there, Ginger. I was just making a point.

Alright. Now, if you throw that horness on the harse wrong you're in deep trouble. I have to say that. You'll lose an hour getting it all straightened out. So, ponder hard. . .

Hey there, you. Over there in the pink shirt, you're dozing off. No sleeping, hear that?. . .What's that? You say you're pondering? Well, ponder with your eyes open and pointed right here. I say that because you'll never make it any other way. This is scients. Remember that.

Alright. Now, as you see right here, a horness has two hames. These right here. Now, the word 'hame' comes out of books, hard books; and hame scients is deep as well water. I could get away off into hames, of course, but you'd have to be a big student of harse scients to get it, and you wouldn't. So, I'll just pass it all and keep it simple by saying that the hames are these two, two-foot-long, inch-thick posts that all the front straps of the horness buckles onto. The hames, as you see here, are a bit curved at the bottom ends, and up close to their tops, they're held together by this six-inch-long strap. Now, the hames fit onto the collar, one on each side - into this groove, deep groove, that goes all the way round the collar. . .

Hey, you. You're leaving, too? How's that? You in the black shirt. Come on back here, you. . .Well, go on, then. Go.

Alright. Now, as I said, the hames, here, fit into this deep groove that circles the front of the collar, all around the harse's neck, you see. Now if you're hornessing a harse and you can't see that collar groove, stop. S-T-O-P. You've put the collar on backwards. Remember, now, the grooved side faces the harse's ears. . .up here, not his tail. . .back here. . .

Whoa, Ginger. Whoa, there, whoa. I was just making a point. Whoa.

Alright. Now, as I was saying, ears, not tail. Memorize that principle. You'll be glad you did. I'm glad I did. Now, the hames, once more, fit into this collar groove, one hame on each side of the collar. . .like this. Ohh. . .wheew. Smarts. . .oowww. Got my thumb pinched there in the groove under the hame. . .wheew. We'll now pause 'til the smarting stops. Wheew.

Alright. Now, with the hames in the groove, the curved ends fasten together down at the bottom of the collar with this strap and buckle, which are hanging here for that purpose only. . .Hey, where's the strap? Hey, you in the green shirt. Did you. . .? Oh, here it is. I missed it.

Alright. Now, this next principle is important. It's lofty scients, so ponder it. There aren't words even in thick books to describe the mess you'll be in if you ever put the horness on in such a way that you're trying to fasten these curved ends of the hames together at the top of the collar. . .up here. So ponder hame work down deep. It low down scients. A guiding principle is that most hames have these nice metal knobs on their tops. One knob on each hame, just one, as you see. . .right here. Fancy, aren't they? Now, underline this in your brains, dark. The purpose of these knobs is to catch your eyes in the hornessing procedure. Remember that. Ponder it. Now, to keep the hames in the upright position when hornessing a harse, just keep your eyes on the knobs at all times, and keep those knobs up. You'll be glad if you memorize it. I'm glad I did.

Alright. Now with the hame principle as clear as spring water, we go to the tugs. Tugs. All hornesses have two of 'em. No more, no less. Two. Pay no attention if somebody tries to tell you different. Two. Now, the tugs, as you see right here, attach to the hames, one on each side of the horse. Not over or under, on the sides only. . .as you see.

Now, the other ends of the tugs have got metal links on them for purposes of hitching onto singletrees. We'll get into singletrees presently. Not the leafy kind of growth, you understand, but the horness variety.

Hey. . .you, there in the spotted shirt. Where're you off to?. . . Trees give you hayfever? Well, good nightshirt. Go, then, go.

Alright. Now I'm going to veer around the deeper scients of tugs by just saying that with the two of them on each horness, harses pull wagons, harrows, swill carts and various assortments of conveyances, and when the tugs are not in use, the links, here on the ends, as you see, clip onto these hooks up here on the backstrap. Right here. . .

Whoa, Ginger. Steady, there. I was just making a point.

Alright. Now, this long strap up here, as I said, is called the back strap, and it has purposes. Big purposes. As you will note, there's one backstrap per harness, only one. It starts up here at the hames, up here at the top of the collar, and it runs along the top of the harse all the way along the hairy spine to the top of the tail. . .right here. Here. . .you see.

Ginger! Whoa, there. Whoa. I was just making . .whoa. . .a point.

Alright. Now, as you see, there's a half-circle of cushioned leather here at the end of the backstrap. It's made circlish because it's got to be slipped under the harse's tail. . .right here at the top of the tail, and it buckles in place. I will demonstrate this presently. . .

Hey. You're going, too? You in the yellow shirt. . .You're leaving in protest of harse discomfort? Goodnight. What next? Go, then. Go.

Alright. Now, this half-moon of leather at the end of the backstrap, as I said, goes under the harse's tail. . .like this. . .

Whoa. Whoa. Ginger, settle down. Whoa, there . . .

Now, you buckle it. Just so, to give the backstrap just the right tension. Ponder that word, 'tension'. It comes out of books. . .

Ginger! Easy, there. Settle down. Whoa. Step back, you over there in the gray shirt! Watch out!

Alright. Now, that cushioned leather is called the crupper. Crupper. Ponder that word. Hard. Now, if you buckle the crupper, here, too tight. . .like this. . .you've got trouble ahead. You can tell if it's too tight if it holds the harse's tail up unnaturally. . .like this. . .

HAY! GINGER! WATCH OUT! HE'S BROKE LOOSE! GRAB HIS ROPE, YOU IN THE WHITE SHIRT. HEY! WHERE'S EVERYBODY GONE? OH! GINGER! COME BACK HERE! GINGER!!

18

Harse Scients II

Now, conditions hereabout being what they are and coming to,I don't know what, and people being no better and myself being a man of scients and of a steady mind, I'm writing all this down for purposes of erudition. Now I know that 'erudition' is a heavy word and that it doesn't bounce easy off most tongues, but it's needed here to get us down to meanings and clarifyings, as you might say. Now for purposes of edging easy into the subject and keeping it light so's it won't go flying off over everybodys' heads, I'll start back a bit, when I and the misses was out on an evening with folks of a fairly high cut, including the water master and the milk tank driver, and there was one or two with bits of college cluttering up their minds and clouding their thinking, and there was some assorted others not needing clarification.

Well, sitting around the Heaterola, talk got plentiful, as you might say, warming up on such useless subjects as yogurt and cow pox and how much snow fell in two days last winter. Now, seeing a bleak evening coming on, I just laid out a word or two, you might say, on scients, in the vain of harses and hornesses and how those two forks of thinking go just like a hand in a jersey glove, and I said it exactly that'a way, being one to keep a deep subject simple. But like I thought it would be, the subject was too heavy for 'em and went over their heads like a puff of wind over a wet, plowed field, not stirring a weed or a grain of dust, you might say, and the light talk proceeded knee deep into weedy canals, and whey vats. So, I lifted the volume and put out something like: "Anybody here ever hitch up a team to a wagon?" But the liquid trains of thought still didn't give an inch. So I laid it out louder and to the point, you might say, and this time scients got into every ear, causing two or three of the lady folks to lurch a bit, and it brought on a sharp elbow to the rib area on my wife's side, causing me to grunt as I added on these words: "Five dollars not one of you knows how many rings on a neck yoke." Now I knew that any word leaning toward cash takes priority over all subject matter, and I was right because with that said, the creamery and the headgates shut down and I got eyes and answers - answers that'd turn a man of scients and thinking out to pasture.

"Diamond rings or telephone rings?" tee-heed the milk tanker's wife, acting upity.

"Rings in an egg yoke?" twittered a female of the assorted group, with a smart pucker.

"You mean jingle bells?" says another, veering clear off the subject. "Ting-a-ling!" she goes on, smuckering at the geek sitting by her. Good night, that sentence just about sent me home mad, so I spoke up.

"Good night," says I, "the erudidity hereabouts is thin as holstein milk." Now, knowing that strain of milk to be blue-white thin, I could say that. And I put in the word 'erudidity' of a purpose, because it's out of books and used sometimes on bunches like this one to test out the deepness and flow of the stream of scients in the brain and thinking. Well, just like I thought, it flowed thin as holstein milk and went noplace. Well, any man of a settled mind would know something had to be done about such a thin state of knowledge, and seeing the milk driver with a word about whey on his tongue, I said loud and quick, not having time to think it all the way through, you understand.

"Now," says I, "you come down to the place tomorrow and I'll give you all a light run through on the scients of neck yokes and assorted subjects of namely the harse and horness variety, leaning a bit toward hitching up to wagons." That said, I see the geek who spent upwards of a month or two over at the Normal School smuckering up to put out a smart syllabel, so I headed him off, not thinking it all the way through, you understand.

"Now," I says, "I've got a nice Christmas present of a sack of spuds and a squash for each of you who comes down, and we'll take a wagon ride for pleasure, as you might say, an' the misses'll have a round of hot cider waitin'." I felt a sharp elbow in the rib area on the wife's side again, causing me to gulp and giving the water man his chance to slip in his thin thoughts on the moisture properties of dew. But I got some nods, and having some culled-out spuds and squash that needed to be moved out of the shed, I felt good about it and settled back. Not being interested in the subject of liquids, as I afore said, I just layed back and yawned and worked the numbness out of a leg that was cramping in the soft chair, following the scientific approach to pain treatment by kneading the leg like it was bread dough, then slapping it sharp. In the midst of this I felt the elbow in the rib area again on the wife's side. But what's a man to do?

Well, we held on 'til dessert, then making a passing reference to spuds and squash again, I edged toward the door, favoring the game leg, the misses objecting, of course.

Well, now, next day, being of a Saturday and four days afore Christmas, they come down to the place, most of 'em, with their eyes sizin' up the sacks a' top-rate spuds and the pile 'a banana squash that was just waitin' to be loaded on the wagon and hauled up to Johnson's produce stand for purposes of selling in the Christmas shoppin' rush, you understand. Nice spuds, they were, all sorted and washed up, and the squashes was a yard long, each one, just right for crackin' open for the oven. Now, the culls, which I had in mind to give to the bunch as Christmas presents, was in a pile in the shed, they being knotty and broke in two and a bit soft, soft applying to the squash and the spuds. I had a shovel and some bags in there for 'em to sack up all they wanted. And I had it figured that after they got all the nutriments they cared for, they sure wouldn't mind giving a hand in loading the good spuds and squash on the wagon and take a nice ride up to Johnson's and then help unload.

Alright, as I said, they come down and began hinting for cider and looking anxious over at the bags of nice spuds and squash, ready for Johnson's. Now, I had Ginger and Homer hornessed and ready for purposes of demonstrating the scients of hitching a team to a wagon, a natural preliminary to haulin' the produce to town. But I see right off that the water master's wife was anxious to pick up her spuds and leave the premises, so I put her at ease with some thoughts on philosofee, you might say, on assorted subjects, but leanin' toward harses and hornesses. Now, not wanting to get in too deep, I finished the subject matter in fifteen or twenty minutes, thereabouts. That's all the philosofee most can handle at one time. I found that out.

Now, it was a bit sharp, it being into Christmas time, but setting your back to the wind and covering one ear after the other with your hand, nobody could complain, and I see they was doing that so I hit the subject hard, as you might say.

"As you now see," I say, "I will hitch Ginger, here, and Homer, over there, to the wagon, which you see right here," keeping it simple to that point, but then putting on two heavy words, one right after the other, which isn't often done except in higher levels of scients. "Now, harses and hornesses," I says, "is both utilized to give wagons locomotion." That's just what I says and it caused the normal school geek to screw up his eyebrows into some pondering, he getting just a thin glimpse of the scients referred to. I proceeded:

"Alright," I says, "now, as you will observe," keeping, as you see, right on with the thick words, "I am leading Ginger, here, over on this side of the wagon tongue, here. . .right here. Now, that's a principle. Ponder it. Now, the wagon tongue, as you see, is this pole sticking out from the front of the vehicle, attached to the axle, right up there between the wheels. . ."

"What's that you're tryin' to say, you there with the red nose," I says as I see the milk driver's wife tryin' to head me off with some irrelovant thoughts.

"Why's the wagon sticking out its tongue," she says real snipity.

"Good night," I says, "what kind of a question is that? We're into scients, here, not frivolary! Ponder that!" She pondered, and smuckered and they all twittered and some began to dance on one foot and then the other to keep the blood flowing, it getting a bit sharper with sundown coming on.

"Alright," I say, "now, I'm leading Homer, here, to 'tother side of the tongue, his tail pointing at the wagon. That's a principle. Tail. Memorize it. You'll be glad you did. You hitch up a team with their noses pointing at the wagon and you're in trouble where even thick books can't get you out. So ponder." I give 'em a minute to ponder and to stir the blood up in their fingers with some arm windmilling.

"Alright, now," I said and proceed to the neck yoke. I hold it up and eggzibit the three rings, two on the ends and one in the middle, all of which have big purposes. I buckle the outside rings, one to Ginger's collar, and one to Homer's, then I slip the end of the wagon tongue into the center ring very smooth, then somebody horned in again with frivolous talk.

"What's that you say," I said, disgusted, "you with your hand over your ear...? Speak up. . . When're we having cider? Good night," I say, "We're into scients, deep. Cider and scients don't mix- never have."

"You promised," she hung onto the subject. But not caring to get into the matter of the misses giving a flat 'no' and a sharp elbow to the rib area at the mention of cider, I went right on and was just getting into the scients of tugs and singletrees when the wife calls from the steps that Johnson wanted some words about the spuds and squash, which were now just a trifle over due. So, leaving the bunch a minute or two to ponder and to windmill and dance, I went off to the house.

Well, now, I was gone no more than five minutes, fifteen at the most, and do you know, and remember what I say in the preliminaries, about people comin to I don't know what? Well, when I get back out to the wagon, they was all gone. They had left the premises. Every one. Now, I didn't care much about that, but then when I see that all the sacks of good spuds and the nice banana squash was gone, I see red. Gone to the last sack and squash, it was! And all the culls was still untouched in the shed. Now, I was of a mind to call the sheriff, but the wife said a flat 'no'. It made me good and mad, though, and came near spoiling my whole Christmas.